I0760987

GRIM

K. LORAINE
USA TODAY BESTSELLING AUTHORS
MEG ANNE

This book is a work of fiction. The names, characters, places, and incidents are products of the author's imagination or have been used fictitiously and are not to be construed as real. Any resemblance to persons, living or dead, actual events, locales, or organizations is entirely coincidental.

ISBN:

978-1-961742-59-8 (Paperback Edition)

978-1-961742-60-4 (Hardback Edition)

No artificial intelligence was used in the creation of this work of fiction.

Edited by Mo Sytsma of Comma Sutra Editorial

Cover Design by CReya-tive Book Design

Photographer: Juliana Andrade

Model: Wander Aguiar

For our Kat, You've been on this journey with us since the beginning. We saw this quote and thought of you.

'Walk on, walk on
With hope in your heart
And you'll never walk alone'
Oscar Hammerstein II / Richard Rodgers

"Hell is empty and all the devils are here."

—WILLIAM SHAKESPEARE, THE TEMPEST

GRIM

AUTHORS' NOTE

Grim contains mature and graphic content that is not suitable for all audiences. Such content includes scenes of dubious consent, captivity, role playing, disasters and more. **Reader discretion is advised.**

As always, a detailed list of content and trigger warnings is available on our website.

CHAPTER ONE

GRIM

"Grim, you absolute motherfucking shit stain of an excuse for a man."

I stared at my reflection in the gilt mirror that hung over the fireplace in my quarters. She'd laid it all bare for us, and what had I done? Taken her soft and vulnerable heart and crushed it in my palm while she watched. But what else was I meant to do? She'd been wrong to place such importance on us. We couldn't be what she said we were.

It wasn't possible.

My gut turned to a stone as dread overtook every other emotion coursing through me. I'd fucked up. I'd known it the instant the words of denial left my lips and that shattered expression crossed her face. I might be correct in my position, but I'd cocked everything up. And now I was fairly certain there was no coming back from what I'd set in motion.

Even if Merri did eventually forgive me, she'd never trust me again.

I clutched at my chest, feeling like something had clawed its way inside and was currently squeezing whatever vital organ might reside there. My breaths came in tight gasps as the squeezing continued, now accompanied by the flood of ice through my veins. What the fuck was happening to me?

I felt Sin's energy before he spoke, fury radiating into the room the same way Merri radiated lust. "You know, I really try to understand you and all your moody bullshit, but this is entirely your goddamn fault, Grim. I thought I was done yelling at you, but now that I'm back and we still can't find her, I'm just more angry. You . . . you . . . twatwaffle."

I couldn't find it in myself to turn and face him. I deserved every insult he hurled my way and then some. "Are you done?" I asked, not quite able to keep the defeat from my voice.

"No!" Sin snapped, like the petulant arsehole he was. I could just make out his reflection in the mirror as he took a few more steps into my room. His expression morphed from righteous fury to concern as he got a look at me. "Dude. Are you okay? You look like shit."

"Thanks," I grumbled, dragging a hand over my nape as I took in my appearance. I did look like shit. Deep furrows marred a forehead that was never smooth to begin with, the weight of every wrong I'd ever done settling across my skin like a roadmap of my transgressions.

He continued to study me, eyes narrowed until he snapped his fingers and a crazed euphoria lit up his face. "You *do* care! All this time, you've been going on and on about duty and priorities, but you're just as in love with her as the rest of us, you fucking faker."

The fight that had eluded me came roaring back to life as I spun around and sent a few of the objects on the mantel flying. "Of course I fucking care!" I bellowed.

Sin leaned against one of the posts of my bed, crossing his arms over his chest. "Could have fooled me. Too bad you won't be able to fix this with her. And what's worse, by the way you told it, none of us cared. You broke her with your indifference and ruined it for all of us. She's never going to trust us again."

Shame burned its way up the back of my neck. He was right. I knew it, but it didn't make the facts any easier to accept. Exhausted by my emotional outburst, I couldn't summon more than a gusty sigh.

"If you came here just to rail at me, I'm not interested," I muttered, waving a hand at him dismissively. "Feel free to see yourself out."

"Fuck no. You aren't getting rid of me that easily, Grimsby. I see straight through you. You're just as torn up as the rest of us."

"So?"

"So the question now is, what the hell are you going to do about it?"

"I'll talk to her. Explain the situation. She'll understand if she lets—"

The man made an annoying buzzer sound, cutting me off. "Ehhh, wrong answer. Try again."

I sighed. "What would you have me do?"

"You're going to need to grovel, my dude. Big time. We're talking mega gesture here. Meet on the top of the Empire State Building level of gesture."

"The Empire State Building was destroyed in th—"

"It was just an example! Have you never read a romance novel?"

"No."

Sin groaned and dragged a hand over his face. "Well, it fucking shows!"

"What the fuck is this?" Chaos growled, his violent energy permeating the room and causing everything not bolted down to shudder. "She's fucking run off, and you two are in here doing nothing to find her."

"Hey! I'm doing something. I did a lot of somethings and then came in here to yell at him when my search yielded no results." Sin stood straight and gestured at me like I'd have any kind of helpful response.

"She's probably hiding in a bloody tree and nursing her wounded heart. Give her time and she'll come around."

The two of them looked at me like I'd just suggested we braid each other's hair or shave each other's balls. With a straight razor.

Now I was the one who shuddered.

"Listen," I sighed, scrubbing a hand over my face. "We know she's on the premises because there hasn't been a breach of the wards. She'll calm down, and then we'll deal with it like adults. Until then—"

"Get your bloody arses down here!" Malice's shout sent a bolt of icy panic straight through me.

Without another thought, I materialized in the foyer where Malice stood, heaving for breath, expression stricken. Chaos and Sin followed only a heartbeat after me, both of them tensed and ready for a fight.

"What is it?" I breathed, but I already knew the truth.

Deep down, I knew.

Malice steeled himself, eyes locking on mine. "The wards have been breached. Merri is gone."

CHAPTER TWO

MERRI

The scrape of ceramic across wood pulled my focus from the surreal beauty of the lake beyond the window. A mug of cocoa, complete with melting marshmallows, sat in front of me, steam curling from the top.

"Here, drink this. My mom always said hot chocolate could fix almost anything." Cole's voice soothed my frayed nerves.

I accepted the cup with a mumbled, "Thanks," stealing a few surreptitious glances at my new housemate. He was way more handsome than I had expected, but not in a knock you over way like the horsemen. Cole was normal guy handsome. He was giving Henry Golding vibes. Like polished and cultured, but it wouldn't be weird to see him doing DIY projects around the house. Business suit in the streets, but he has flannel sheets.

"Are you okay? You looked rattled when I answered the door." He took the seat across from me but didn't move to touch me. I probably seemed a lot like a scared stray cat at the moment.

"No. I'm not. Not by a long shot."

"Do you—"

"I don't want to talk about it. Not yet."

He held up both his hands in a placating gesture. "No worries. I'm down to listen whenever you're ready. In the meantime, why don't you enjoy the hot chocolate, and I'll get back to work. When you're ready, you can come find me, and I'll give you the nickel tour."

I cocked a brow. "Nickel tour?"

He smirked, flashing me a heretofore unknown dimple. "I just meant there's not a whole lot to see. Grand tour felt like it would be misleading."

A genuine smile graced my lips for the first time since I'd had my heart crushed by Grim. "With a view like this, it's already pretty grand."

He turned and looked out the window at said view. The lake water was so still it resembled a mirror, reflecting the fire-streaked sky. It was as beautiful as it was eerie. Nothing was in bloom, but the evergreens made up for the lack of foliage. Due to the lake, their roots must have had enough water even with the raised temperature.

Just like at the château, there was not a flake of snow to be found. So much for winter.

"You should have seen it a week ago," he said, still looking out at the lake. "The snow all melted because of the heat, and the whole thing was overflowing."

I peered out the floor-to-ceiling windows. "Looks normal to me."

"Yeah, now. All the runoff evaporated. Who knows what it will look like next week."

"Sounds like par for the course with an apocalypse," I muttered.

"What was that?"

Shit. The humans had no idea what was happening. I wasn't going to burst his bubble. Poor Cole had enough on his plate with me invading his life. "Nothing." I flashed him a brighter-than-normal smile before picking up my hot cocoa and bringing it to my lips. He was right; it was delicious. "Can I bring this on the tour?"

"As long as you don't dump it on my typewriter," he teased.

I gasped. "I would never."

He winked at me before offering his elbow. "Ready?"

"As I'll ever be," I said, accepting the proffered arm.

"All right. This, as you can see, is the kitchen-slash-dining room. Where I've enjoyed many a TV dinner while writing."

"Shnazzy."

"I do love to embody a stereotype."

An unexpected bubble of laughter escaped me. "And what stereotype is that? Bachelor?"

"Starving artist."

I snickered. "Fair. Well done, then."

He gave me a little bow and then pulled me into the living room. "And here is where I sit alone and watch my stories."

Another giggle escaped me. "Stories? Like soap operas?"

"Reality TV mostly. I'm partial to the real estate shows. The drama. The houses. The backstabbing. It's really great for plotlines."

"What exactly do you write?" I glanced at the bookshelf and caught sight of a row of hardbacks with the name C.J. Hardy.

"Political thrillers. No one is more diabolical than a politician. Trust me."

"Was that a secret? Because I'm pretty sure everyone knows that."

He laughed. "No, I guess it's not. It's why we're in this mess now. Climate change."

"Totally," I said, taking another sip of my drink to avoid giving anything away.

Cole tugged on my arm again, pulling me into a long hallway. "So this is the"—he paused for dramatic effect—"hallway, where, as you can see, I've pulled down every awkward photo of me as a teenager. I did leave this gem, though." He stopped beside a picture of what I had to assume was him as a child, dressed up in a devil costume and beaming at the camera with his mother beside him.

"I really like the 'stache."

He grinned. "I'm partial to the goatee. I drew that on with my mom's eyeliner."

"Very professional."

"I know," he said with a sigh. "I could've been a Lucifer impersonator, but I chose the life of a creative instead."

"I suppose one could argue they aren't that far off."

"Hey now."

"Do you know how many romance novels I've read that made me wonder if the author was secretly the devil? Those cliffhangers can be brutal."

Waggling his brows, he nudged me with his elbow. "That's what we're going for."

Something about being here with him, pretending everything was normal, made me feel less devastated by what had happened only an hour ago. I was still missing four pieces of my heart, but Cole's presence steadied me and distracted me from the pain I knew would come the moment I was alone. Suddenly, I found myself wishing this tour would never end.

Coming up to the first door, Cole waved a hand. "This one's my room." Instead of opening it up and taking me inside, we avoided the whole awkward *I'm in your bedroom and you've seen me naked* moment and kept walking. "This one used to be the guestroom, but I converted it into my office a few years ago after my folks died."

"So you inherited this place?"

"Yeah. My parents bought it before I was born. I've been coming here every summer since I can remember."

I could picture the little devil running on the shore, splashing in the water while his mom watched. "How nice."

"Yeah. It was. They used it less and less the older they got, so I made it into a writing retreat until recently. Once things went to hell in a handbasket, this seemed like the perfect escape. It's where all my best memories are. We even buried my dog under the big tree by the lake. Charlie was the best. So loyal, but what else can you expect from a border collie?"

Before I could react to the sad story about his dog, he opened the door at the end of the hall and flipped on the light, revealing a simple but cozy bedroom.

"This can be your room. The bathroom is shared with my office, but I never use that one. I have my own. You'll have all the privacy you need."

I couldn't help but notice that he remained in the doorway, respecting that this was now my space. It shouldn't have been a surprise. Cole had always been a gentleman with me. I mean, until he wasn't, but that was different.

"Well, I'll let you get settled. Give me a holler if you need anything. Or if you get hungry. I don't have much, but I do make a mean grilled cheese sandwich, and I'm pretty sure there are a few cans of soup floating around in the pantry."

As soon as he left, I closed the door and sat down on the bed. Taking a deep breath, I sank into the reality of my situation. He was the last person I'd be going to when I got hungry. Feeding was one problem I currently had zero solutions for. With the grid down, camming was out. And with Cole being human and not supernatural, there was no way I could risk his life. Not to mention I couldn't toy with his emotions like that. He thought he loved me. It would be cruel to play on those feelings. I was going to have to come up with another solution. And soon. Maybe I could find someone safe to snack on in a dreamwalk? I guess we'd find out.

Shoving that problem away for now, I took another calming breath. The human pheromones were strong even though this was just a guest room. Honestly, it took the sting out of not having my horsemen. If they'd rejected me, but I'd stayed? Fuck. Their pheromones would have broken me. Even now, just thinking of them sent pain slicing through my chest. How could they do that to me? Grim with his words, the rest of them with their silence.

A single tear slid down my cheek, my lip wobbling in its wake. If I gave in, I'd start really crying. Not soft, gentle whimpers either. Great racking sobs. A faint knock had me swiping the offending tear away as Cole pushed open the door. He stood there with a laundry hamper in his hands.

"Sorry. I just thought you'd like some towels and a change of clothes. They're mine, so they'll be big, but you can't stay in those forever."

So much for not crying. Tears burst free, and I let out a keening wail.

"Oh shit, I'm sorry. I was just trying to—"

"I-it's . . . n-not . . . y-you," I forced out, though I wasn't sure how coherent the words were between my sobs.

He dropped the hamper and rushed to my side, pulling me against his warm chest as I continued crying. Gentle hands rubbed my back as he made soothing noises.

"What happened, Merri? Was it that guy? The rock star?"

Again, that pang of deep loss hit me, and I nodded, inhaling a shuddering breath.

"What did he do to you?"

My lip quivered as tears continued spilling down my cheeks. I hadn't thought this far ahead, but I should have. I was so focused on getting away that I never came up with a human-safe version of events to explain my arrival. Not knowing what else to do, I went with the opening Cole provided.

"I was stupid. I caught feelings, and I thought he did too."

"Of course you did."

"Yeah, but he's a rock star. I should've known better. Instead, I was delusional."

He pulled back and stared into my eyes. "Merri, I need you to listen to me. Any man who doesn't see what a treasure you are must be blind. He lost you because he was stupid. Not because you were. He doesn't deserve you."

I sniffled and Cole reached up, brushing a tear off my face with the pad of his thumb. "Thank you for saying that."

"I mean it."

His eyes were so kind. *He* was so kind. It was such a shame Cole hid himself from society. The world needed men like him.

He tucked a stray lock of hair behind my ear and offered me a shy smile. "Why don't you get some rest? I'll be here when you need me. Just say the word."

I nodded as he stood. Before he left the room, I called, "Cole?"

"Yeah?"

"Thank you."

Expression serious, he said, "Anything for you, Merri."

CHAPTER THREE

ASHER

"So the last place we tracked the horsemen was here," I said, pointing to the red thumbtack Gavin had shoved into the map on the wall. "The ruined penthouse."

"Correct. We haven't found any trace of them since the explosion, but a car was missing from the garage. If it weren't for the CCTV in the city being down, we would have more to go on."

I spared the Duke of Tears a glance. "Careful there, Count Orlok. You're starting to sound like me."

"An insufferable know-it-all?" he mocked.

"Tech savvy."

Rosie's vampire mate let out a long-suffering sigh. He did that a lot. Especially when Remi and Kingston were around. Which was part of the reason he'd banned them from our makeshift Situation Room. If you'd asked me a few years ago, I never in a million years would have pictured this stuffed shirt British duke and I working together. But what could I say? The Bridgerton knock-off and I made a hell of a team. We were a modern-day Starsky and Hutch. Mulder and Scully. Regis and Kathy Lee. Bert and Ernie.

No, not like Bert and Ernie. This wasn't that kind of partnership.

"More like Seigfried and Roy." Pan's lazy drawl pulled me out of my jumbled inner ramblings, causing me to snap my gaze to his. He was manspread in a chair in the corner, fingers curled around a glass of brimstone whiskey as he watched us work.

"Did I say that out loud?"

Pan tapped his temple. "Group chat."

"Fuck," I muttered. I'd gotten pretty good at keeping my inner thoughts to myself, but I was stretched so thin these days, my mental barriers weren't nearly as solid. And not just mine. The amount of weird shit the rest of our group accidentally sent to each other in the last couple of weeks was the stuff of teenagers' nightmares. We're talking wet dreams. Badly delivered one-liners. Pimple popping. The group chat, as we called the telepathic connection between Rosie and all of her mates, was more beneficial than detrimental, but sometimes I really hated it. I was a very private person. A hermit, actually. That was, until Rosie found me.

But that was a different story.

"You didn't have to eavesdrop," I grumbled.

Pan waved a hand. "It was a welcome reprieve from translating."

"Translating what?" Gavin asked. "The need for that vanished with Lilith's arrival. Your position on this team is redundant. You're little more than a pretty hood ornament."

Pan narrowed his lavender gaze on the vampire. "How very dare you? Need I remind you, none of you would be here without me."

Gavin groaned. "Not this again. Every time someone puts you in your place—"

"Nobody puts baby in a corner," I murmured, sad Remi wasn't here to appreciate my epicly timed reference.

"—you burst out in a one-man show about how you saved the day."

"Well, I did."

"Debatable. We all fought. We wouldn't have been in the position to require it if you hadn't been so self-serving and devious."

Caleb cleared his throat from the rickety folding table where he was investigating his never-ending notes. "As much as I expected you all to start your incessant bickering sooner, would you mind bringing it down a notch? I'm trying to concentrate."

"Now you made Daddy mad," I muttered, the quip only serving to add to my longing for Remi and his levity.

Before we could continue, Lilith materialized in the center of the room, her power sucking all the air from my lungs for a moment. She was a force of nature on her worst day, devastating on her best.

"Arts and crafts time, is it?" she asked, clocking the red strings webbing across two of the walls.

"Cute," I said, taking in her apocalypse-chic attire.

It was the first time I'd seen her in anything other than her fuck-me femme Domme outfits. Not to say she wasn't exuding sex. Lilith would do that in a paper bag. But this was definitely not her usual corset and pencil skirt situation. It was more of a military-esque catsuit like you'd see Black Widow wear. Form-fitted, showcasing her curves, but covering every inch of her skin save her hands and a small triangle of exposed flesh at her throat. She wasn't even wearing her signature stilettos. The boots on her feet were sturdy, utilitarian, but as she strolled toward me, I noticed they still bore the red-bottomed soles she was so fond of. Designer shitkickers . . . I didn't know they made those.

"Going somewhere?" I asked, wondering at the shift.

"This old thing?" she asked, tossing me a wink.

"Strap a gun to your thigh and you could go to war."

"Darling, we *are* at war. Haven't you been paying attention?"

An icy chill ran down my spine even though her tone was playful. If Lilith was dressed to fight, that could only mean one thing. She knew she was going to have to get involved in the fray. Lilith used her power, her cunning, her massive influence to manipulate the circumstances around her to her benefit. She never actually got her hands dirty. She hadn't needed to. Nor had she been allowed to, technically speaking. At least not when it came to the horsewomen and their games. I had no doubt that in a physical altercation with the original demon, I'd lose. Badly.

"Where is your annoyingly handsome faerie pet, Auntie Lilith?" Pan asked, a smirk on his lips.

"Says the man who looks like an annoyingly handsome faerie himself," I said under my breath.

Pan glowered at me. The loss of his demon form was a sore spot for him. He didn't mind the pretty purple hair and human-colored skin, but as soon as it came up, he was bemoaning the lack of his stupid tail and horns.

"You wouldn't dare speak to me that way if I still looked like myself," he snarled.

"Easily remedied," Lilith said, snapping her fingers.

In a puff of glitter and—I shit you not—rainbows, Pandemic the Demon was back in all his seven-foot, purple glory. His horns were still gone, but the stumps remained as silent effigies to his sacrifice. And he would never let anyone forget the sacrifice.

Ever.

"Great. Now we have to deal with him like this," Gavin grumbled. "Insufferable."

Pan stretched, his tail curling upward and taking hold of the glass in his hand. "Oh, hello you. I've missed you so." His gaze flicked to Lilith. "Can I keep it for a while?"

"As long as you like, darling."

"Why is he still here? He's outlived his usefulness." Caleb's eyes narrowed as he took in the demon. He'd been front row center for Pan's possession of me; it was clear there would always be very little trust between the priest and the demon he'd tried to exorcise.

"He's the only one of us with inside knowledge of demonkind," I said.

Lilith cocked a brow and served me a cool stare.

"I'm sorry, but it's true. It's common knowledge that despite your ties to the Hellscape, you remain in this realm. Pan, on the other hand, was still in the thick of things until this last year. He has valuable insights about the way demons fight, how they think, where they might strike. And since we have no outside access to information anymore, he's the closest thing to an encyclopedia we have."

Pan blinked at me. "That might be the nicest thing you've ever said about me."

"Don't get used to it."

Brotherly love was a complicated dance, and as Remi once said, I didn't know the steps. But I did know that Pan and I understood each other in a way no one else could, thanks to our bitch of an egg donor. And that counted for something.

"To what do we owe the pleasure of this visit, Lilith?" Gavin asked, adjusting his shirt cuffs like he was preparing to go to some kind of event. It was the literal apocalypse, and the vampire was in a three-piece suit. What was wrong with him?

"In answer to your earlier question, Drystan is working on security with Nord and Lina. The Novasgardians are security experts, as is my prince. As for the four of you . . . I was hoping you'd made some headway."

"On locating the horsemen? Negative, ghostrider," I said, gesturing at the wall. "With the grid down, collecting intel is basically impossible. We have no idea what's going on up there. Unless your angel friend wants to come back and start giving us the headlines. He can be our celestial news anchor."

"Evander will love that," Lilith said with a smirk.

"Everyone has to pull their weight. Including angels," Caleb grumbled.

A strange look crossed Lilith's face as she held out her empty palm, revealing a dark curl of energy that sparkled in the light, wavering like a mist over water. Then a black envelope manifested, and her blue eyes blazed with anticipation.

"Hello, what's this?" she murmured, turning the envelope over and inspecting the wax seal.

"Wait!" I shouted as she moved to break the seal and open the letter. "It could be a trap."

"He's right. It might not be safe," Gavin warned, backing me up like a true partner should.

Lilith laughed. "Sweet poppets. Just because your network is down, doesn't mean that mine is."

"What are you talking about?" Gavin asked.

"You're just mentioning this now?" I said, almost on top of him.

She blinked at us as if we were a bunch of naughty children. "A girl must have her secrets."

"Not during the apocalypse," Caleb said, coming to stand with Gavin and me.

Pan, the clever little duck, clearly knew what was going on because he just grinned. "Devious as always, Auntie Lilith."

Pan's voice echoed in my head without warning. *"Call me a duck again and I'll have your balls for breakfast."*

I couldn't help myself; I snorted before sending back, *"You wish. Also, stay out of my head if you don't want to hear things you won't like."*

"Boys," Lilith snapped. "Care to share with the class?"

"You first," I tossed back. "You're the one with the secret messages."

She raised a brow, clearly unimpressed with my temper. "I have a network of informants spread throughout the realms."

"And you trust them."

She rolled her wrist and fingers, like a dancer doing elaborate hand choreography. "I own them. They could no more lie to me than they could ignore my summons."

A light bulb went off in my mind. "They made deals."

She winked. "Just so."

"And how is it safe for them to send you communications?" Gavin asked, still suspicious as ever.

"The bond magic protects it," she said simply.

"How?" I demanded.

She shrugged. "Not every trick should be revealed. Suffice it to say, it's a special sort of magic that has its own rules. It cannot be tracked or monitored the way elemental or even spellcraft can."

"Am I the only one annoyed that she is just now mentioning this?" I asked the others.

Caleb was less interested in the details of how it was possible and more interested in what the message contained. "None of that is relevant. What's it say?"

Gavin scoffed. "Of course it bloody is. We are in hiding. Do you want a sloppy trail to lead them straight to us? To your mate?"

Caleb's chiseled jaw worked as he ground his teeth and stared Gavin down. "Lilith has been operating in secret for millennia, Donoghue. Don't discount her power. I trust her more than anyone in this room. What does the note say, Lilith?"

She opened the envelope and quickly scanned the contents, a frown pulling at her lips the more she read. "The Princes are gathering demons to find the children of the horsewomen."

I let out a disbelieving laugh. "Oh? Is that all?"

"No, actually. Three of the four members of the Siren coven have been taken."

I gulped, not having expected her to have an actual answer. "Shit."

"Why are they coming after us . . . again?" Pan asked.

Lilith's eyes went hazy, as if she were weighing dozens of options. "I'm not sure, but it's not for anything good."

"And the witches?" Gavin prompted.

"The Siren coven match the Belladonnas in power. With that kind of magic at their disposal, there's no telling what the Princes will be able to do."

"Locator spells," Caleb murmured.

"Very likely. Especially if they're looking for us."

"Why would they willingly help the Princes?" I asked, but I knew the answer. It was always the same thing.

"What wouldn't you do to save the lives of those you love, Asher?"

Nothing.

That was the answer.

I'd throw away every scruple I had if it meant saving Rosie or Remi. Our kids. Our family.

"Okay, so they're looking for us. Why? What purpose do we serve them now? This isn't their fight, is it?"

Lilith shook her head. "One could argue that they started this apocalypse and they want to see it through."

"Great. Fucking wonderful."

"What can we do?" Caleb asked.

"Besides sit here and cower," Gavin added.

Lilith tapped the edge of the card against her lips.

"Drystan!" she called, magic pulsing in the air as she summoned him.

The man walked through the door moments later, long black hair shiny and slick as oil down his back. "You called, Lilypad?"

"Care to give us an update on our security measures? We've received word the Princes are coming for us all. Some of us are a titch antsy."

"We've established traps in various locations, portals that look like they'll bring them to us but send them elsewhere. Some to their deaths, others to cages where we can intercept and question them. It's all very elaborate and impressive, really. You're welcome."

I didn't know much about Nord and Lina's abilities, but Alek said that his mother was a reality shaper and his father had spent several centuries as something called a Guardian. I could only assume their skills in those regards were what made such things possible. Especially if they were able to do things on that scale with only three people.

"That's great, but we need to be doing more," I said. Trapping them and killing them wasn't going to work in the long run.

Crombie glared at me. "Be my guest, human."

I narrowed my eyes right back, not appreciating his tone. "Technically, I'm not a human." With a horsewoman for a mom, and a fallen angel for a dad we weren't exactly sure what I was.

"Oh? Do you suddenly have useful magical skills to offer?"

I didn't answer, because no, I didn't. Unless you counted purple laser beams that showed up whenever the fuck they wanted and a healing ability I still hadn't fully learned how to master. Power was only useful if you could control it, and I, unfortunately, could not.

Crombie smirked at my continued silence. "Hmm. What's that mortal saying? If it walks like a duck, and quacks like a duck . . ."

Pan's snicker filled my mind. *"Now who's a duck."*

"Fuck off," I shot back, before returning to my earlier point. "We can't keep sitting here waiting to be found. If enough of them find us at once, we'll be cooked. We have the numbers to start patrolling, to get ready for the big fight ahead and keep watch so we'll know if they do get close to our hideout. And it's a way to get our own info about what's happening in real time."

"You're suggesting strategic strikes?" Gavin asked.

"Yes. We find them before they find us."

Lilith nodded, a smirk playing on her lips. "Look at you, Asher. Coming into your own. Who shall lead the army of our resistance?"

"Alek and Tor, along with Jensen and Finbar. They're all fighters. The fae are commanders of the Shadow Court's army. They can work together and train our people to be real warriors. Give us a chance to survive."

"Why the twins instead of their father?" Pan asked. "Wasn't he Odin's warrior? Seems like he would be an obvious choice."

I nodded. "Yeah, but he's busy doing magic shit with Crombie. And he trained his sons, so they're basically the same thing."

"Fair enough," Pan murmured.

"Go on, then. Gather your warriors, Asher. I'll keep you abreast of any further intel I'm given." Lilith took her pet's hand and the two of them vanished from the room, leaving me looking from Caleb, to Gavin, to Pan.

"Well, clearly we're done here," Pan said before turning on his heel, tail swishing behind him. "I've got a date with a vampire queen in desperate need of a good choking."

"Pan!" I shouted behind him. "She's pregnant. You can't play the same games you . . . Goddammit, why do I even bother?" I asked the room as he stalked out, ignoring me and my warnings completely.

Seconds later, shouts rang out as our allies clearly came face-to-face with his demon form.

"God grant me the serenity," I intoned, knowing I was going to have to deal with the fallout of Pan's little stroll.

Caleb chuckled behind me. "Ah, one of my favorites."

CHAPTER FOUR

CHAOS

"Merri is gone."

Malice's words hung in the air like a fucking grenade in the seconds before hell rained down on all of us. A range of emotions flooded me all at once: fury, disbelief, shame, and above all, fear. She couldn't be gone. If she were, that meant I'd failed her in every sense of the word.

"What do you mean, she's gone?" Grim asked, voice low and measured.

"Exactly what I said. Just beyond the gate, I found evidence of heavy magic use."

"What kind of evidence?" I asked.

"Residue on the ground. It was a portal."

Jaw clenching tight enough to send a spike of pain through my temples, I took a long, slow breath. "Where to?"

"How the hell should I know?" Malice snarled.

"So there's no way to track her?" Grim asked.

Malice shook his head, a slight feathering of a muscle in his jaw the only outward sign of his agitation. Sin was unusually quiet, but I was too consumed by my growing fury to care.

"Don't just fucking shake your head. Do something useful." I stepped forward, getting in his face as I confronted my brother.

"What else would you have me do?"

My vision turned red. "The words of a true coward. Giving up at the first roadblock."

"How is this on me? I chased after her while the rest of you stood around with your cocks in your hands."

My hand wrapped around Malice's throat without my brain giving permission. "This is your property. Where are all your fucking cameras? Where is the security you promised when we came here? She's just gone. Vanished. And we have no recourse? This is all your fault. We don't even know if she took off on her own or if someone snatched her." The walls shook as my power lashed out, the thin thread of control I had on my violence stretched too far.

"You think someone took her?" Sin finally piped up. There was a soft undercurrent of hope in the question, as if it was somehow better that she was kidnapped than fleeing on her own. I guess in a fucked up way, I could understand the logic. Kidnappers meant enemies to fight. If she left on her own . . . well, that was just on us for making her think she had no other options.

"No," Malice wheezed as I tightened my grip.

"Release him, Chaos," Grim commanded. "He can't tell us anything with a crushed trachea."

With a growl, I released him, but not before shoving him away and causing him to stumble backward.

"Why don't you think foul play was involved?" I spat.

Malice rubbed his throat. "The wards were only breached once. If she were taken from within, I would've known. There would have been at least one more breach."

Sin's shoulders slumped as his hope was snuffed out.

"So what the fuck do we do now?" I demanded, fists clenching and unclenching at my sides. Lamps and other knickknacks rattled as my power filled the room. If I didn't get ahold of it soon, walls would start coming down. But since that was the least of our problems, I didn't give a fuck.

"She's not so stupid as to leave the property, surely."

As a unit, Malice, Sin, and I all swung our gazes to Grim, who stood at the base of the stairs with his arms crossed over his chest.

"You have to be joking," Sin said, incredulity bleeding from every word.

"Why would I be?"

"Because if it weren't for your callousness, she would still be here with us, safe and where she belongs," Malice said.

"My callousness? Convenient for the rest of you to forget the part you played."

"What fucking part? You were the one who yelled at her," Sin reminded him.

"And what did the three of you do? That's right. Nothing. Your silence was your complicity, so don't you dare put all of this on me. Every one of you is just as much to blame."

Sin's face cracked as Grim's shot struck true. I knew that each of us was beating ourselves up for the part we played, but I had little interest in self-flagellation. My anger was firmly pointed in a different direction.

"We have to find her. She is in danger out there, wherever she is. There is no scenario in which our Merri is safer than when she's with us. Her *mates*."

I may have spoken to the group as a whole, but my focus was on Grim, driving home the point that we belonged to her. He might not be ready to accept the truth, but I could no more deny it than I could the mantle I'd taken up. I was War, *and* I was hers. To Grim, those two truths were mutually exclusive. But they weren't. I was proof.

"How do we do that? Mal said she's lost like dust in the damn wind. You can't track a portal's destination." Sin took a seat on the second stair and rested his head in his hands, murmuring to himself, "Fuck, kitten, why didn't you give us a chance to fix this?"

"Christian." Our heads snapped to Malice, his eyes flashing with renewed purpose as he elaborated, "He can do a locator spell. We don't need to know where the portal went if we can find the object of our desire herself." He moved toward the front door, only stopping when I scoffed.

"Why the hell should we trust him? His wards are shit and frankly don't fill me with any confidence after what's gone on the last few days. Do you think he's even up to the task?" I snapped, my rage taking on a new target.

"Do you have a better idea?"

No. I didn't.

"Even if it fails, we have to try."

Grim's voice was so soft that I knew his facade was finally breaking. Death was proud. Perhaps even more proud than any of us. But when push came to shove, none of us would let that cause our fall.

"He'll need something of hers to help track her."

Sin was on his feet before Mal had finished his sentence. "I'm on it!"

He blinked out of existence and then, in the span of a breath, reappeared with Merri's hairbrush and a pair of lace panties.

Without a word, I snatched the panties from him and shoved them into my pocket. "You're not giving these to Christian."

"Dude. Finders keepers. By rights, those should be in my pocket."

"You wanna try and take them from me?" It might have been a playful challenge, if not for the tremor that shook the floor hard enough to crack the marble beneath us.

Sin held up his hands in a placating gesture. "Brush it is."

"You're going to fucking pay to repair that," Malice growled at me.

"Put it on my tab."

We filed out of the door, our current goal giving us purpose and, frankly, a sense of control I knew we desperately needed. If we had a next step, it meant there was still a chance of finding her. Of getting her back.

The part that worried me, though I refused to admit it aloud, was what happened when we ran out of steps. The horsemen with a purpose were terrifying. But when all hope was gone? When there was nothing left to lose? I didn't think anyone wanted to be around if that eventuality came to pass.

In moments that felt like years, we found ourselves standing outside the groundskeeper's modest cottage. I'd never darkened his doorstep for a multitude of reasons. Chief among them, I had no need to interact with him beyond what was unavoidable. I wasn't what you'd call a people person.

"Why isn't he answering?" I grumbled.

Malice frowned. "He was in his garden a while ago."

"Maybe he's taking a shit," Sin offered.

We all glared at him.

"What? Humans do that. It was a perfectly reasonable explanation."

"So was the shower," I muttered.

"Wrong," Sin said with a smile that made me want to punch him. "We'd hear the water running. Unless he was destroying the toilet, a shit would be mostly silent."

"Your brain is an exhausting place to exist, isn't it?" Mal asked.

"Nope. It's very exciting. Just ask—" The light dimmed in Sin's expression as he swallowed back the rest of what he was going to say.

Merri.

For a second, everything felt normal, but just that fast, we all remembered what we were doing here.

"Fuck this," Grim said, shoulder-checking the door and stepping inside.

His body stiffened not two feet past the threshold, the shift in his energy filling the small space. I knew what I'd find before Grim stepped to the side simply based on his countenance.

He confirmed it not even a second later. "He's dead."

Yes. Dead was the only explanation for the husk on the floor in the middle of the small living room. Christian's face was locked in a scream of horror, eyes bulging, cheeks sunken, mouth opened impossibly wide due to the way his lips had receded.

"What the fuck happened to him?" Mal asked, approaching the corpse slowly. "I just spoke to him less than an hour ago."

"Well, it's safe to say he didn't die of natural causes." Sin nudged what was left of Christian with the toe of his boot. "He had every ounce of his life force sucked out of him."

I moved closer and crouched down, recognition dawning as Sin's earlier words landed. "It was Merri."

"No. She wouldn't do that," Sin protested.

"Who the fuck else can suck souls out of bodies? We already established that no one else entered the wards, so that leaves you and Merri. That's it. Did *you* kill him?"

Sin deflated, sighing and dragging a hand through his hair. "Fuck. It was her, wasn't it?"

"But why would she?" Malice asked.

"Is it really so hard to believe? We've all seen what humanity is capable of when backed into a corner." Grim stood to one side of the corpse, gaze locked on Christian's eternally screaming visage.

All I could manage was a grunt of assent. Something he'd said struck a nerve within me, unearthing memories long since buried.

"You'll do it if you want to live. Or we can just end this right here and right now. It's all the same to me in the end. Your corpse is as good as any other when we release the lions."

I barely had the energy to sneer up at the Roman guard standing outside my cell, his burly arms folded over his chest.

"I will not perform for you," I snarled, the shackles binding my wrists and ankles clanking ominously as I shifted my weight. The goal was to keep my muscles loose and ready, but after weeks of travel and captivity with barely any food or water, there was only so much I could do to fend off the pain.

"You will. They always try to resist before we send them out, but trust

me, once you are in the arena, there will be no other choice. Kill or be killed."

The bastard had been right. Memories of bodies swam through my mind. Friends. Innocents. Slaughtered by my hand so I could live another day. Oaths meant very little in the end, especially when all that remained was your mortality. I broke my word time and time again, even after my escape. The survive-or-die mentality was the only thing I held on to.

And once I finally met my death, lying atop a pile of those I'd killed in battle, I found myself faced with one last choice. The ultimate test of the theory.

"Not where you expected to end up, is it, Spartan?"

Blood bubbled up my throat as I coughed to clear it. My breathing was nothing more than ragged, shallow drags as I slowly drowned. I'd killed the man who'd managed to strike a blow before I could dodge his spear, but this time I wasn't fast enough. He had run me through and dealt me a mortal blow.

"It's what I deserve," I spluttered.

The man hovering over me swam in and out of focus as he made a musing sound low in his throat. "That's a matter of perspective." More blood dribbled down my chin, and the man squatted down, his body blocking the sun. "You're running out of time."

I wanted to say something cutting, but it was getting harder to form words. I settled for a glare and hoped it conveyed all that I couldn't say. Every beat of my heart came slower and slower, but the sound of it in my ears was overwhelmingly loud. I knew the truth. With each valiant pump, my heart was speeding along my demise, my blood flowing into the earth below, filling my lungs, going everywhere but the places I needed it to.

"It's very important that you listen to me, warrior. This is your only chance for survival."

I tried hard to focus on the man's face, but it was cast in shadow. Why wouldn't he leave me alone and let me die? Again, I attempted to force the words past my lips, but all that came out was a wet grunt.

"War is in your blood. It is what you were born for. Are you ready to

lay down your sword for good, or would you like a chance to continue what you started? To right the wrongs, punish those who deserve it, topple empires, and mete out justice when needed?"

This time I blinked, and apparently that was enough to indicate that he had my attention. Meting out justice seemed pretty fucking great right now.

"You will be immortal, Spartan. But in order to gain such a gift, you will have to sacrifice. You will never again fall ill. Never again know a killing wound. But you also will never again live as a human."

Humanity had proven to be the most terrible part of the world. Why would I miss it?

"Unfortunately, this is going to require more than blinks and gurgles. I need to hear you accept. A simple yes will do."

With every passing second, my vision dimmed until all I could see was a pinpoint of light. It was now or never. I didn't have the luxury of time to weigh my decision.

"Y-y-yesss," I rasped, just as the light faded.

"He has the same residue on his fingers that I found outside the barrier," Malice said, snapping me out of my reverie.

"So he provided Merri with the portal spell," Grim concluded.

"Do you think he helped her willingly?" Sin asked, eyes trailing over Christian's corpse.

"Doubtful." My response was low and filled with frustration. "What good would killing him do if he gave it to her?"

"So she killed him, stole the spell, and fled." Malice paced in front of the body, his distress mirroring my own. "Where would she go?"

"Not to Lilith. Too obvious," Grim answered.

I glanced around at the others, waiting for someone to offer an alternative. But there wasn't one. Merri didn't have other friends or family to turn to. Which meant she was out there alone, with more enemies after her than I could count.

"We can't know where she's gone, but we have to find her. There is no other option."

"How do you suggest we do that, Chaos? Do you have a locator spell in your pocket? Any secret magic up your sleeve?"

I ignored Sin's jabs because he was right. We were woefully unprepared for something like this. Glancing from man to man, I sighed before finally admitting, "I have no idea."

CHAPTER FIVE

FAMINE

"This band of pathetic rebels still thinks they beat me."

I listened to my sister drone on and on as I checked my manicure. The long, pointed, crimson nails suited my ensemble, the color nearly matching my tresses and contrasting beautifully with my black leather catsuit. God, it was good to be back in my body.

"I can't wait until Sunday sees my face again and realizes how wrong she was."

I rolled my eyes, stifling a loud sigh. War had always been too confident, somehow able to twist her failures into successes when the tides began to turn.

I stood outside Lucifer's main hall, where he'd most recently tortured me for no damn reason. Now he was gone and my sisters were here, plotting like the mischievous hens they were.

It was nearly time for my grand re-entrance, but if I'd learned anything during these games of ours, it was that information was priceless. I'd been away for a while, and this meeting was a perfect opportunity to bring me up to speed. Especially since they might reveal something they may not want little old me to know. The second thing I'd learned is never to trust these scheming bitches farther than I could throw them. That went double for Death.

"We have to find them first. My army has been scouring London for any sign of Lilith or her lackeys. We're sure she has her claws in this." A male voice filtered to my ears, causing me to perk up. Pride. How interesting. What were the Princes and the Horsewomen doing colluding without their boss around to tell them how high to jump?

"Lilith isn't important. She can be dealt with. It's finding our children that matters. Where are we with gaining the Siren coven's cooperation? Without their locator spell, we're not going to find them. They have too many magical allies who can shield them." Death was the smartest of them. Always had been. She was honestly the only one who could give me a run for my money.

"They've been annoyingly tight-lipped," Greed answered. "We've tried our most persuasive techniques, but they aren't taking the bait. Thankfully, Sloth will be free in a few more days, and then they won't stand a chance."

A little shiver rolled down my spine at the mention of the final Prince. Sloth had a reputation, and not just for being lazy. Laziness was the mother of all invention, and Sloth had a sadistic streak that made my sisters and me look like pussycats. If he was going to deign to do something, he'd damn sure make it count. He'd strip your skin slowly and keep you awake for every long, drawn-out moment of it. When it came to torture, he wasn't just a prince; he was king, and everyone knew it.

Now was my time. A lull in conversation while the group pondered their next topic. The perfect entrance. I stepped over the threshold, the echoing of my heels on the stone floor calling their attention from one another.

"Well, well, well. Look who finally decided to show up," Death said with a smirk.

"Where have you been?" War demanded.

"Who fucking cares?" Pestilence muttered, ever the petulant bitch.

"Lovely to see you all as fucking always." I gave them a saccharine smile before settling myself at the head of the table, where Lucifer normally sat. Mmm, it felt nice to be here. Powerful. "I've been doing what none of you were capable of while you sit around staring at each other and complaining."

"And what's that?" drawled a Prince I didn't recognize, though his green eyes gave him away. Or maybe that was the aura of jealousy he couldn't quite hide.

"Envy, is it?" I asked, making a show of it as I eyed him up and down.

His lips twisted in a sneer, though he gave me a little nod.

"Well, darling, prepare to live up to your name, because I found them."

"Who?" War snapped, sitting forward with her elbows on the table. She fucking hated the idea of someone getting one over on her, which frankly just made me want to do a little dance in my chair.

I smirked, leaning back and kicking my feet up onto the table. "Take your pick. The horsemen. The vessel. All of them."

"What? And you're only just sharing this now?" Pestilence snarled. "How typical."

"I've been working my way into her heart. You would've been smart to try that tactic yourself, Mayor *Delta Dubois*. If you had, maybe you wouldn't have ended up as a victim of your two sons." I shook my head, tutting. "No one likes a politician. Why on earth you'd take the form of one is a mystery to me." Then I offered her a wicked smirk. "Oh, wait, I know. It's because you're fucking stupid."

Death snickered and rubbed her hands together in glee. "I think I missed you."

"I wish I could say the same," I crooned, tossing her a toothy smile.

The Princes were not impressed by our posturing. I could feel their impatience permeating the air. Honestly, I didn't get it. They'd already been waiting centuries to be released, what was a few extra days?

"Why are we sitting here discussing this? If you know where the vessel is, why haven't we brought her to Lucifer? Our king has given us many tasks, but this one is the most important." There Wrath went, bursting into the conversation with about as much tact as a bull in a china shop.

"Well, I don't know where she is right this second. But I do know she left them. She's more than likely on her way to find the one man who can offer her a place to stay. Sweet, sensitive Cole."

"Who the fuck is Cole?" Pestilence blurted.

I tsked softly and shook my head. "Careful, sister. Our sweet Lucifer might take offense to you speaking about him that way."

"She's with him?" Lust crooned, perking up from their slouch in the corner. I hadn't had the pleasure of meeting this particular Prince, but they were a bit of me, and like always recognized like.

"If all went according to plan, yes. Our king will be on his honeymoon until further notice."

Death eyed me suspiciously, her shrewd gaze narrowing as she asked, "How do you know all of this?"

"Because, sister, while you were here doing fuck all, I was hiding in plain sight. Helping them all with every pathetic need they had. Counseling Merri in matters of the heart. All I had to do was bide my time, manipulate her just right, and the idiot horsemen played right into my hand. They broke her. I gave her the wings she needed to fly." My lips curled up in a grin as I thought of our last moment together. "Allons-y, mademoiselle," I murmured, mostly to myself, frankly missing the French accent I'd had to keep up while wearing the handsome Christian like a cheap suit.

Emotions rippled through the room, a delightful bouquet of interest, jealousy, and my personal favorite, respect.

A slow clap started, Death giving me her signature simpering smile. "Brava, sister. You always were a clever little cookie."

Ignoring the patronizing compliment, I stood and braced both arms on the table. "While the king is away, we are in charge."

"Wait just a damn minute. Why are you in charge?" Pride

protested, eyes flashing with righteous indignation as he jumped to his feet.

"Because, you silly muppet, my sisters and I are the only reason the rest of you are here. Now sit down and be a good puppy."

My sisters snickered while I watched Pride wilt like a flower left in the hot sun. Pretty, but useless. Just like him.

"Now that we've gotten that out of the way. There is still a very real threat to the success of our endeavors. Everything hangs in the balance, and we must be prepared to topple the scale in our favor."

"So what do you propose?" Greed asked, eyebrows lifting.

"I'm so glad you asked. We do anything and everything required to ensure this apocalypse goes our way. No matter the cost."

CHAPTER SIX

LUCIFER

"How does one coax a skittish creature out of her hiding place? Why, with treats, of course." My delicious houseguest was playing the hermit role far too convincingly at present. After a day of her being locked in the guest room, I had to take matters into my own hands.

Lucifer would have stormed in there by now and confronted the situation head-on, but *Cole* was much more of a gentleman. *Cole* was safety and comfort. A man who would give her space and gently bring her out of her shell. So . . . cookies it was.

Yes, Lucifer Morningstar knows how to bake. Of course. Why do you think they call desserts sinful?

Also just, come to think of it. But I suppose that's neither here nor there.

I glanced around the counter, tallying up the ingredients listed in the classic red and white gingham-covered cookbook. "Sugar, flour, eggs . . ." I murmured, nodding along. Perfect.

After a quick flourish of my hand, everything appeared before me. Let's see *Cole* do that, hmm? You think a regular mortal like him would have a line on eggs? During the apocalypse? Pfft. Unlikely.

It didn't take long before I had the dough mixed, and now I stood there, adding the final ingredient with a smirk twisting my lips. I watched as the chocolate chips came pouring from the bag into the mixing bowl like a waterfall of pure delight. One greased cookie sheet and a preheated oven later, we were in business.

This would get her to come out. No one could resist the scent of freshly baked cookies. Not even me. Although, I wasn't really a poster child for resisting temptation. I practically invented the concept of giving into it.

"Let's see how long it takes you to follow your nose, darling," I murmured, leaning against the counter as I watched the clock. "My money's on two minutes."

It took her three. But she came. The sound of her door creaking open, followed by soft footsteps down the hall, had victory singing in my veins. I was so bloody good.

"Are you making cookies?" she asked, hovering in the hallway like she hadn't fully made up her mind whether she wanted to come and join me.

"Sure am," I said, plunking the dirty mixing bowl into the sink I'd just finished filling with sudsy water.

She took a few hesitant steps forward.

That's it. That's my brave girl. Now sit down and let me win you over with my compassionate spirit.

"They're chocolate chip. Your favorite."

Her eyes flared wide for just a moment before a faint blush filled her cheeks. Cheeks that were pale and looking a little gaunt, if I was honest. But that was to be expected for a succubus who hadn't recently fed.

"You remembered."

"Of course I remembered. I remember everything you've told me."

Her eyebrows lifted, and for a second, I thought she might ask me to prove it. But she didn't. Instead she took a seat, perched on the edge like she could still flee at any second.

"You haven't eaten much since you got here. I thought I could tempt you with something you liked."

"That's really sweet of you, Cole."

Yes. Yes, it was. Thank you for noticing.

"I . . . I'm sorry I'm not great company right now."

Hmm, what would *Cole* do right now? Go to her and sweep her into my embrace? No. Too aggressive. Ignore her and make her come to me? No. She was too fragile at the moment to play that game.

"I told you I'd take care of you. That's what I'm doing. You don't have to entertain me in order to stay here."

There we go. Security. Safety. Reassurance.

She made a soft sound, but I couldn't figure out what it was supposed to mean.

"Where did you find the ingredients?" she asked.

Shit. Was she on to me?

"Most were on hand in the pantry and deep-freeze," I answered vaguely.

"Even the eggs?"

See? Even Merri knew Cole wouldn't be able to get fucking eggs.

"Neighbor," I said with a tight grin. "They have some chickens. But if you're hoping for milk, I'm afraid I have to disappoint you. No one has a cow or goat that I'm aware of."

There. That was plausible. And by showing her there was something she'd have to go without, I made the lie more believable. The Master of Lies wasn't a title I'd gained by tripping over my words.

"I see. Well, I don't like milk anyway. I'm honored you'd use your eggs on cookies for me. Even with a chicken coop nearby, they can't be that plentiful."

"The world could end tomorrow, so we might as well have cookies today."

Merri looked at me far too shrewdly. I thought back over my words, afraid I'd slipped up, but no. I just said it *could* end, and that was true. As far as humans were concerned, everything could come to a screeching halt at any moment.

"I guess you have a point," she finally said, settling back in her chair.

"We've got another few minutes before the cookies are ready," I said, pretending to eye the timer. "How should we spend them?"

She stood without answering me and walked to the sink before grabbing a sponge and starting in on the few dirty dishes I'd placed in the soapy water.

"I'll wash, you dry?"

Her words were soft, and she wouldn't look at me, but it was something, so I joined her dish towel at the ready.

It was the closest we'd been since our initial hug, and I was not remotely immune to the proximity. Maybe it was because of what she was, or what she represented. Or maybe I'd just been waiting so long for us to be together. Whatever the reason, I, Lucifer Morningstar, was completely and utterly distracted.

"Hel-lo? Earth to Cole?"

I blinked and caught Merri waving a dirty spoon under my nose. "Sorry," I said with a nervous chuckle. "My mind wandered. What did you say?"

"I said, if I'd known you would be so easy to be around, I might've taken you up on your offer sooner. Honestly, I probably should have."

Yes, you should have. You should have come to me the moment I offered. You should have been with me all this time. Not with *them*. Did I say that out loud? No, of course not. I'm not an idiot.

"You came when you were ready. And like I said, it was an open offer. I'm just glad you took me up on it." The smile I offered her was lopsided and one hundred percent boy next door, golden retriever vibes. Maybe I was laying it on a bit thick, but I didn't want to give Merri a single reason to mistrust me.

With a ghost of a smile on her pretty pink lips, she handed me a clean measuring cup. Did I take the opportunity for our fingers to touch? Absolutely. I wanted every possible bit of contact I could get with her, and I needed her to crave me in the same way.

For my plan.

The plan to impregnate her.

No other reason.

Her eyes locked on mine at the brush of our skin, and I thought for a heartbeat I had her. But then a frown pulled her brows together as she assessed me.

"Your eyes."

"Yes. I have two of them."

"You said they were green."

My stomach clenched. Fuck.

"They're a shade of green."

"Uh . . . no. Those are definitely blue. Well, blue-gray if we're being technical."

"I mean . . . depending on the light."

She raised a brow.

"And you know, what I'm wearing."

"I guess. Mine never change. They're always this." She waved a hand at her face.

"So, beautiful?"

Those cheeks flushed again. I loved making her do that.

"Yours are too. Gorgeous really. The starburst in your iris is almost metallic. I've never seen anything like it."

I was devil enough to admit that I preened a little under her praise. It was the first compliment she'd given me. The real me. Not stupid Cole. Somewhere in my donning of his meat suit, I'd forgotten to update that detail and allowed some of the real me to shine through. I *never* forgot such details. I'm sure the more discerning of you are going to try to tell me that I subconsciously wanted her to care about and notice me. And my response to you is, butt out.

"They suit you. I don't know how you're single, Cole. I really don't. You're kind, charming, handsome."

"And I never leave the house. Pretty hard to date when you're eternally alone."

Fucking Cole again. I hated his name. I hated his face. It should be me she was calling handsome. Not this reclusive shut-in who could barely be bothered to put on a swipe of deodorant. I'd made him the man she saw before her now with the goal of seducing her, but now the thought of succeeding in this form made my skin crawl.

Oh, don't go looking at it too deeply now. It just didn't feel like a true victory if I wasn't my authentic self. That's it.

"Well, I rarely left my . . . apartment and still got my heart broken, so I guess I'm not qualified to give advice." She handed me the clean mixing bowl and pulled the drain in the sink.

A flare of protectiveness caught me by surprise. How dare they hurt her. They had her, had everything I desired, and they broke her. Those overgrown rodeo clowns.

Wait a tick. Why was I frustrated with how they treated her? Their actions put her right where I wanted her. They drove her to me. I should be thanking them.

"You deserve so much better than what you got," I said, my voice low and measured because damn if I wasn't feeling actual emotions over what happened to her.

The timer went off before she could respond, forcing us to turn our focus to the fucking cookies neither of us needed to—or frankly, wanted to—eat. At the last second, I remembered to grab a towel before pulling the hot tray out of the oven and setting it on the stove to cool.

"Those smell amazing," she said, her eyes falling closed as she inhaled. "I can't remember the last time someone made me cookies."

Using a spatula, I cut a small piece off one of them and blew on it, making a show of cooling the chunk off. "Here," I said, offering it to her. "The true test. How'd I do?"

She smiled as she took it and popped the piece into her mouth. "Still hot," she said, laughing. "But if this were a baking show, you'd get star baker for sure."

"Don't go getting too excited. I'm a one-trick baker. Cookies are all I got."

"Do you really need other tricks when you do cookies so well?"

she asked, the question sounding oddly seductive. I suppose that was just a side effect of Merri being part succubus.

She sighed and leaned her head on my shoulder as we waited for the rest of the batch to cool. "Thank you, Cole."

I stiffened at the name, but then asked, "For what?"

"For being the friend I need."

A heavy stone lodged itself in my stomach. *Friend.*

She'd gone and done it now. Here I was trying to be the man she needed, and she went and *friendzoned* me. Was there anything worse? It was a damn death knell.

Snagging the rest of the cookie she'd sampled, she walked away from me, hips moving in a mesmerizing sway that could bring anyone to their knees. I probably would have done so myself, but I was too busy fuming.

Friend. Fucking *friend.* No way was that going to stand. I was not her *friend.* I was her *destiny*. She was made for me.

"Oh, sweet darling, you have no idea what you've done, do you?" I crooned beneath my breath.

No one, and definitely not the personification of sex and sensuality, was allowed to friendzone the devil. The gloves were officially coming off. It was time to make her a deal she couldn't refuse. And who knew more about making deals than me?

CHAPTER SEVEN

SIN

"So that's it then?"

My voice rang out loudly in the fucking vacuum of the billiards room. The four of us had been sitting here for hours in silence, no closer today than we were yesterday to coming up with anything constituting a plan. Not even a hint of one.

"What do you want us to say? We have no magic that can trace her. We aren't omnipotent. Merri left us with nothing to help find her." Grim's usually fierce voice was subdued, defeated, almost.

"If you have any ideas, Sinclair, then by all means enlighten us."

My angry gaze flitted to Chaos. "There has to be some way. A hint about where she ran off to. Something from a conversation, or hell, I dunno, a text message." I pulled at my hair so hard a few strands came out.

"She took her phone with her."

My glare was now aimed at Malice. "Don't you have your fancy spyware or whatever? Can't you ping her location even with the grid being down? You're the tech wizard here. Do some wizard shit."

"With what computer, Sin? What satellite? They've crashed into the ocean. Even if everything weren't dead, the internet may as well be a thing of the past. Those avenues of investigation are closed to us."

Frustration burned through me. I hated being so helpless. Merri was out there with God knew what chasing her down, and all I could do was sit here and stew. No way. That was not acceptable. "We don't know how to find her, so we just do nothing? That's fucking ridiculous!"

"What do you suggest, Sin? That we roam the city streets and call her name like she's a lost cat?" Chaos asked.

"Maybe. It would be better than just waiting for the world to end."

No one responded, and all I could do was sigh and flop back in my chair, staring up at the ornate ceiling of the billiards room.

"If we had another witch, we could try a locator spell," I grumbled after a minute.

"And where are we going to find one of those? The supermarket? The yellow pages? We're as likely to find a needle in a haystack," Malice drawled.

"A needle would be easier."

I shot a scathing look at Grim. He wasn't helping either. "There have to be some covens around who can help."

"Where?" Malice demanded, throwing his hands up. "Anyone sane has gone to ground. We don't exactly have a well-established network to rely on for access to information. So how do we suss out someone who doesn't want to be found?"

He could have been talking about Merri or the witches.

"I don't know. I haven't had a lot of experience with people wanting to have nothing to do with me. Usually *I* have to push *them* away."

"Fucking incubi," Chaos said under his breath.

"You're just jealous."

"I'm really not."

"Stop fighting or I'll send you to your room," Grim snarled, fed up with all the bickering.

Frankly, so was I. I was crawling out of my damn skin just sitting around waiting for an answer to fall into our laps. And watching everyone around me sink further into their own personal pity parties wasn't helping.

"Great idea. That sounds a lot more productive than staying here in this room looking at you three. At least there I can take a fucking nap."

Without waiting for anyone to acknowledge me, I stormed out of the room and beelined for the stairs. Moving felt good; it gave my body something to do. A way to channel the excess energy pounding through my veins.

"Stop fighting or I'll send you to your room," I muttered, adopting a pretentious British accent for the full effect. "Fucking Grim. Who does he think he is, my dad? I'll go to my room, but not because you suggested it."

Did I sound like a petulant teenager? Sure. But it was warranted. Didn't they miss her like I did? Weren't they sick with worry over our girl being out there alone? Every second that passed was one more opportunity for Lucifer to get his hands on her.

"Fuck."

Almost of their own accord, my steps slowed as I neared Merri's door. Without talking about it, the four of us all sort of decided to leave her room alone, like it was some sort of weird fucking shrine. As if keeping the door closed would somehow make her disappearance less obvious. Well, fuck that. It wasn't working anyway.

I turned the knob and stood on the threshold, my heart aching as I breathed in her lingering scent. It was already fading, and that fucking hurt.

She'd left her bed unmade, the pillow still dented where she'd lain. Exactly as it had been when I first discovered she wasn't there.

"Dammit, kitten, why didn't you just give us time to get our heads right?" I whispered as I moved deeper into her space. "Did you leave any clues for me? Anything that might help me get to you?"

I wandered over to the bed, just wanting to be close to something that she'd touched. I ran my fingers over the cool linens, a heavy sigh escaping me as I did. Even though I knew better, that Merri wasn't magically going to waltz into the room or just appear beside me, I climbed into her bed and pulled her pillow into my arms, squeezing my eyes shut and breathing in as much of *her* as I could.

I'd hoped she might visit my dreams last night, that subconsciously she missed me enough to seek me out. Sadly, no matter how much I wanted it, she hadn't appeared. Who would feed her now? Some random prick who was none the wiser?

The only silver lining was that I was pretty sure Merri wouldn't break her No Sex With Humans rule.

Unless she gets so hungry her succubus forces the issue.

A shudder of pure revulsion rolled through me. I fucking hated the idea of Merri with anyone but us. It was wrong. Like pineapple on pizza wrong. But she had no choice in the matter after a certain point. Her hunger eventually would take over. That was where we differed.

Though I was going to have to feed eventually. And without her here, my options were bleak as hell.

I'd never invaded someone else's dreams to get the sustenance my body required. Until Merri's nocturnal visits started, I hadn't even known it was an option. I simply siphoned from the people around me. Bustling cities were always full of lust-addled creatures I could snack on without leaving a trace.

The apocalypse changed the rules of the game, though. Cities were no more. Any large groups of people would be in hiding, and I'm ninety-nine percent sure lust was the last thing on their minds. If push came to shove, I might have to test out the dream thing.

"Oh, fuck. Sinclair, you idiot." I smacked my palm against my forehead. "You're an incubus. You can dreamwalk with her. She doesn't have to run the show all the time. And the ladies appreciate a man who takes initiative. She's probably been waiting for me to shoot my shot, and I'm over here totally fumbling the ball."

Closing my eyes, I burrowed deeper underneath the covers and took a few centering breaths. Then I waited.

And kept waiting.

Okay, how did she kick-start these things? Should I think of her? Think of her naked? Think of us naked?

All that did was make me hard.

Fuck.

Come to think of it, I probably should have asked her some technical questions about how the dreamwalks worked. I'd been more wrapped up in reaping the benefits than trying to recreate them myself, and now it was too late. She was gone, and the only other succubus I knew familiar with the practice was Lilith. And it wasn't exactly like I could call her up for an assist.

Why didn't anyone send me to incubus school? There was a lot to learn, and apparently no one taught me anything useful.

I adjusted my position in the bed a few more times and tried to calm my racing thoughts. Those couldn't be very conducive to conjuring a line to my Merri. If she was out there—which she absolutely was—I'd find her. I didn't have any other option.

Somewhere between my spiraling thoughts and my getting comfortable, my breaths evened out and my mind started to drift. Instead of falling into a dream, like I assumed I usually did, this time I just sort of floated in this hazy pink cotton candy type realm. It wasn't clouds per se, but it wasn't *not* clouds. It was like a veil, maybe?

A flicker of lavender lightning flashed in the distance, calling my focus there. Someone was in the mist, I could feel it, feel them calling to me.

"Merri?" I whispered, following the pull of their consciousness.

Time and distance had no meaning here. I simply thought about going to the lavender flicker, and I was there.

Or I guess here.

In the middle of a . . . tea party?

An enormous stuffed octopus sat at the head of a long table, which was decorated with an array of cupcakes and cookies, jars of Skittles and gummy worms, and a tureen filled with what looked suspiciously like tomato soup. That was quite the combination. My stomach hurt just thinking about it. Before I stepped any closer, a small child's voice floated through the air.

"Mister Wiggles, don't ignore our new friend."

As one, the half a dozen other stuffed creatures at the table turned and locked eyes with me. But not human or animal-like eyes. That would be acceptable. These were creepy glass and, in some cases, overly large button eyes. Then Mister Wiggles turned and reached out for me with one long tentacle.

I sucked in a horrified breath and noped myself the fuck out of there.

I don't know what the hell that was, but that was no dream. That was a damn nightmare.

Shuddering as I blinked my eyes open, I took a moment to pull myself together. Kids had the most terrifying brains.

Shaking off the vestiges of my first attempt, I settled back into the bed and willed myself to the dream realm. I had proof of concept; now I just needed to perfect my technique. Maybe it wasn't as simple as diving headfirst into any random cotton candy cloud. There had to be a way to sort them since Merri so easily lasered in on us. My focus drifted from one cloud to another, attention homing in on one that felt familiar.

Music hit my ears the moment I walked into the dream, and I knew beyond the shadow of a doubt I wasn't with my girl. That didn't stop me from moving forward, though, because I knew this person. In another life, I'd been in a band with him. I hovered on the periphery, watching as my old bandmate relived his glory days. He had to be well in his eighties now, his fingers long past able to do the complicated riffs he was currently showing off. At least here, in his dreams, he could still hold on to his greatest passion.

Backing out of the dream, I returned to the pastel realm of possibilities and frowned. I'd recognized Scott's energy, the unique signature of his soul, something I hadn't understood at the time but Merri had mentioned once in passing. If I'd taken more time to focus on it, I was certain I'd have realized who he was before I entered his dream. That was good. That was progress. I just needed to be able to do that with Merri. But maybe she wasn't sleeping. I knew from my chats with the others that being awake wasn't a deal breaker. Merri was able to induce sleep in her intended target. She'd done it with Chaos and Malice multiple times. So I should be able to do it too.

Figuring out how to reach an awake consciousness when I was still working on finding a specific person was a bit like trying to run a marathon before really learning how to walk, but I didn't exactly have time to fuck around and find out.

A flicker of recognition tingled in the back of my mind as I once again searched the clouds. This time I snagged it, the thread thin but growing stronger the longer I held on, like it had simply been waiting for me to notice it this whole time. It was her. I knew it as surely as I knew I was still lying in her bed and that the thread was our bond. The more I focused, the more I could feel her soul, the connection we had linking us together.

"Merri," I breathed as my yearning for her eclipsed everything else. I wasn't here to feed. I was here to find her and get her back where she belonged.

The clouds parted, revealing Merri standing on a dock overlooking a picturesque lake. Her crimson hair cascaded freely all the way to her waist as she looked down at the water. Fuck, I missed her.

She didn't turn away from the view, but I knew she felt me join her. It was just the barest tilt of her head, but it was all the acknowledgment I needed.

"Pretty view," I murmured, wrapping my arms around her waist as I came up behind her.

"It is."

"I wasn't talking about the lake."

With a sigh, she sank into my hold, and I allowed myself a moment to breathe her in.

"I missed you, kitten. Where did you go?"

"Go? What do you mean? I've been here the whole time."

"Tell me how to find you, Merri." Desperation clawed at my chest. If I could get an answer from her, we would be able to bring her home. "You belong with us."

The gentle breeze changed to a biting wind as dark storm clouds rolled in and thunder rumbled overhead.

Merri stiffened in my arms, turning around and staring into my eyes. All I saw was hurt, betrayal, and distrust reflected in her gaze.

"You shouldn't be here."

"What are you talking about? Of course I should. I'm your mate. My place is with you."

"No. You don't get to do this. You rejected me."

"No," I insisted, the wind pushing so hard that it was a struggle to remain standing.

A tear rolled down her cheek. "Your silence was your rejection, Sin. Trust me, it spoke volumes."

"Merri, I—"

"Go."

"No, Merri. Please—"

"I said leave!" she shouted, the storm turning violent. I had to let go of her to protect my eyes. When I opened them again, I was no longer on the dock but back in her room. In her bed. Alone.

"Fuck."

I immediately returned to the dream realm in hopes of forcing my way back into her mind, but the path was shut. There was nothing from her. Not even a glimmer.

She'd locked me out of her mind as effectively as slamming a door in my face.

I'd had her right there with me, in my arms as she should be. I'd been so close to getting her back there for real. All I'd needed was for her to tell me how to find her. But now, knowing the depth of her hurt, I'd never felt so far away.

Despair twisted inside me, its hold on me so tight I could hardly breathe. I'd been so certain that seeing me coming after her would have been enough to show my true intentions. That she would have taken one look at me and forgiven me because she could feel how deeply I'd fallen for her.

But she hadn't.

This whole time, I'd been sure that Grim was the only one responsible for her heartbreak.

But he wasn't. In Merri's eyes, we were all villains.

And now I was finally faced with the reality that, no matter what, we may never win her back.

CHAPTER

EIGHT

MERRI

Aside from the flaming streaks across the sky, Cole's property was truly stunning. I could see why he came here to recharge, why his family kept the cabin and used it regularly. If I needed to get off the grid and away from people, this is where I'd come too. Each step I took on the path down to the lake centered me a little more, the crunch of twigs and leaves underfoot reminding me of simpler times. A little hint of normal during an anything but normal situation.

When I was a kid, I used to spend a lot of time in the backyard, playing pirate and hunting for buried treasure or pretending to be a brave adventurer seeking new worlds. No princess in her tower or damsel in distress for me. I'd been an only child, entertaining myself most of the time because my parents both worked full-time. I was the definition of a latchkey kid from far too young an age. It was kind of sad to look back and realize my solitary lifestyle never really ended.

Not until I was taken by the horsemen.

Nope, not going there, Merri. They never really wanted to be yours in more than duty. You were just a means to an end. A job. So there's no point in dwelling on them. They aren't worth your time, tears, or thoughts.

Easier said than done, but the hope was that if I reminded myself enough, it would become true. That's what they said, right? Tell yourself a lie often enough and it turns into your reality?

God, I was fucking lonely. With no way to reach Andi, all I had was Cole, and as sweet as he'd been so far, I was too worried about killing him to lean on him for emotional support. That kind of connection was my gateway drug. Look at how things played out with Sin. Spooning leads to forking and all that. Emotional intimacy was a dangerous thing.

I could imagine what Andi would tell me.

"The last thing you want is for a client to break down your boundaries. If you fall in love, it's all over, baby girl."

"Tell me about it," I grumbled, kicking a rock so hard it went flying down the path. I'd barely gotten a handful of days after admitting I loved the horsemen, and not even a full hour after realizing they were my soulmates, before it all came crashing down around me.

"It's their loss. Idiots. You are a fucking delight, and they should be so lucky to be loved by you."

"Yeah. You're right." My chest tightened at the thought. "Maybe I said too much too soon. I went too fast. I mean, men in general are rarely great when it comes to feelings or commitment. And these guys aren't even technically men, which makes it an even bigger hurdle."

Imaginary Andi snorted and scoffed immediately after. *"Fuck that. You were exactly who you should always be. Yourself. It's not a you problem, it's a them problem, and if you were too much or too fast for them, it's their fault. Not yours. It's like I always say, if I'm not your cup of tea, don't drink me. They drank you right down, girl. It's not on you that they couldn't handle everything you gave them."*

Andi and her words of encouragement might be in my head, but the relief I felt at hearing them was not. The fist around my heart loosened its grip, and I was able to take my first full breath all morning.

"Thanks, Andi."

I'm not sure why I was carrying on this conversation, or what it said about me, but fuck it. The world was ending. I could talk to my bestie if I wanted to.

My head swam as I walked onto the small dock, a sharp pain behind my eyes accompanying the dizziness. Dammit, I was starting to get hungry enough that we were going to have a problem. Cole had busied himself working in the mornings, dropping off meals and water at my door, and generally giving me my space, so his presence hadn't tempted me too terribly. That was going to change soon.

No wonder Sin and I had dreamwalked. My succubus wanted to feed, and he was a surefire way to sate any hunger I had.

With the internet down and the whole "killing humans" part of my history, I wasn't keen to find out what would happen when my succubus forced the issue. Fuck, I really hadn't thought this whole escape to Cole's thing through. I might have put him in far more danger than either of us realized.

Dreamwalks could be an option, but Lilith's warnings about how they impacted humans were still true, so unless there was a way to keep Cole from becoming a mindless sex slave, I wasn't convinced that was possible. And my pride would simply not allow me to run back to the horsemen. In our dreams or otherwise.

I wondered if it would be safe to visit Christian's dreams? He liked me. I could probably tell him the truth of my situation and he'd be happy to help . . .

But again, did I want another soul bound to me simply because I needed to sustain myself? Because I *was* going to need to figure out how to sustain myself.

A cold sweat broke out across my skin, leaving me clammy and vaguely nauseated. It reminded me of the way I'd felt that time Grim found me in the wine cellar. The last thing I wanted was for Cole to find me passed out on his dock. If he touched me while I was out of commission, there was no guarantee I wouldn't accidentally begin to feed.

I turned away from the lake and started the short hike back up to the house. What I needed was a nice nap, maybe a long soak in that tub I saw.

My breaths came in labored pulls as I closed the distance from the lake to the back patio. "Why are there . . . so . . . many . . . stairs?" I complained. The tragedy of it was, a few flights of stairs shouldn't have bothered me. My stamina was way more impacted than it should have been, given how regularly I'd been feeding up until now.

Panic gripped me as I placed my palm on my stomach. I was finally understanding what it meant to be Famine's daughter. My hunger was endless. No wonder fate had seen fit to give me multiple mates. There was no way one being could possibly supply everything I needed.

The house was quiet when I entered, not even the tap of a keyboard from Cole's office filtered to my ears. So far he'd spent the mornings working on his new book. I didn't have the heart to tell him the world really was ending and he'd never publish again. It seemed cruel to take that from him when he loved it so much.

"Cole?" I called tentatively, not really wanting to run into him while I was in this state. Relief washed through me when there was no answer. He must also be having a nap or something.

That potential land mine avoided for now, I turned down the hall and headed toward my room, my steps faltering when I approached the bathroom. Light spilled out from underneath the door, and the unmistakable sound of running water hit my ears.

The image of a wet and naked Cole bloomed in my mind, and I swayed as a pang of hunger slammed into me. I had to shoot my arm out to catch myself on the wall.

"Fuuuuck."

I held my breath as Cole's obvious groan of pleasure came through the door. Oh, no. He wasn't doing what I thought he was doing, was he? I knew what it sounded like when Cole jacked off. I'd listened to him do just that more than once. But a girl could hope, right?

"Merri," he moaned. "Yeah, baby, just like that."

Shit. I was so screwed. The temptation to give in and feed on the sexual energy Cole was about to put off would be my undoing. I had to get out of here before I did something really stupid and accidentally killed the only friend I had left.

"You weren't supposed to use this bathroom," I hissed as I sprinted to my room and slammed the door closed behind me.

The urge to let loose and feed on every ounce of his lust had me squirming in discomfort. I wouldn't kill him. I. Would. Not.

"I'm so close, baby. Fuck, you're so beautiful."

Oh, this was terrible. All of it. He was using me to get himself off, and unknowingly tempting a shark with a freely bleeding arm. My mouth watered, my body ached, and I had to get the fuck out of here before I did something I couldn't take back. A single wall between us was not nearly enough to ensure his protection. At least, I wasn't sure one way or the other, which meant I couldn't risk it.

As I flung open the door and raced down the hall and back out of the house, I gave in to the frustration throbbing in my chest along with each beat of my heart.

"Damn you, Grim. Why did you have to go and fuck everything up? If you hadn't gone and broken my heart, we could all be happily fucking our way through this stupid apocalypse. But noooo."

I couldn't feel any lust from Cole from this distance, but the damage had been done. I was a ticking time bomb, and if I didn't figure something out soon, I would be burying Cole right next to his family dog.

CHAPTER NINE

LUCIFER

Merri was in quite a state this morning when she woke. I could feel the hunger radiating from her in waves. Sweet creature she was, she wouldn't give in and take from Cole without permission. Or perhaps at all. But that just wouldn't do. I needed her strong and willing, able to accept me into her body so she could carry my child. None of that would happen if she starved herself.

Which meant it was time to take matters into my own hands. Literally.

I timed my plan perfectly, starting the shower the second I spotted Merri turning up the path to head back to the house.

"Places everyone," I murmured, stepping under the steamy spray.

I glanced down at my already swelling cock and smirked. "Well done, you. Rising to attention like a good soldier."

Listening intently so I could time everything just right, I waited for the sound of her footsteps coming down the hall. Angelic hearing was certainly a gift I'd made good use of every day of my long existence. Today was no exception.

Reaching down, I grabbed my throbbing dick and gave him a nice hard squeeze. The pulse of pleasure that shot through me was far more intense than I anticipated, telling me that this show of mine wasn't all an act. I wanted her. But that wasn't a surprise.

Outside the bathroom, Merri's steps faltered, and I heard the impact as she hit the wall, followed by a tight gasp.

I've got her right where I want her.

A long, slow stroke from base to crown and back again had me grunting and throwing my head back before I released a loudly groaned, "Fuuuuck."

She stayed put, and dare I say . . . whimpered faintly?

I could picture her, giving in to her need for me to sate her. She'd open the door, strip out of her clothes, and join me under the hot water.

As I fantasized, my strokes grew more fevered. Now I was chasing release as much as I was baiting her. Who said work wasn't fun?

Time to break out the big guns, as they say.

"Merri. Yeah, baby, just like that."

She sucked in a breath.

Bullseye.

But then she said, "You weren't supposed to use this bathroom."

She sprinted away, the slam of her door hard enough I imagined the walls rattled from the force.

Ooh . . . Looks like I touched a nerve.

Knowing that I was getting to her only fueled my desire for this game of cat and mouse we were playing. She wanted me. Craved me.

Me.

Well, technically, Cole. But only because she didn't know better. Yet.

It was cute that she assumed going to her room would keep this moment from affecting her. There was a door connecting the bathroom to her boudoir. And I wasn't quiet when I came.

Honestly, I didn't understand men who wouldn't make noise.

How else was your partner supposed to know you were enjoying yourself?

Cock pulsing, I shot one hand out and braced myself on the tile wall. I hadn't planned to actually get myself off, but I was all in now. Why not enjoy the fireworks?

"I'm so close, baby. Fuck, you're so beautiful."

Just when it seemed victory was in reach, I caught the fumbling at her door and the rush of her feet back down the hall.

"Bollocks," I snapped, my true voice slipping out due to my frustration.

I'd been *right there*. Not just with tipping Merri over the edge, but myself as well. The loss of my audience was, well . . . deflating. In more ways than one.

"It is never advisable to leave the devil with blue balls, little minx. You'll just have to take care of that later."

Shutting off the water, I stepped out of the shower and toweled off. I needed to lean into the forced proximity of our situation now that I'd gotten her so worked up she'd had to run. We were never going to conceive my antichrist without her letting me—and my cock—in. She was too in her head, too worried about feeding off Cole or about her stupid horsemen, to give herself what she needed. What she truly wanted.

Me.

Wrapping a towel around my waist, I wiped my hand over the fogged-up mirror. Cole's face stared back at me, all but the eyes. I had to keep my beautiful irises. They were too stunning to hide. A sneer curled my lip as I looked at the man these circumstances forced me to pretend to be.

"Prepare for your final act, Cole. If this face isn't enough to get the job done, then perhaps it's time to retire it." As I spoke, my reflection rippled in the mirror until I was looking at my true self, the one I'd shown her in her dreams. "And I just so happen to know she's a real fan of this one."

It had been nearly an hour before she returned. I'd settled myself in the living room with a surprisingly well-written thriller to pass the time. It was adorable that she thought she'd be able to sneak behind me on her way to her bedroom, and I gave her enough grace to let her skulk by before calling over my shoulder, "Everything okay, Merri?"

Look at me, sincerity dripping from every word.

She froze, indecision radiating out of her.

I turned so I could see her fully, not giving her the option of ignoring me or the question.

Clearing her throat, she ran a hand through her long hair. "Um, yeah. Fine. Just wanted to stretch my legs."

"Are you hungry? I can give you something to eat." Standing, I began closing the distance between us with slow, purposeful steps. She, in turn, backed away, eyes darting toward the hall.

"I . . . I'm good. I'll take care of myself."

My expression was filled with concern. Sweet Cole, heart on his sleeve, desperate to help her. And truthfully, she looked miserable. The poor thing was starving. Her eyes had purplish bruises forming beneath them, cheeks pale, skin lacking its usual luminous glow. She *needed* me.

"Merri, you and I both know that's a lie."

She visibly startled. "What?"

"You can't give yourself what you need. Only I can do that."

Her mouth dropped open. "H-how—"

I was close enough now that I was able to reach out and place my finger against her lips. "I know what you are."

"What are you talking about?"

"You're a succubus."

Her eyes were so wide I could see the white on the top and bottom. "How did you . . ."

"You know I'm good with research. I looked you up when you first started your page."

"There's no record of me. Especially not as a succubus. The humans don't know we exist."

I grinned. "Meredith Devereaux. Foster parents abandoned you after your boyfriend died from an aortic aneurysm when you were in high school. You disappeared after that, but it wasn't hard to figure out the rest. Especially after I learned to identify what succubi deaths look like. The dark web isn't all insidious and nefarious."

She shook her head, at a total loss. So I pressed my advantage.

"Let me help you, Merri. I want to. I told you I'd take care of you."

"No. You don't know what you're suggesting."

"Yes, I do." Sliding my fingers into the hair at the base of her skull, I drew her into me. "I know what you need. I know how to give it to you. You won't hurt me."

"I will, Cole. I will drain you dry."

"I'm not Jimmy. I'm not a human."

"You aren't?" she asked, cocking her head. I could practically see the wheels turning in her mind as she tried unsuccessfully to figure out what I was.

"I'm Nephilim," I breathed, my lips hovering just over hers. "Part angel."

Technically *all* angel, but she wasn't ready for all my secrets just yet.

"I'm not agoraphobic. I'm in hiding, same as you. They don't want me to exist. If they could, they'd trap me in a cage for eternity." Also not a lie.

"An angel?" she whispered.

Taking her hand, I pressed it against my chest. "In the flesh."

"So I won't be able to . . ."

"Suck my soul from my body and kill me in the throes of passion?"

Her gaze left mine and dropped to the floor. "Something like that."

"You won't. It would take a lot more than a succubus feeding to kill me."

She huffed out a disbelieving laugh. "I've heard that line before."

Taking her face in my hands, I lifted until her eyes were locked on mine. "Merri, don't you get it? We were supposed to find each other. How else do you explain me stumbling onto your page all those months ago and how you and I ended up here in the middle of the apocalypse?"

She jolted a little at the word.

"Yes, I know about that too." I snickered. "My kind are sort of hardwired to know the signs."

Her breath was sweet where it fanned over my lips.

Pressing my forehead against hers, I delivered what I hoped would be the killing blow in terms of her resistance. "I feel like I've been waiting my whole life to be right here, in this moment with you. You're the one I've been looking for."

Ooooh, I was good. Knee-buckling, panty-incinerating, swoon-inducing. She wasn't going to be able to deny it now. Not when I said all that to her. Not when I knew it was what she most craved.

A voice in my mind whispered, *and not when it's the truth.*

I shot that down instantly. She was my purpose, yes, but that purpose was to claim the world as my domain and get out of the depths of hell.

Time to bring it home.

I leaned in and brought my lips a breath away from hers. One kiss and she'd be mine; I just knew it.

But she pulled back, denying me.

"I'm . . . I'm sorry, Cole. I'm not ready for something so intimate."

A snarl formed in the back of my throat, but before it could take shape, she looked me dead in the eye and added, "But you're right. I do need to feed."

"So . . . Pretty Woman rules? No kissing on the mouth?"

She smirked. "Yes. Nothing on the mouth. But trust me, there are other ways to get what I need. You'll enjoy them all."

CHAPTER TEN

CALEB

"You're holding out on us. You seraphim are notorious liars via omission. Worse than demonkind ever has been." Pan's bitterness couldn't have been more clear if he'd spat poison at Evander.

"That's where you're wrong. Respecting the concept of free will without interference is *not* omission. Demons are too selfish to appreciate the nuanced nature of the notion." The angel's cool dismissal was completely on par with his unbothered persona. It was only our second time meeting him, but he'd certainly made an impression on this group of hotheads. The less emotional his reactions, the more it seemed to fire up the shifters, demons, Vikings, fae, and, well, frankly, pretty much everyone in the room.

"How can you be so nonchalant about this?" Asher asked. "The rest of us are chalant as fuck over here. Because, you know, the world is ending and you aren't helping."

Evander stood, eyes blazing bright with the threat of a low-boiling temper. It would seem the angel had a button to push after all.

I slammed my palms on the table between us. "That's quite enough of that from you three."

A few guilty glances cut my way, along with a few appraising ones.

"Are we boring you, padre?" Asher asked.

"We've been in here for over a fecking hour and still haven't gotten to the main point of our meeting."

"This is why I suggested an agenda," Moira stage whispered to Kiki. "It's the only way to keep these guys on task."

"I don't know if that even works anymore. There are a lot of cocks in the hen house these days."

"Too many, if you ask me. Lilith was right; we need more feminine energy in the Hades Society."

Lilith smirked but didn't say anything in response to the witch.

"As Miss Belladonna has so kindly pointed out, there is an agenda we need to be following. Where are we with the—"

"Look at him over there with his slutty little glasses on like he needs them," Kingston muttered under his breath to Alek.

"What was that, Kingston?" I snapped, taking off the glasses I'd forgotten I was wearing and folding them up before slipping them in my pocket.

"We all know you have perfect eyesight. You were only wearing those because Sunday likes them. No need to rub it in."

"Well, we know what he was doing prior to the meeting," Kiki said with a snort. "Get it, preacher man."

My neck prickled with embarrassment, but only because I'd been so caught up in my time with Sunday I'd forgotten to remove them. I'd wear anything she wanted if it made her come the way she had earlier.

"I assure you, I got it. And I'll be getting it again as soon as we're done here."

"Showoff," Kingston grumbled.

"I don't know why you're complaining. You snuck your way into our date night again just the other day," Thorne pointed out.

"And mine," Alek said with a pointed lift of his brow.

Kingston smirked. "My girl's pregnant with my pup. I can't help it if she needs me."

Thorne, Alek, and I all rolled our eyes. The alpha had been absolutely insufferable now that Sunday was starting to show.

"Anyway," he continued, holding out his fist, "wankmates for life, right, buddy?"

"Fuck off," Thorne growled. "I never should have agreed with you. You've been lording it over me ever since."

I sighed. "Kingston, before you interrupted me, I was going to ask for an update on the demon raids. Do you think you could put your cock away and stop measuring it against Thorne's for a moment and bring us up to speed?"

"Wasn't he measuring it against yours?" Crombie asked, gesturing to me. When we all turned to look at the fae, he shrugged. "I'm just trying to follow along with this little soap opera you insist on playing out in front of us. But by all means, please do go on wasting our valuable time. It's not like the world is ending or anything."

Lilith placed her palm on his knee, her lips quirking with laughter.

"It's no contest," I said, holding his gaze for several heartbeats before looking back to Kingston. "Report."

Kingston snapped to his feet and saluted me. "Sir, yes, sir."

Alek grabbed him by the bottom of his flannel shirt and tugged him back down. "Sit the fuck down." As Kingston settled in his chair, Alek stood to his full, considerable height.

"Why do you get to st—"

Thorne covered the wolf's mouth, but he continued on, mumbling behind the vampire's hand.

"We should always use that function," Moira said. "Sunday told me I can't use my mute button on him anymore. It's a real shame. It would make these meetings so much faster."

"Y'all are the ones who picked him to be here. His rambling is as much your fault as his," Hades chimed in.

"For the love of God," I sighed, pinching the bridge of my nose. "Alek, can you please just give us the fecking update so this misery will come to an end?"

"Of course. The demon riffraff seem to be growing in number. During our last patrol, two of our best fighters were nearly caught and taken prisoner, but luckily Kai was able to dispatch them with his dragon fire."

The dragon in question offered a curt nod. "Aye, they got the drop on Devon and Lincoln. The two of them are fine, their injuries only minor and their fae blood accelerating their healing."

"What kind of demons were they?" Pan asked, sitting forward and bracing his elbows on his knees.

"Lust demons," Kai and Alek answered together. The two looked at each other, Kai gesturing for Alek to continue. "Sorry. You go ahead."

Lilith made a soft musing sound. "You're lucky you got them free. Lust demons are notoriously tricky. Most willingly allow themselves to be ensnared."

"It was a challenge. The two of them are the most vulnerable sort—unmated males. Young and full of piss and vinegar."

Lilith and Pan nodded, as if that was not at all surprising.

"Would you say the number of demon encounters has gone up?" I asked.

Alek nodded. "Exponentially. I think it's safe to assume that more are coming through the hellmouth every day."

"It will be even worse in a few days," Hades said.

Evander caught his gaze and gave a sharp nod. "Sloth is coming. He and his ilk are rumored to be the worst of the lot."

"How so?" Asher asked. "Shouldn't they be too lazy to bother with us?"

"You would think so, but Sloth is a sadist. Cruel for cruelty's sake. He was Lucifer's prime torturer, skilled in extracting information as quickly and painfully as possible. Where most would assume he's lazy, he's actually quite adept at being efficient. He's trained his Knights to be the same."

"Then his name is a misnomer, don't you think?" Kingston asked.

Alek, Thorne, and I all shot him a disbelieving look, but he simply shrugged.

"What? I've been using the Word a Day calendar Glinda got me for solstice last year. Thanks, witchy-poo." He winked at Moira.

"More misleading than inaccurate," Lilith mused. "Laziness can be an excellent motivator."

"He'll take his time flaying the skin off your bones after you've given him what he wants. His methods will be efficient to accomplish his goal, and then long and drawn out afterward until you're dead. It's not that he prefers to do nothing, it's that he prefers to maximize the amount of time he spends doing what he loves. That's why he's called Sloth."

A chill ran down my spine. For a vampire, that would mean an eternity of torture.

"How do you know all of this?" Thorne asked, and I could see my own fears echoed in his eyes.

"Because I'm one of the angels who hunted down the Princes and sealed them in their prisons."

"Geeze, Lil. You didn't mention we were in the company of celestial royalty," Kingston said. His voice was light, but the awe on his face wasn't feigned.

"I told you he was important."

My brows lifted when Lilith didn't correct Kingston for using a nickname. Normally, the succubus was quick to nip that in the bud.

"Yes, yes. Very impressive. But how many people did he take out with a single plague?" Pan asked, fussing with the cuff of his shirt. Apparently a line had been drawn in the sand between those two.

"Do we have the manpower to fight them?" I asked, bypassing Pan's comment.

"For now," Alek said, but his expression was grave. "They are powerful, but their armies are small enough to handle at the moment. If they grow, which we can only assume they will, we might be telling another story."

A bleak silence filled the room.

"Great. I love an underdog story," Asher muttered.

Since there was nothing more we could discuss on that front for the time being, I decided to switch to the next topic. "Where are we with locating Gabriel or the horsemen?"

"We're exactly where we were the last time you asked, Caleb." Lilith's eyes narrowed as she focused on me.

"So nowhere."

"Not exactly nowhere," Evander offered. "Gabriel is fully hidden with no trace."

"How is that *not* nowhere?"

"As one of his brothers, I should be able to find at least a trace of him. A whisper of his grace. But there is nothing. Not a hint. That means he's being hidden, whether by choice or by force."

"Who's powerful enough to manage that?" Kai asked.

"There's only one being powerful enough to hide an angel's grace from his own kind."

"Lucifer," I whispered. I could've kicked myself for not putting it together sooner, but I had a lot on at the moment. Pregnant mate, looming demon attacks, apocalypse.

"Correct," Evander said.

"And what of the horsemen?"

Hades cleared his throat before flicking his gaze to Kiki, who stood in the portal to the underworld.

"Oh, me? Thank God. I've been waiting for my turn for-fucking-ever," the ghostly woman said, tossing her long hair over one shoulder. "So, my initial investigation turned up pretty much nothing, unless you count the ghosts telling me they haven't seen or heard a peep from Mr. Death in weeks. That seems important, right?" She cocked her head, sending her hair flying in the other direction. "I'm pretty sure that's weird."

"It's strange," Hades agreed. "Death is always looming. He can't help himself."

"It isn't strange. Not if he and his brothers are trying to keep Merri shielded from sight." Crombie inspected his nails as though he were fully nonplussed.

Lilith nodded her agreement. "It's very likely they are warded in a similar manner to Gabriel."

"So we're fucked then, is that what you're saying? Gabriel's untraceable, and the horsemen might as well be ghosts. Oh wait, ghosts would be easier because at least then we have a chance at contacting them," Asher spat, sitting back and crossing his arms over his chest.

"Perhaps not," Lilith said, voice musing. "I have a way to pass on a message to the horsemen *if* we can determine their location." As she spoke, she turned her gaze to Moira. It was too pointed a look not to relay some sort of silent message.

"And how are we supposed to do that?" Kingston blurted.

"I can get my coven behind doing a spell. Remember how we found Alek? It's more complex than a basic locator spell, but powerful enough to find him in another realm." Moira's eyes were bright with excitement at the possible solution.

"Why the bloody hell didn't we try that from the start?" Thorne asked.

"Because you don't break out the big guns when something less dramatic will do. It calls way too much attention, for starters, and could be an unnecessary power drain. There's nothing worse than blowing your load early and then being at a disadvantage when said power could have been the difference between a W or the Big L."

"Premature Bazooka," Kingston said with a knowing nod.

"Precisely." Lilith smirked. "We didn't realize the extent of the protections keeping them from us. Gabriel pops in and out all the time, and he's not exactly a trained dog who runs to us on recall. The horsemen . . . They're serving a purpose. Until now, searching for them would have put that mission at risk. Things are different now."

"Tell us, Ms. Belladonna, what do you need to perform this spell?" I asked.

"Well, it's not as simple as just having something that belongs to one of them. Yes, I need that, but this magic requires a celestial event. The next one is in three nights."

"Okay, oracle of the stars, how do you know that?" Asher asked, sarcasm thick in his tone.

Moria shot him a deadly look. "Have you been paying attention? Every time a Prince is released, there's a shift in the universe. They've been coming once every week like clockwork. Like the angel just said, the final one is due."

Evander nodded. "The witch is correct."

"Thanks, angel daddy."

He gave her a strange look, but remained silent. If I had to hazard a guess, I don't think he fully understood the nickname. He still had much to learn about the ways of mortals.

"So you need something of Gabriel's and something of the horsemen's?" Kingston asked.

"Yep. Since the guys are all together, one of their possessions should do the trick if their magic is trackable. I can't guarantee anything, but this is a spell so powerful we were able to pull Tor out of Novasgard."

"How the fuck are we supposed to get our hands on a possession from any of them? It's not like they leave items lying around." Pan's jaw ticked as he waited for an answer.

Between one breath and the next, Evander disappeared from his chair and returned, this time standing before Moira with a silver-tipped feather in his outstretched hand. "Will this do?"

Moira blinked as she accepted the offering. "Is this one of Gabriel's feathers?"

Evander dipped his chin in the barest hint of a nod.

"But he doesn't have wings. Lucifer took them decades ago."

"Every angel submits one feather to the registry upon induction into the ranks."

“Like some kind of celestial AFIS situation?” Asher asked.

Evander narrowed his eyes in confusion and continued with his explanation. “Strictly speaking, I’m not supposed to remove this from the files, but the greater good is more important.”

“Ask for forgiveness instead of permission,” Kai murmured.

“Exactly.”

“Well, that solves the Gabriel issue. What about the horsemen?” Alek asked.

Hades cleared his throat. “I might be able to assist with that.”

I shot a glance at the god of the underworld. “How’s that?”

“I need to take a little trip on the River Styx. Give me a day, and I’ll have what you require.”

“Lovely. Are we done here?” Crombie asked, glancing around the room. When no one immediately spoke, he slapped his hands on his thighs and stood. “Perfect. Come on, Lilypad. We have a date.”

CHAPTER ELEVEN

MERRI

I had to hand it to Cole; he was a gentleman. It was obvious in more ways than one that he was eager to help me with my little hunger problem as soon as I gave him the green light, but when I pressed pause and told him I needed some time to get things set up, he bowed out with grace.

His exact words were, "Just call for me when you're ready. I'll be there."

I took a final glance around the room, appreciating my setup. I'd found a folding privacy screen and some extra lamps and worked some magic. Now he'd be able to see my silhouette through the white rice paper framed by the wood, and I would hear everything he did as clearly as if we were right next to one another. It was basically an in-person version of our private chats. All the benefits of sex without any of the touching. A perfect balance, if you will.

As much as I liked Cole, I was not remotely ready to jump into bed with him. This staging of mine would allow us to keep the focus on feeding without it having to become physical. Which was an important distinction for me, because my heart might be broken, but it still belonged to the horsemen. Love wasn't something you could just turn off like a light. It burned inside you like an ember, weakening over time, but lasting long after the flame was doused.

I opened my door and called out, "Cole, I'm ready for you. Come in and take a seat."

Cole was there only moments later, desire in his eyes, and anticipation rolling off him in waves. "I was worried you'd changed your mind there for a sec."

Shaking my head, I reached out and took him by the hand, gently leading him to the chair I'd positioned in front of the screen. "Sit there."

There was no missing the flicker of disappointment as it crossed his face. "We're going to be on separate sides?"

I gave his hand a squeeze. "We are."

"I was really hoping I'd finally get to touch you."

We were next to the chair now, so I placed my hands on his shoulders and gently applied pressure until he sat down. "Don't worry," I said, chucking him under the chin. "You're going to feel right at home in no time. I need to ease into this, and some separation is the most familiar thing for us."

"I understand, but I'm not going to lie to you, I've been aching to touch you from the moment you walked through the door."

My heart skipped a beat at the urgency in his voice. He didn't understand the complexities of my heartbreak. I might appear single to the rest of the world, but I had four mates out there. Their rejection didn't make it any less true.

"Just relax and enjoy what I have planned." I winked and moved to walk around the partition, tossing a sensual stare over one shoulder. "Do me a favor?"

"Anything," he said, his voice already tight with arousal.

"Don't hold back. I want to hear you."

"Y-yes ma'am," he rasped.

"Good boy," I said with a wink before disappearing behind the screen. I'd set it up in front of a dresser that housed a single lamp and a vintage record player. With the press of a button, the turntable began spinning, and the sultry, bluesy number I'd selected filled the room. The whole vibe I was going for was something between burlesque show and voyeur room.

Before Lilith had relegated me to isolation, she'd trained me to dance at *Iniquity*, hoping I could control myself enough to feed on clients she specifically sent me. That hadn't panned out, but I still learned a thing or two that I'd used in my camming sessions on occasion.

After a little testing, I'd been able to figure out the best place for me to stand and had marked it with a small X in lipstick on the floor. I didn't think Cole was using it, and I doubted his mother would mind that I'd borrowed it.

"Comfy?" I asked, getting into position.

"Something like that."

"What would make you more comfortable?" I began slowly swaying my hips as I ran my hands along my body, grabbing the hem of my shirt and carefully lifting it.

"Taking off these pants."

"Then you should do that. The whole point of this session is pleasure. I want you to enjoy yourself."

The sound of his belt, followed by a zipper, had me grinning. Then he grunted in relief as his jeans hit the floor.

"Better?"

"Fuck, yes. I'm so hard."

"Perfect."

I peeled my shirt up over my head, making a point to stand sideways so he could see the curves of my body.

"Merri, you're so beautiful."

Humming in response, I moved my body in a mesmerizing wave before reaching behind my back and unhooking my bra.

I caught his hissed intake of breath as my breasts fell free from the lace and underwire. Making a show of it, I held the bra by one strap and dropped it on the floor in front of me.

"What color was it?" he asked.

A soft giggle escaped me. “Red lace with no lining.”

“So your nipples would have been visible if we didn’t have this screen between us?”

“Yes.”

He groaned. “You’re torturing me.”

“You’re loving it.”

“Fuck me, I am.”

I chuckled again and turned so I was facing the bed. This time I slowly spread my legs and bent over, making a point to run my hands up the insides of my thighs.

Cole whimpered.

In one smooth motion, I flipped my hair as I stood upright and hooked my fingers in the band of my panties, then I shimmied out of them.

“Are you wet, Merri?”

I didn’t need to touch myself to know the answer. “Yes.”

“Fuck, I want to smell you. Taste you.”

His desire permeated the room, but I couldn’t get past the mental walls he had up enough to feed deeply. Why was he blocking me out?

Tossing the scrap of lace over the screen, I waited for his reaction.

The hitched breath that came from him was so satisfying my nipples tightened in response and lust sparked in my lower belly.

“Tell me what you’re doing.” I had a pretty good idea, but I wanted to hear him say it.

There was a rustle of fabric and then a deep inhale followed by a rumbling moan. “Committing your scent to memory.”

“Does that mean you like it?”

“Fuck, baby, you smell incredible. I bet you taste even better.”

I bit my lower lip, enjoying myself more than I thought I would.

“I’m not giving these back, by the way.”

“You should use them.”

“Use them?”

“To get yourself off,” I clarified. “Wrap them around your cock and get as close to my pussy as you can.”

"Fuck."

The song changed to another equally sensual rhythm, and I cupped my breasts, making certain he could see from the angle I chose.

"God, I wish these were your hands," I said, rolling my nipples and undulating my hips.

"They can be. Just say the word."

The need in his voice was delicious, but I still couldn't get a good enough hold on him to feed. I had to find a way to break through his walls. If I'd learned anything from Malice, it was that the more you could make someone focus on the moment, the less likely they'd be able to maintain their mental barrier.

"Relax and make yourself feel good, Cole. That's the best way to take care of me."

He groaned.

"And you want to take care of me, don't you? You like knowing you're giving me everything I need."

"Yes. I want you to want me. I want to provide you with everything."

His breaths were coming faster now, and that hold he had over his walls was weakening.

"You're so good to me. I should have seen it before. You make me feel so safe, like I can really just let go." I moaned for good measure as the sound of his palm shuttling along his cock became my only focus.

"Yes, fuck, Merri. I'm so close."

The barrier was crumbling, but it needed a little nudge. Sending out a tendril of my power, I pressed against the bubble of his consciousness the way Malice had taught me. It popped easily, and a wave of his sexual energy flooded my senses.

Trap sprung, I latched on to his mounting pleasure, but something didn't feel right. This energy I'd grabbed was familiar, but it wasn't because of my sessions with Cole. It was from my dreams.

Of Luc.

Oh. Shit.

Ice filled my veins as the reality of my situation came crashing down around me, and I tore all the threads connecting us out of his mind, taking the lust with me and ruining both my feeding and his orgasm.

Grabbing the robe I'd hung on a hook behind me, I covered myself and stepped around the partition to face the impostor that was most definitely not Cole.

As I watched, his expression changed from frustrated to concerned, erection angry and swollen in his hand.

"Is something wrong?"

I narrowed my eyes. "You know exactly what's wrong. Put your dick away . . . Luc."

A terrifying smile stretched across his face, and with a snap of his finger, Cole turned into the golden-haired smoke show from my dreams.

"Well, I guess the devil's out of the bag."

CHAPTER TWELVE

LUCIFER

I always knew it was only a matter of time before sweet Merri found me out. What I hadn't counted on was being on the precipice of greatness, shall we say, when it happened. I was all for delayed gratification, a little edging, a moment of denial before the reward, but not when I was the receiving party.

Merri stared at me with fury blazing in her bright blue eyes, hatred clear on her face. That was fine. I could handle hatred. It was only a breath away from love, after all. Two sides of the same coin. Not that I required Merri's love, but a little passion would make the fathering of my antichrist far more pleasant for all parties involved.

"What did you do to Cole?" she asked, voice shaking.

I snorted a laugh. "I killed him, of course. Buried him under that tree right next to the family mutt."

"How did you know about him?"

"Know about him? Darling, who did you think you've been talking to this whole time? I found him lurking online, talking to dozens of cam-girls just like you. He wasn't a good man like you thought. Cole was a pathetic creature, cyberstalking five other women so badly they banned him from their sites. One even had a restraining order. You should really be thanking me. I did you a favor when I intercepted him before your first session really got going."

The little furrow between her brows deepened. I could tell my words were getting to her, but the mistrust in her eyes was only growing stronger. She didn't know what to believe. Who can blame her, I guess. I did have a bit of a reputation when it came to my handling of the truth.

"What reason do I have to lie to you now? You've found me out. All my cards are on the table. It doesn't serve me or my needs to alienate you further. You're far too precious to me."

"Because all you do is lie. Everything you've done and said has been based on a lie. It's who you are. Literally."

She tightened the robe's sash around her waist and stormed toward the bedroom door, but now that I didn't need to hide my true self, I slammed the wood shut with a flare of my power.

"Ah, ah, ah, no escaping right now. Not until we talk about the predicament you're in."

She snorted, but there was no humor in her expression. No, she was all fire and brimstone, and I swear my dick gave a happy twitch. We did so love to play with fire.

"I can't believe how stupid I was. I should have known Cole was too good to be true."

"Oh, don't be so hard on yourself, love. You found yourself in a pickle and needed an escape. I knew it was only a matter of time before those four buffoons mucked things up. So I played the long game. If Luc couldn't win you over in your dreams, Cole would be there waiting for you with open arms."

"You couldn't seduce me without pretending to be someone else. That must've really hit you where you live."

"Nah. The first time I seduced a woman, I was a snake. It's pretty much my MO at this point."

Standing, I adjusted myself in my tailored trousers, thankful I could stop wearing Cole's insultingly low-effort sweats and T-shirt combinations. Honestly, would it have killed the man to up his wardrobe game?

"What are you doing?" Merri asked, backing away as I approached.

"You don't need to fear me, my sweet. Give me what I want, and I'll make you a very happy woman. You have my word."

"No," she spat.

A sneer twisted my lips. "I could just take what I want, you know. I don't need your consent."

Something flickered across Merri's face too fast for me to name it. She straightened her spine, determination radiating from her stance. "But you won't. Because you might not need my consent, but you want it."

I raised a brow. "An expert on me now, are you?"

"I've gotten pretty good at reading people. And this whole time, in every iteration you've taken, you've always tried to win me over. You want me to choose you."

I covered the distance between us in three long strides, moving forward until she was pressed against the door and our faces were inches apart. Anger and frustration burned inside me because she was right. Slamming one palm on the wood next to her pretty face, I released a snarl.

"And why shouldn't you? I'm God's favorite. The most beautiful angel ever created. Powerful beyond measure. A king in my own right. You would be so lucky to be my consort."

"Would I?" she whispered through gritted teeth. "Or would I be your whore?"

"Technically you'd be my baby mama, though I personally hate that phrase. It lacks a certain *je ne sais quoi*. Consort sounds far more classy. Has the proper gravitas for the position. Though I suppose if titles really matter to you, we could go with . . . *wife*."

Merri bared her teeth. "Fuck you."

"That's what I've been saying. Finally, we're on the same page."

I must've gotten soft in my old age, because I absolutely didn't see her slap coming. The crack of her palm across my cheek filled the room a moment before the sting registered. Eyes wide, I took her in. Oh, she was beautiful in her rage. Cheeks flushed, eyes bright, lips just a little swollen, as she shook from the adrenaline of our play.

"Was that supposed to put me off you? Because joke's on you. I like it rough." My words were a sensual hiss against her lips.

She brought her hand up again, but I was ready this time. I easily caught her wrist and let out a disappointed sigh. "Merri, Merri, Merri. The sooner you accept your situation, the more pleasurable it will be for all of us."

Without waiting for a reply, I scooped her up into my arms. She struggled like the delicious little wildcat she was.

"Put me down," she insisted as I strode into the bathroom.

"My pleasure." I deposited her in the shower, once again using my power to turn on the cold water and douse her.

"What are you doing, asshole?" she screeched. "It's freezing!"

"You should have thought about that before you got so heated. Actions have consequences, darling. I know that better than anyone. Perhaps it's time you learned the lesson." I spun on my heel, prepared to let her . . . cool off.

"You're leaving? Just like that?"

I paused in the doorway and looked over my shoulder at her dripping wet and shivering in the shower. "Why wouldn't I? It's not like you have anywhere else you can go."

And with that, I tossed her a wink and left, locking the door to her bedroom behind me. It wouldn't stop her for long, but it would make a point.

Merri was mine, and now that I had her, I would never let her go.

CHAPTER THIRTEEN

MALICE

"Bloody useless," I muttered as I screwed the front panel on the radio I'd been attempting to fix for the last six hours.

The sky was still dark, but a soft glow tinged the horizon, somehow signaling my abject failure. I was at a loss, unwilling to sit around and do nothing while we worked out our next steps, so I'd had the bright idea of using the radio to seek out news of the state of the world. It was better than inaction.

Even if I got it working and found no one on the other end, it gave me something to *do*. Knowing Merri was out there somewhere without the four of us to protect her had me twisted up in so many knots it was a damned miracle I could function.

As I dropped the fiddly piece of metal in my hand for the seventh time, I let out a frustrated growl.

"See! This is why I didn't want to have feelings. Now I'm bloody useless."

I slammed my palm on top of the radio, my heart lurching when static blasted from the speakers. That was progress. Hope ignited faster than a wildfire within me. I twisted the knob, on tenterhooks as I sought a live signal. Seconds passed, my palms growing sweaty with each turn, but all that awaited me was more static.

"Fuck it all!"

Dropping my head into my hands, I forced long, slow breaths. Rage mixed with disappointment, creating a bitter cocktail in my gut. I was not used to failure. I allowed myself time to wallow, my face pressed to my palms. Frustration wouldn't lead to anything other than mistakes. I didn't have time for mistakes.

The static flickered in and out, and I knew it was only a matter of time before the old radio finally gave up the ghost and shut off on its own.

"Mal? Mal, are you there?"

Every muscle in my body tensed at the distorted sound of Merri's voice. I snapped upright, staring hard at the radio.

"Merri?"

I grabbed the radio, holding it so tight my fingers turned white as I desperately played with the knob again. "Merri? Hello?"

No answer.

"Dammit!" I growled.

A gentle tap on my shoulder had me nearly jumping out of my skin before I turned my head to find my hellcat perched on the desk, a wry grin on her lips.

"I'm right here."

Relief flooded me, followed closely by confusion. "You're back?"

She shook her head. "Not quite. Any other guesses?"

The whiplash of emotions was making a mess of me. I sat back with a grunt of disappointment. "I'm dreaming."

Merri offered me a wan smile. "Surprise."

Getting to my feet, I took all of her in. The fall of fiery locks that tumbled over her shoulders, those big blue eyes, her full, tempting lips. Seeing her, after fearing I may never again be afforded the privilege, was like handing a cool glass of water to a man dying of thirst. Or perhaps I was more akin to a man in a desert stumbling across a mirage. I couldn't quite trust she was real.

"You came to me." The words spilled from my lips as soon as they appeared in my mind. This was a dreamwalk. She chose to be here. With me.

"Yes."

"But why? Sin said you shut him out."

As badly as I wanted to hear her say she missed me, I knew that alone wouldn't be enough to sway her. Studying her a bit more carefully, I caught the little smudges below her eyes and the hollowness of her cheeks. She needed to feed. She didn't want me; she needed me.

I'd fucking take it.

"You're hungry, aren't you?" I asked before she could answer my previous query.

She bit her lower lip and looked away from my eyes, then flicked her gaze back to me. "Yes. But I'm not here for that."

"Then why?" I asked again, fearing the worst.

"I don't know how to say it."

"Just spit it out."

"Lucifer found me."

My chest constricted as the one thing we'd been fighting to keep from happening became a reality.

She continued softly, "Well, found is a bit misleading. I sort of, um, walked directly into a trap."

"Explain," I ground out, forcing myself not to raise my voice.

"I thought I was going somewhere safe," she haltingly began.

"Where are you?" I demanded.

She gave me the address.

"I'm coming for you."

"Wait, there's more you should know first."

"What else do I need to know? You're with Lucifer, the one man we swore to protect you from. We know him. You have to get away as fast as you can."

Her soft, warm palm rested on top of my hand. "He's done something to the house. I can't leave. I've been trying for hours. Every exit is spelled. I tried to step off the porch and ended up back at the front door. Same with the windows. I think it might be a ward or, I dunno . . . I've never seen anything like it. But I have no way out on my own. I . . . You broke me, and I'm so angry with you all, but I need your help."

I tucked the information away to share with the others. The need to get to her was an insistent itch beneath my skin.

"We'll be there as soon as we can. Whatever's waiting for us, we'll handle it."

"And if you can't?"

I hated the little wobble in her voice, that she had any reason to doubt us or our ability to protect her.

"We will."

"Mal . . ."

Threading our fingers, I squeezed her hand. "I won't rest until you're back with us. None of us will. But you need to feed, hellcat. You're starved."

She released a heavy sigh, her eyes dropping to her knees. "I know."

"Have you fed at all since you left us?" That question tasted like ashes in my mouth. The last thing I wanted was for her to be feeding off anyone other than the four of us. We were meant to be her providers and protectors.

"I tried. That's how I found out the truth of who he was, but after that . . ."

"Take from me," I insisted, pushing away the jealousy that rose like a tidal wave at the thought of Lucifer getting everything he didn't deserve.

She opened her mouth like she was going to deny me, but I stepped closer and placed a finger against her lips.

"You need this. If, for some reason, we can't get to you, keeping your power topped up is the only hope you have to fight him. I know things are a mess between us at the moment, and I'm not going to deny the role I played in that, but this is bigger than either of us. This is literal life or death. So I mean it, Merri. Take from me. Take as much as you need."

Uncertainty flickered across her face, but she nodded. "Okay."

I sat down, sliding the chair across the floor just enough so I was directly in front of where she was perched. The need to touch her had me trembling as I reached out to run my fingers along her ankle and then up the side of her calf.

Merri flinched, and regret ate away at any possible excitement I might have been feeling.

"Merri—"

"It doesn't have to mean anything, Malice."

"But it does mean something. Every time with you means something."

Her expression shuttered, her lips no longer soft but drawn into a tight line. "That was before. Now you're basically a taco."

"A taco?"

"Would you prefer if I called you a hamburger?" she asked with an arched brow. "You're a way for me to eat, Malice. That's all this is. You made it clear."

Anger got the better of me. "I did no such thing."

"Yes, you did. You sat there and looked at me like I was crazy. You watched Grim crush my heart, and you did *nothing*."

Guilt sat heavy along my neck and chest. "I know, Merri. Trust me, I know exactly how badly I fucked up. But my silence was never because I didn't believe you. I was so shocked by the truth of what you said, of what it meant, that I got lost processing it."

There was a glimmer in her eyes that I couldn't quite read before she swallowed. "It doesn't matter anymore."

My hand was at the top of her knee now, and I squeezed gently to emphasize my point. "Of course it matters. You're my mate, hellcat. That's just about the only thing that matters."

Her gaze met and held mine, and I swear an entire novel's worth of longing and regret passed between us, but she didn't say a word. She just held my stare and sighed, her shoulders slumping a little.

"Horsemen don't have mates," she finally whispered.

It was going to take more than a single apology to undo the damage we'd caused. That was okay, it was what I deserved. I didn't mind proving myself to her.

"I'm not a hamburger," I said firmly, running my palm up her thigh. "If anything, I'm a fucking five-course meal."

She uncrossed her legs and parted her knees minutely, the tension in her muscles easing ever so slightly. I took that for the opening it was, needing her in the worst way.

"Merri, I've missed you," I murmured as I leaned in and kissed the soft flesh of her inner thigh. "Your taste, your smell, your touch."

A sigh escaped her as I moved up her leg, taking the hem of her skirt along with me.

The first hint of her arousal hit my nose, and I inhaled greedily, nipping at the sensitive flesh I'd just exposed. I was nowhere near close enough to where I wanted to be, but after days without her, it felt like I'd just found the fucking promised land. Tingles raced down my spine as she threaded her fingers through my hair, her nails scraping my scalp before she fisted the strands.

"You smell divine. Lie back and let me have you, hellcat."

Her breath hitched, but her voice was firm when she said, "No."

"No?"

"That's not how I feed. I need to taste *you*, Malice."

My cock gave a very happy twitch in my trousers, as if eagerly volunteering for the job. I leaned back in my chair, spreading my legs wide as I slid my zipper down. "Then do it."

As she hopped off the desk, I pulled my dick free and slowly stroked from root to tip, sucking in a sharp breath at the intense desire already building at the base of my spine. She needed me to come, but I wanted this to last. What a conundrum.

Watching her stare at me as I stroked myself was almost enough to settle the matter for both of us. The hunger that burned in her eyes ignited within me, like it was the answer to a question I'd been afraid to ask. If this were just about feeding, surely it wouldn't feel this way.

We were mates, after all. That didn't cease to be true because of a bump in the road.

No matter what either of us claimed in the beginning, or perhaps in this moment, it would never *just* be about feeding her. We were more than a means to an end. Grim may have denied it, but he was wrong.

Merri got to her knees, and I welcomed her between mine, reaching out with my free hand to stroke her face before I wrapped her hair around my fist.

"You look so beautiful on your knees for me," I rasped.

"Bet I'll look even better when my lips are wrapped around your cock."

Fuuuuck me.

"Prove it."

"Yes, sir."

And, fuck me two times.

She leaned forward and replaced my palm with hers around my jutting length, her touch somehow so much more sensual than my own. With deliberately slow strokes, she worked me, precum beading on the tip almost instantly. Fuck, I was weeping for her, and she wasn't even using her power on me.

Holding my gaze, she opened her mouth and started to swallow me down. I hissed in a breath, my fingers flexing in her hair. "Fuck yes, just like that. You take me so well, hellcat. You were made to suck my cock."

Part of me wanted to talk her through it, to tell her exactly what to do, but she had other plans. Merri had me seeing stars and losing the fight against my orgasm within minutes. It was unfair, really. She was born for seduction, and I'd been denying myself for centuries. I'd lost the battle before we even started.

And I'd never been so happy to lose.

"Merri," I gasped as I fell over the edge, coming down her throat.

My pulse pounded in my ears, and it was several shuddering breaths later before I managed to open my eyes.

All I wanted was to pull her into my arms and keep her with me, but as the room came back into focus, I realized two things simultaneously. I was awake, and Merri was gone.

A wave of conflicting emotions hit me all at once: disappointment, confusion, despair, euphoria . . . love. It was entirely too much to make sense of.

But one thing was abundantly clear. One of us was in denial.

I just wasn't sure if it was Merri . . . or if it was me.

CHAPTER FOURTEEN

HADES

It'd been too damn long since I'd visited my realm. What with the apocalypse taking every moment of our time and collective efforts, and all. But by the looks of things, my crew was keeping things running like a well-oiled machine. The lines had never been longer, but that was to be expected with all the death and destruction Earth had seen the last few months.

"Now serving soul number 7,568,989,001 at counter ten," an automated voice said over the din of people waiting their turn.

"What the fuck is that garbage?" Asshole asked, pawing at my leg.

"I have no fucking clue," I muttered, his question mirroring my own. "Shouldn't you know? You're the one who's been holding down the fort."

Asshole scoffed. "How very dare you imply I've been slacking when you know I've been on a super important mission with my girl Keeks."

"Who gave permission to change the way we do things? Who are all these people at the counters?" I scanned the ten kiosks that had replaced Janine's desk. Each soul behind the impersonal glass barriers looked less than thrilled to be there. Complexions ashen, eyes sunken, expressions grim. They appeared more like prisoners than willing volunteers.

"Not exactly Miss Argentina, are they?" Asshole asked.

"From Beetlejuice?"

"Fuck yeah. She was my favorite shade of blue, and those stems . . . Mmm, I bet she gives a real good walk."

I groaned before storming past the people waiting to be processed and headed toward the kiosks.

"You haven't met your quota yet, Al. I told you, if you want to avoid the infernal fires of floor seven, you have to process at least fifty percent faster than you have been. Time is money, pal. Stop wasting mine."

Janine. I turned in the direction of her voice and made a beeline for my number two.

"What the fuck is this?" I asked when I came up behind her.

Janine jumped and spun toward me, one hand pressed against her chest, the other clutching a clipboard. After sucking in a breath, she righted her cat-eye glasses and gave me a stern glare. "Boss. You really gotta stop sneaking up on a girl. You gave me a fright. If I wasn't already dead, I might've had a coronary."

"Who the fuck are these souls you have doing your job?"

"Now serving soul number 7,568,989,002 at counter seven."

"And what in Zeus's name is *that*?" I gestured wildly at the space because the computerized voice seemed to come from everywhere all at once.

Janine smacked her gum as she looked upward with a grin. "Oh, that? Isn't it nifty? It really saves my voice."

"What happened to the personal touch? To welcoming the downtrodden?"

She blinked up at me. "Boss, maybe you've been too busy enjoying your honeymoon, but the world is ending. Do you have any idea how many souls Charon is bringing over per day? Hell is full. At capacity. Bursting at the seams. I was talking to myself during my off time, 'Welcome to the underworld, name, death date, and papers' over and over. It's just too much for a single gal to manage on her own. I had to call in reinforcements."

"She makes a good point," Asshole said.

I nodded. She really did.

"Yeah, fair enough."

Janine squinted at me. "Pretty sure you aren't making a house call for funsies, so what is it this time?"

"First, I need you to elaborate on all this," I said, looking toward the kiosks. "Who are they, and why do they look like they're being tortured?"

"Like I said, hell is full. These guys are all destined for eternal damnation with nowhere to go. What better way to serve their sentences than to have to see all the good and kind people passing on to the Elysian Fields?"

Janine was, dare I say it, diabolical.

"Miss Argentina would never. She was an angel," Asshole muttered.

Janine rolled her eyes. "Feel free to leave a suggestion in the box. Oh, wait, there isn't one."

"Do you see how she treats me? She's on a power trip, boss man. You gotta do something."

"Well, someone has to be in charge. You're off frolicking with Kiki, and the boss is on vacation."

"I wouldn't call it vacation."

Janine talked straight over me. "I'm trying to keep our realm running smoothly. I still see souls to their final destinations on a case-by-case basis. For instance, I just helped an adorably confused Frenchman find his way to his heaven not long ago. He was so lost. But Famine sucking your soul from your body will do that to ya."

I blinked and held up a hand. "Famine? Which one?"

"How am I supposed to know? It wasn't exactly part of his paperwork. Does it matter?"

"It might."

"Then I guess you'll have to go and ask him, won't you?"

I sighed, feeling like I was being pulled in a dozen different directions. I'd come here to collect an article of Death's, but I couldn't leave without finding out about this soul's run-in with a horseperson. No matter which one it might be, the information was pertinent to the resistance's mission.

"Where is he?"

"Right this way." Janine took off her glasses and let them hang like a necklace as she strode down the endless hallway lined with doors to various celestial realms.

Asshole made to follow, but I turned and squatted down so I was at his level. "I need you to do something for me."

"Name it, boss. You want I should bite her ankles for getting sassy?" He wagged his little tail so hard he couldn't sit still.

I chuckled and couldn't help but give him a few scritches under his fuzzy chin. "No. She'd probably poke one of your eyes out with her pointy shoe. I need you to go to my office. There's a bundle wrapped in leather tucked in the false floor under my desk."

"Oh, the one where you try to hide things from me?"

I should've known my dog would be able to sniff out any and everything. He did have three noses in his normal form, after all.

"That's the one."

He lifted a paw in what I thought was supposed to be a salute but just looked like a sweet as hell wave. Then he trotted off the other way.

"He's in here. Just be gentle with this one. He's new, and death really did a number on him. Unexpected doesn't even begin to describe it." Janine pointed to a door, her demeanor more tender than was typical.

"Thanks, Janine."

I reached for the handle, but Janine stopped me with an uncharacteristic touch. "Boss? I'm sorry about the changes. I didn't know what else to do. There's just so many of 'em."

"No apology needed. You did what I asked you to do. What I *trust* you to do."

She gave a little sniff, the only indication that my words affected her. "All right, well, if that's everything, I have work to do."

I winked at her. "Best get to it."

"Yeah, my boss is a real pain in the drain." Her laughter chased her down the hallway as she tossed me a finger wave over her shoulder. "Make sure to say bye before you go."

"Why? So you know when you can slack off?" I called after her.

"So I can release the strippers. A whole truckload of them just came in from Vegas. I'm considering putting in a theater just so they have somewhere to use their skills."

The sad part was, I couldn't tell whether or not she was joking.

With a shake of my head, I turned my attention back to the matter at hand. I hadn't interrogated a soul in a long time. I had people who did that sort of thing for me now, but every once in a while, I found cause to dust the old skill set off.

"It's just like riding a bike," I told myself as I opened the door and stepped inside what could only be the French countryside.

I found him sitting under the shade of a tree. He didn't hear me approach, which was common for the newly dead. They weren't aware of much aside from their inner turmoil as they processed their demise. Especially if it was sudden or traumatic.

Settling in the grass next to him, I stared out at the gently flowing creek as it glistened in the perpetual late afternoon sun.

"Beautiful, isn't it?" I asked, never looking away from the water.

"Oui."

"It's designed to set you at ease. This realm. It adjusts to fit your memories, recreating your favorite place."

The man finally looked at me, brows furrowed as he assessed me. "I'm sorry, but who are you?"

"My name is Hades, and this is my world. Well, yours now too."

Eyes widening, he scooted away as if he might try to run from me.

"Easy, I'm not going to hurt you."

"Then why are you here?" he asked, still giving me a wide berth.

"The manner of your death left me with more than a few questions."

He huffed out a laugh. "You and me both."

"Yeah, I imagine so. What'd you do to piss Famine off?"

Shaking his head, he glanced down at the grass between his bent knees and began plucking at the blades. "I have no clue. One moment I was making myself a coffee, the next she had overtaken me and made me a prisoner in my own body."

She. Well, that was one question answered.

"What did she want with you?"

"I think it was proximity. She wanted access to my master and his friends."

"And who was he?"

"Monsieur Laurent. He wasn't who I thought he was, though I only know that thanks to her. He was like her. A horseman. They all were."

A frisson of excitement raced down my spine, causing me to straighten and turn toward him. I'd come to the underworld to find the horsemen, but what were the odds information about them would fall so easily into my lap?

"You were with them all? Where?"

"Oui. And sweet Merri. Oh, that poor girl. She trusted me, and I unwillingly led her to her doom."

That sounded exactly like the kind of underhanded shit the horsewomen would pull. They loved to manipulate and mastermind situations. The horsemen were far more direct than their female counterparts.

"She's gone?"

He nodded, despondent. "She is probably dead by now. It's all my fault. But Famine was too strong. I couldn't fight her. Not when she whispered in Merri's ear and sowed doubt about the horsemen, not when she lied and drew false wards of protection. I had to watch it all happen and was helpless to stop it."

I recognized a doom spiral better than anyone, and I knew I had to stop this one before I completely lost him.

"Merri's not dead."

"How do you know?"

I raised a brow. "This is my realm. I'd know if she were here."

"Right." He blew out a heavy breath. "Well, that's one bit of good news."

"Where are the others? I can help them."

He gave me a suspicious glare in response. "How can I trust you? You're Hades. I have heard the tales of your trickery and dishonesty."

I snorted. "Handed down by my brother, Zeus. Untrustworthy megalomaniac. I have a vested interest in keeping our worlds as they are, not ending them. The horsemen are an integral part of that."

He studied me for several heartbeats before giving me a little nod. "I suppose it doesn't matter much to me one way or the other. I'll be dead regardless."

"That's true. But helping the horsemen means helping Merri. You could still right a wrong. Or at the very least, toss a spanner in the works of the one who killed you."

After a long pause, the man heaved a sigh and stood, me following suit. Then he turned to me and gave me everything I needed to locate the Four Horsemen of the Apocalypse.

I was gone between one thought and the next, appearing at the gates of a secluded château in France. Wards that should have stopped me dead in my tracks didn't do more than tickle as I pushed through them and onto the property. Famine had laid herself a devious trap. A cursory search of the premises revealed an unfortunate truth.

They were gone.

Thankfully, I still had an ace up my sleeve. It would have been a nice change of pace for things to be easy, but I wasn't returning empty-handed. It was impossible to know whether the horsemen planned on returning to this place, but now that I knew it existed, I could always pop by and check.

One way or the other, we would find them.

It was only a matter of time.

CHAPTER FIFTEEN

GRIM

"He's a real twat, you know that?" Sin's voice filtered into the hall as I approached the billiards room where they were all waiting for me.

"You've made your feelings known," Chaos muttered.

I stood outside the room, listening in just so I could let Sin have his gripe. I'd earned it.

"Don't act all high and mighty. You two agree with me. And he's being even twattier than usual. Admit it."

"So what if he is? It doesn't matter. You're focusing on the wrong thing." Malice's voice joined the others. I crossed my arms, resting my shoulder against the wall as I contemplated my entrance.

I was typically the one to call these meetings, the natural leader of our group, if you will. Never had I felt less than confident about striding into a room and commanding a situation. Until now.

"And what's more important than a unified front?"

"Getting Merri back," Malice deadpanned.

"What do you think the unified front is for, Sherlock?" Sin shot back. "He can't even make it to book club on time."

The children were fighting. It was time for me to make an appearance.

Pushing through the partially open door, I held my head high and put my mask of confidence firmly in place.

"Ah, look, it's the king of the assholes, finally gracing us with his presence." Sin's face was always punchable, but right now, he'd never been more so.

"Why did you call this meeting, Mal?" I asked, ignoring Sin simply because we didn't have time to fuck around, and as satisfying as breaking his nose would be, that would delay us longer.

"Merri came to me," Malice said.

"Wow, man, way to bury the lede."

All three of us glared at Sin.

"What did she say?" Chaos asked.

"Why you?" I said on his heels.

"Firstly, fuck you," Malice said, eyes narrowed as they met mine. "Secondly, it's not good news."

"Oh, so you're delusional now too?" Sin asked. "Merri is always good news."

"She told me where she is."

"See? Good news."

Malice shot Sin a withering glare. "If you'd let me finish . . ."

Sin mimed locking his lips.

"She's with him."

Sin mimed plucking a key out of the air and quickly unlocking his lips. He gasped dramatically. "Him who?"

"Well, that was too good to last," Chaos muttered.

Rage burned through me as I growled, "Lucifer."

"Okay, but you found her. We can go get her." Sin's words were filled with a hope I couldn't feel.

"Yes. She's tried to escape but has been unable due to Lucifer's magic. She hasn't been feeding—"

"Whose fault is that?" I snapped.

The others all looked at me with varying degrees of incredulity.

"It's yours, dumbass," Sin sniped.

"She would have been taken care of if she hadn't run off."

"She wouldn't have run off if you weren't such a festering turd."

Malice cleared his throat. "We're getting off topic. I took care of her last night."

"Does that mean she forgave you?" Chaos asked, his hope so pathetically obvious I couldn't stand looking at him.

"No," Malice answered with a slow shake of his head. "She's absolutely furious with us. She called me a hamburger."

Sin snickered. "Burn."

"I'm sure you'd be a stale croissant."

"Watch your mouth, hot pocket."

"What the fuck is a hot pocket?" Malice asked.

Sin made a considering face. "They're actually pretty good, to be honest. So I take it back. You've been demoted to a soggy, day-old french fry."

Malice made the V sign.

"Don't you British middle finger me."

This was getting out of hand. The reality of our situation was bleak. Merri was with the enemy. Trapped with him and at his mercy. We were lucky he hadn't taken her against her will and planted his seed inside her already. My stomach churned at the thought as jealousy raged within me.

Worse still was that I was the reason for all of it. I might downplay my guilt in front of the others, but I couldn't afford to appear reticent. If I gave them even an inch, they'd never cease with their pestering. The truth was, Merri couldn't be my mate, and she was mistaken, but I should have handled my response to her confession differently. I should never have been so cold and callous. She left because of me.

Which meant Lucifer's capture of her sat squarely on my shoulders.

We had to get her back.

I had to get her back.

"Where is he keeping her?" I finally demanded as they continued their childish bickering.

Everyone stopped at the sound of my voice, then Malice turned his focus on me. "She gave me an address. A lakeside cabin in Illinois."

"So what are we waiting for?" Sin demanded.

"We are not going in guns blazing without a battle plan," Chaos snapped.

"That sounds like exactly what we're supposed to do," Sin countered.

"This is Lucifer. We have to be smart or we'll lose before we step foot on the property."

I nodded my agreement. "Chaos is right. No running about half-cocked."

"Excuse me, I am fully cocked at all times." Sin glanced down his front. "That should be obvious by now."

"I will muzzle you if you do not get a hold of yourself. Things could not be more dire, do you understand?" I snarled. "This is not the fucking time for your dick jokes."

"Shall we summon the horses?" Chaos asked under his breath.

He was always trying to summon them so we could ride into battle, but this time it was warranted.

"Horses, armor, weapons," I said. "We'll face Lucifer with all the power granted to us so we can take back our woman."

That earned me a couple of raised eyebrows.

"A bit late to care about that, don't you think?" Sin asked with a pointed glare.

"Not this again," I grumbled.

"She wouldn't be gone if you—"

"Enough of this bullshit!" I shouted, at my wits' end. "I admit it, all right? I cocked it all up. I'm the reason it's all gone pear-shaped. I broke her heart and ruined everything. Now we have to fix it. We have to clean up my mess and bring her home where she belongs."

"With her mates," Sin pressed.

"With us."

"Her. Mates."

I heaved a sigh and dragged my fingers through my hair. "You know that's not true. We don't have mates."

Sin shook his head in disgust. "Lie to yourself if you have to, but never say that to Merri again. You don't speak for the rest of us."

Chaos and Malice took up position behind him, silently echoing their support of his assertion.

"Fine," I growled through gritted teeth. I was entirely too tangled up in my feelings. It was damn near impossible to reclaim my usual unbothered facade.

"Now that we've got that cleared up," Malice said, "can we get back to the strategizing portion of this meeting?"

While we didn't require an elaborate strategy for this recovery mission, we did plan for a few of the most likely scenarios. Each of them ending with Lucifer incapacitated and one or all of us escaping with Merri. Either way, Lucifer Morningstar would rue the day he crossed us. Mark my words.

Sin clapped his hands and rubbed them together. "Okay, let's get to summoning our steeds already. I haven't seen my horse in too long. She's such a pretty girl."

"Not here!" Malice cried. "This house is not a stable."

I nodded. "Outside then. Time is wasting."

We shouldn't have expended the energy to teleport to the main drive, but we did it anyway. All of us shared a looming sense of urgency now that we finally knew where Merri was being kept. It had been hard enough to focus long enough to pull together a strategy, but we knew what was on the line. And who we were up against. We wouldn't get a second chance at this.

No one uttered a single word. No one had to. We simply called for them in our minds and they came.

The clouds darkening and swirling until they boiled with frenetic energy was the first sign our loyal steeds were heeding their summons. Elation built within me at the knowledge that we had all finally been restored to our full selves after that bitch Hel drained us. If we hadn't, our horses wouldn't have been able to reach us.

As always, Pestilence's arrived first, breaking through the clouds at breakneck speed. His horse was a gorgeous animal, its white coat and mane pristine, almost gleaming. War's followed, its rust-colored hair reminiscent of dried blood, made only more terrifying once you realized its mane and tail were made of freshly flowing blood. Next came Famine's, a black-on-black nightmare of a beast that was garishly skeletal, the only life within it coming from the glowing white orbs in its eye sockets. Bringing up the rear was my pale steed. Many believed that I was the one with the white horse, but she was actually a pale green, meant to mimic a corpse's deathly pallor. Her mane and tail were a soft, cloudy gray that flowed behind her like mist over a graveyard. Beautiful, but eerie. Not a creature that belonged on the earthly plane.

"God, I've missed them," Sin whispered, waiting for his steed to touch ground.

"As have I," Malice agreed.

"We haven't been ourselves without them." Chaos strode forward, his red armor materializing and replacing his clothes.

The rest of us followed suit: Malice in his bone-white armor, Sin in his black, and me in my striking silver. Unlike the others, I also wore a cloak, its hood hanging low to obscure my face, the misty gray color an echo of my horse's mane.

We took our mounts, weapons at the ready in the blink of an eye. The weight of my scythe in my palm grounded me in a way I hadn't realized I'd needed. I was certain it was the same for the rest of them. With a flourish, Chaos rolled his wrist, his sword materializing before he completed the move. Malice's bow appeared on his back, the quiver filled with never-ending arrows tipped in poison. And Sin, the newest of us, watched on, anticipation on his face as he waited for his own weapon. He held out one hand and manifested an ornate golden scale. His shoulders slumped, expression twisting to pure incredulity.

"What the fuck am I supposed to do with this?"

Chaos rolled his eyes. "Swing it, kid."

Sin's eyes narrowed with distrust, but he lifted the scale above his head and gave it a tentative swing. As the two plates of the scale moved, they stretched, and the entire thing lengthened into a two-headed flail.

"That's more like it," he said with a proud smirk.

"Ready?" Chaos asked, looking around.

We nodded as one.

"Let's fuckin' go, boys!" Sin whooped.

Locking eyes with Mal, I jerked my chin at him. "Lead the way."

"I always do."

We arrived at the coordinates between one step and the next. The ramshackle cabin had seen far better days.

"Are we sure this is the right place?" Chaos asked, staring at the front door, which was only half-hanging on its hinges.

"This is the address she gave me," Malice affirmed.

Tattered curtains waved in the slight breeze, coming out of the broken window that had been infiltrated by vines and other foliage.

"There is no one here. Not a single spark of life." That sense of dread in my gut I'd been nursing since the moment she left grew to the size of a boulder. "She was never really here."

"Lucifer planned his trap well," Chaos murmured.

My horse huffed and stomped at the ground, sensing my frustration.

"What do we do now?" Sin asked.

"We have to tell her she's not where she thinks she is, and we keep looking." Chaos brought his horse around to face us all.

"Where would Lucifer take her?" Malice asked.

"Nowhere good."

"And in the meantime? It's not going to be easy to find her," Malice pointed out.

Chaos answered. "We keep her safe the only way we can. Feed

her when she comes to us, help her stay strong. Strategize alongside her."

He was right. As much as I hated the idea, dreamwalks were the only way for us to reach her. Merri would have to fight Lucifer on her own until we could find our way to wherever she was.

I could only hope she'd learned enough during her time with us to do so.

Unfortunately, hope wasn't something I was overly familiar with.

CHAPTER SIXTEEN

CHAOS

My heavy, rhythmic footfalls and steady breaths were the only sounds that accompanied me as I ran through the wooded area surrounding Malice's château. With little else to do but wring our hands and talk incessantly about what our next move might be, I needed an outlet. That became punishing my body through intense exercise. It was either that or pummel my brothers bloody. And while helpful, at least for me, no one appreciated being a human-sized punching bag.

Following a slight curve in the path, I released a pulse of pent-up power. There was a loud crack immediately followed by the ominous sound of a tree toppling down.

"Timber, motherfucker," I muttered. "Who needs an axe?"

"Are we seriously running?" Merri's voice caught me off guard, annoyance coloring each word.

I staggered to a stop, feet skidding on the dry terrain before I could face her. When I did finally turn around, she had closed the distance between us. Gods, she was beautiful. Skin glowing, hair pulled back in a high ponytail exposing her perfect features. I glanced down at my dirt-streaked legs, baggy basketball shorts, and sweat-soaked tank with exaggerated arm holes that left most of my ribcage exposed. I could not have looked worse.

Tugging at my shirt, I pulled the fabric up and off, attempting to mop up as much sweat from my face as I could.

"You're here," I said stupidly.

Merri pressed her lips together, but to her credit, she didn't laugh at me. "I am."

"We tried to come for you, but the house was vacant. You aren't where you think you are."

"What are you talking about? I'm at the lake house. I can see the lake from the kitchen window."

I stepped closer to her, desperate to feel her skin on mine, but she took a hurried step backward. "Merri . . ."

"I need you to explain what you mean when you say the house was vacant."

"Exactly that. The four of us came for you, weapons and horses at the ready, but the house was nothing more than an abandoned shack. The lake was there, now only a dried, cracked pit of rotting fish."

Merri held up a hand. "Back up. Horses?"

My lips quirked. It was such a Merri point to get caught up on. "We *are* the horsemen."

"Well, yeah, but . . . Okay then. Sorry, continue."

"Wherever you are, it's an illusion. He doesn't have you at that address. Not even close."

The color drained from her cheeks as my words sank in. "I . . . But that's where I went. That's the exact address."

"And I'm sure you're right about that, Red. But the facts are the facts. The moment you got there, he sprung his trap. Your reality changed. Malice thinks he might have used some sort of portal that teleported you to a different location or plane as soon as you arrived."

"But wouldn't I have been able to tell?"

"Not necessarily. He could have had the whole property spelled to look however he wanted it. And stepping through a portal is no different than crossing a threshold, so it would have been easy enough for him to do. Liminal spaces hold their own power. Combined with his, you wouldn't stand a chance of noticing."

"Fuck."

"Exactly."

Eyes wide and searching, she asked, "What am I supposed to do now?"

"You need to figure out where he's keeping you."

"And how am I supposed to do that? It looks like a fucking lake house. It's not like there are neighbors I can ask. Or like Lucifer will just hand out the information freely."

"He might. He does love to show off."

"But wouldn't that tip him off that we're on to him?"

A thrill raced through me at her use of the pronoun. She still saw us as a "we." That had to mean something. If nothing else, there was hope.

"He's not stupid. He already knows. He's going to be focused on his goal for you. That's all that matters to him right now."

Merri's gaze had wandered, and she was chewing distractedly on her bottom lip.

"Hey," I murmured, using the distraction to step forward and tug her lip free with my thumb. "It's going to be all right. Between the five of us, we'll figure it out."

"Sure."

"You came to me for a reason, Red. I doubt it was to chit-chat."

She hadn't slapped my fingers from under her chin. That was a good sign, and as she lifted her bright blue gaze to meet mine, I saw a flare of hunger there.

"You know why."

My dick stirred to life, the mesh shorts doing nothing to hide the swelling erection. There was nothing more I wanted to do than help her feed and feel that connection with her again. Since she'd been gone, her absence had been a gnawing hole in my gut. A physical ache I couldn't ignore. I never wanted to be separated from her like this again.

The knowledge should have concerned me. I mean, I'd spent centuries without her and did just fine. But all of that changed. There was no way I could live any kind of life without her in it.

Merri was right. We were mates. It was like that poem. Whatever souls were made of, hers and mine were the same.

I don't know how the fuck it was possible, but that didn't make it any less true.

"Let's get back to the house," I said, my voice deep with longing. "I just need to clean up—"

"Way ahead of you," Merri said.

I blinked, and we were in my bathroom, the room already fogging with steam from the shower. As I watched, she stripped out of the hot pink sports bra and leggings combination she'd worn to drive me crazy, leaving her naked and ready like she was a gift only for me.

"Take off your clothes and get in the shower, warrior."

Usually I liked to be the one in control, but right now, listening to her tell me what to do only added to my arousal. If letting her call the shots was the only way I could get my hands on her, I'd gladly play along.

My shirt dropped to the floor first, having already been removed. Then I sort of kicked off my shoes and shimmied out of my shorts at the same time. Merri watched me with obvious amusement.

"You should take that act on the road, big guy."

"Ha ha," I deadpanned, stalking toward her. I gestured to the shower with my head. "You first, Red."

"You just want me to get wet. Joke's on you," she said, leaning close and dropping her voice to a whisper, "I already am."

Fuck. Me.

I reached between my legs and grabbed hold of my already throbbing cock before giving the considerable length a stroke.

Precum beaded at the tip, and it was all I could do not to wipe it off with my thumb and feed it to her.

"You're always wet for me, aren't you?"

She shrugged noncommittally. "Don't flatter yourself. It comes with the territory."

If things were different, I wouldn't have let her get away with being such a brat, but as things currently stood, I was just too fucking happy to see her, so I let it slide.

"Keep telling yourself that."

"You're still not in the shower."

I gestured to the glass-encased area. "Ladies first. I insist."

Huffing, she turned away from me, giving me a perfect view of her heart-shaped ass as she opened the door and stepped inside.

If she thought I was going to let her call all the shots without fighting back, without trying to reclaim her as mine, she was dead wrong. I'd take control one step at a time, and remind her how much she loved it when I took care of her. I'd earn my place in her heart again if it was the last thing I did.

She might think of these dreamwalks like showing up at a fast-food joint, but I would never be a hamburger, or whatever the fuck it was she called Malice. No matter what any of us claimed, it had never been just about feeding her or knocking her up before Lucifer. It had always been more. *Would* always be more.

The water was a warm comfort as I stepped under the spray, my tense muscles loosening as the heat sluiced over my skin. Merri had already soaped up a loofah and wasted no time in her efforts to get me clean, or so I thought. The bright notes of citrus mixed with a deeper scent of sandalwood as she washed my chest, over my shoulders, and down my arms. But she avoided going any lower just yet, and I wondered if perhaps she was trying to torture me.

"Turn around," she whispered, her voice tight and betraying how much she wanted me.

"Trying to get me to drop the soap?" I teased. "Because I'm not sure you have the equipment for that."

"I have fingers. And a wicked imagination. Wanna try me, Chaos? I can manifest a strap-on."

I wish I could say I wasn't remotely interested in the possibility, but my dick gave a decidedly interested twitch. When it came to Merri, I guess there wasn't much I wouldn't explore.

"I'll try anything . . . once."

Her brows flew up, and a smile teased her lips. "Noted."

Turning my back on her, I waited for the touch of the loofah, but was pleasantly surprised when it was her soapy fingers that found my broad back. I melted into the feel of her touching me, a sense of completion washing over me at the contact. I'd missed her more than I'd been willing to admit to myself. But living without the woman I loved was like living without purpose.

Her hands trailed over my shoulders, down the backs of my arms, and across my hands, until she threaded our fingers in a tender gesture that lasted for the briefest moment. Far too short for my liking.

Before I could catch her fingers, they trailed lower, ghosting over my ribs and abs. She pressed her wet body against mine, her chest to my back as she ran those devilish hands over my thighs.

My legs trembled, fucking trembled.

"Christ," I bit out, pressing a palm against the tiled wall to keep myself steady.

"Tell me how much you want me, Chaos. I can feel it, but I want you to say it," she purred.

Her hands slid to my inner thighs, running up until her fingertips barely brushed my balls.

Fuck. Fuck. Fuck.

"I want you, Merri. I always want you." She grabbed my balls and rolled them in one hand. "Fuuuuck. You're all I've ever wanted."

"Mmm. I can see that," she murmured. Then her other hand wrapped around my straining length, and she stroked me from root to tip.

It was damned lucky I was already bracing myself against the wall because my knees about gave out.

"Feel good?" she asked, a cocky smile in her voice as she continued to work up and down my shaft.

"Slow down," I begged, not remotely ready for this to be over. It would be days before I'd get my turn with her again. I needed this to last.

"Not a chance," she whispered, voice close to my ear. She wasn't quite tall enough to get all the way there, but the effect was the same.

"Red," I warned, but my protest was weak at best.

"Give it to me, Chaos. Give me what I want."

"I will— Oh Gods," I groaned, toes curling as I fought the waves of pleasure that were bearing down on me.

"Now," she ordered.

"Let me inside you," I bit out around clenched teeth. "Let me put my seed where it belongs."

"No," she said, biting down on the back of my arm before releasing a wave of her power and forcing the issue.

I came with a startled cry, jet after jet of my cum coating the wall.

"Mmm, that's better," she crooned. "God, you're delicious."

She released her hold on me and stepped back. That was all the opportunity I needed to round on her. I grabbed her by the throat and walked her backward until she was pressed against the tile, a lust-drunk expression on her face.

"You didn't let me finish inside you," I said, my voice low and tense. "That wasn't very nice, Red."

She looked up at me through hooded eyes. "You lost that privilege."

I blinked at her. "What?"

"You don't get access to my body when you treat me the way you did."

"Merri—"

"No. Don't try and argue this. You fucked up. I get to say who I accept inside me, and I don't accept you."

Frustration burned through me, both at the rejection of the two of us connecting in the most intimate way possible, and at the very real problem this presented. Regardless of how mad at us she was, she still needed to get pregnant.

"And how are we supposed to keep Lucifer from filling you with his hellspawn if you won't let us get there first?" I snarled.

She shoved at my chest. The move alone wouldn't have done anything, but I released her and took a step back.

"Are you fucking kidding me? *That's* what you're worried about?"

"Of course I am."

"Well, maybe you should have thought about that before you four chuckleheads pushed me away."

Guilt hit me in the gut, but I persisted. "Don't be a stubborn little brat about this. It's stupid."

She scoffed, shoving at my chest again. "Stupid? You think I'm stupid because I'm setting boundaries? You think I'm stupid because you broke my fucking heart and I won't let you do it again?"

"I think you're stupid if you think Lucifer won't try anything. He has one goal, Merri. One. He will do anything to achieve it."

"Yeah, well, I think you're a real asshole."

"I don't care if it means that you're safe."

"Safe? You think getting me pregnant keeps me safe? Newsflash, Lucifer already has me. If I'm pregnant, he has no reason to keep me around. The best way to keep me safe right now is to keep that option open."

"So he can take what you won't give him by force?"

I couldn't say it more plainly. Well, I could, but the thought of what he might do to her if she didn't give in made me see red, and that wasn't good for any of us.

"He won't."

I let out a derisive snort. "You're naive if you believe that."

Her eyes narrowed as my words hung between us. "Thanks for the meal, but you can fuck all the way off, Chaos."

And just like that, Merri was gone, and I was awake in a puddle of mud and decomposing leaves in the middle of the woods.

I slammed my fist into the ground, the trees around me quaking in protest.

None of that had gone according to plan. Worse, she was fucking right. Not about Lucifer, but about me. And I didn't even get a chance to tell her I was sorry. I'd gotten so worked up about the danger she was putting herself in that everything else flew out of my head. I was the asshole in this situation. In every sense of the word.

"Motherfucker."

CHAPTER SEVENTEEN

FAMINE

How was it that a glorious being like myself always seemed to be reduced to waiting around for a man? Blech. I didn't waste my time on them if I could avoid it. And for good reason. They always let me down.

Case in point.

Lucifer simply abandoned his throne, leaving us to keep things running smoothly with nothing more than a "See you later" and a wave. After all the torture he'd put me through, you'd think I'd at least rate a heads-up or check-in.

Now here I stood, waiting on another male who was likely just as cocksure. And just as disappointing.

I picked at my teeth, my chrome red nails gleaming in the fluorescent light. I was leaning against a boring cinderblock wall, one stiletto-clad foot propped up against it. I might be stuck waiting, but I looked fucking hot. I'd opted for my demonic form; she was my favorite visage. My long red tresses flowed down my back, nearly to my waist. It was stunning in contrast to my choice of clothing, a skintight black leather bodysuit that matched my delectable little black horns. How could anyone resist me? One glance my way and they'd be sucked into my gaze, lost to the milky white of my eyes and unable to escape my kiss.

Releasing a heavy sigh, I glanced down the long hallway for the eight-hundred-and-twenty-seventh time. You'd think for a guy on a very set schedule, this asshole would at least be punctual.

"No wonder it's taken this long for the apocalypse to unfold. Men will be the downfall of everything. Rome. Democracy. Marriages. The economy. Their egos ruin every—"

The soft scuff of a shoe over concrete was my only warning he'd arrived.

Sloth. The final Prince.

He was disgustingly beautiful, his inky black hair in a perfectly coiffed pompadour. He was lean with chiseled muscles, his face all perfect angles and full pouty lips. Give him a guitar and he could have been Elvis. With a leather jacket, he could have been James Dean.

"What, no applause?" he asked, his voice blessed with a rolling Irish accent *just* this side of cruel.

He was my own personal brand of catnip. Pretty and mean. Exactly my type.

"That's it?" I deadpanned.

"What was that, darlin'? Surely you're not speaking to me in that tone." He cocked his head as he assessed me, acid-green irises pulling me in.

I had to tear my focus from him before I took a step closer. Then I realized what the handsome fuck was doing.

"Don't try and use your charm and magic on me, Sloth. I'm not your target."

"You could be."

"Never gonna happen, hot stuff."

His shoulders dropped. "At least you admit I'm hot," he eventually said with a shrug, sauntering over to me. "You really should afford me the respect I deserve, though."

“For what? Walking into a room?” I offered him a slow, sarcastic clap. “Great job. Well done. I’m soooo impressed.”

Eyes widening, he took a beat before closing the distance between us and leaning in until his mouth was inches from mine. “Give me five minutes and I’ll leave you so impressed you’ll be begging me to stop.”

“You know, you Princes talk a big game, but so far, all I’ve seen is a bunch of pompous asses who show up, make a mess, and then wait around to be told what to do.” I met his dominance with my own, bringing my lips a breath away from his like I was going to kiss him. Then I snapped my teeth, nipping his full bottom lip with my petite fangs. A bead of blood blossomed on each side, and he hissed. “Careful, Slothy. I bite.”

He leaned back, wiping away the blood with a sneer. “Bitch.”

“Aw, that’s the nicest thing you’ve said to me.” I gestured down the hallway with my head. “Come on, I’ve got a present for you.”

He didn’t follow when I started walking. I stopped with a sigh and slowly spun back around to face him. “What?”

“Do you have a death wish?”

“News flash. I can’t die.”

“Perhaps not, but I can make it so you wish you could.”

“Promises, promises.”

“Are you really that stupid?”

“What am I supposed to be afraid of, Sloth? Maybe you’re the one who isn’t showing enough respect. Do you know who I am?”

His brow furrowed as he stood, arms crossed over his chest, posture all masculine bravado. God save me from toxic masculinity.

“I couldn’t care less who you are. I fear no one. My arrival was heralded by a tidal wave so massive it wiped out the entirety of South America. In one fell swoop, I claimed millions of souls.”

I gave him a doe-eyed stare, my hair tossed over my shoulder as I mocked, “What? Like it’s hard?”

He growled, and a little shiver raced up my spine. If I weren’t in such a hurry to get this show on the road, he and I could have so much fun together.

"Are you always like this, darlin'?"

"Like what? Perfect? Amazing? Beautiful? Intense? You'll need to be more specific."

His lips twitched. "Challenging."

"Oh, yes." I turned on my heel and added an extra sway to my hips. "Come along now, handsome. Your services are required. Perhaps when this is all over, I'll find another use for you that will be . . . mutually enjoyable."

His laugh was a sexy rumble. "I don't fuck crazy."

"Yet."

"What was that?"

"You don't fuck crazy *yet*." I tossed a flirty wink over my shoulder, catching his incredulous expression. "The name's Famine, by the way. But you can call me Sabine."

He quirked a brow when I held my hand out, waiting for him to kiss the back of it as one would for royalty. He glanced from my eyes to my hand and shook his head slowly once.

"Fine, suit yourself. But know this, Slothy. If I wanted you to, you'd crawl across a floor of broken glass to kiss the toe of my boot. And you'd *beg* me for the privilege. I make a much better friend than an enemy."

"You're quite confident for a lass who is facing off with a sadist. You know that, don't you?"

A throaty laugh escaped me. "Oh yes. But trust me, my confidence is earned."

"So, tell me, Sabine," he murmured, coming up beside me as we continued down the hall. "What does a horsewoman want with one of the seven Princes of hell?"

We stopped in front of a locked door, and I made a show of unzipping the front of my catsuit all the way to my belly button before I pulled the key out of my cleavage. "It's simple. I want to win."

It took him longer than he probably liked to force his gaze up from my perfect breasts. "You have my attention. I'm not sure that's a good thing."

Unlocking the door, I pushed it open and stepped into the dark room. The soft whimpers coming from within sent glee ricocheting through me. I did love it when they whimpered.

"Get the light, would you, my prince? I want to show you your welcome gift."

With a click, the room illuminated, casting my chosen hostage in a flood of overhead light. His white cassock and red papal shoes gave him away for who he was, but still I asked, "I assume you don't need an introduction?"

Sloth looked from me to his present. Then his lips twisted into a wicked smile before the room filled with his evil laughter.

"Oh, Sabine. This is brilliant."

"Yes, yes, we've established that. Now, do with him what you will, but don't kill him. He's proving to be very stubborn and resolute in his devotion. I want you to change that. We have plans for this one."

"Plans?"

"Ever heard of a mass possession?"

The pope jolted in his bindings.

"Can't say that I have."

"Me either, but doesn't it sound positively scrumptious? Just think about all those souls, corrupted in one fell swoop because they're meek little lambs listening to their holy father as he leads them to eternal damnation." I shivered. "Welcome to the apocalypse, handsome. Now be a good boy and persuade my pope."

"Aye, that does sound right up my alley. Perhaps you and I are more suited than I thought."

I grinned. "I did tell you I made an excellent friend."

Sloth was too busy pulling out a selection of tools to pay me any attention. That was all right. I had business to attend to myself.

"You two have fun," I called over my shoulder. I'd barely made it out the door before screams chased me down the hallway. A giggle escaped, and I clapped my hands together in glee. "Oh, this is delightful. I just love when a plan comes together."

CHAPTER EIGHTEEN

MERRI

Fucking Chaos.

Fucking horsemen.

They knew me better than I wanted to admit, and Chaos was determined to win me back. I might've shut him down the last time, but he was right about so many things. Malice, too. I had to be strong enough to keep Lucifer at bay, so I had to feed, but I wasn't ready to fully let them back into my body or heart yet. Unfortunately for all of us, the best way for me to feed would be to do just that. It was so much more satisfying when my partner finished inside me. Not only did I stay full longer, the power it gave me was exponentially greater.

But doing that opened doors to other things. Namely feelings. I didn't want to end up with my heart even more broken by the time these four were done with me. They'd already hurt me deeply. Could I withstand anything else?

Then there was the not-so-small issue of the devil I knew. As in the literal devil, currently holding me captive. Was I really willing to stick to my guns and risk Lucifer forcing himself on me? My gut said he wouldn't take anything that wasn't offered, but my gut also told me the horsemen were my mates, and we saw how that turned out.

As confident as I was that Lucifer wouldn't force the issue, and that my current lack of bun in the oven was a point in my favor, I also wasn't one hundred percent sure. Would it actually be safer for me to continue with the original plan?

The truth was, I just didn't know anymore.

The one thing I did know? Nothing would change until I figured out where I was. That was priority number one. Well, technically priority number one was staying alive, but the two sort of went hand-in-hand. Which was why I was brushing my hair and giving myself a final critical check in the mirror. It was time to face the devil.

I didn't want this upcoming chat to seem like a complete about-face after avoiding him for the last two days, so I really needed to play my cards right, or he would see straight through me. That would probably be the case anyway—he was a clever fuck—but I didn't need to make it easy for him either. Maybe I could get him to slip up and give me some clue as to where he'd hidden us.

I half expected him to be waiting outside my door, ready to pounce as soon as I stepped into the hall. He wasn't. The house was quiet, cozy, and just as inviting as it had been when I first arrived. A far cry from the prison it really was.

I padded down the hall, warily checking for any hint as to where he was hiding. I swear to God, if that asshole jump-scared me, I would punch him in the dick so hard. It was the soft click-clack of keys that gave him away. Following the sound, I found him at his desk, spectacles perched on his aquiline nose, fingers typing away.

Before I could stop myself, I snickered, causing him to look up at me.

"So you've decided to come out of your room. Miss me, did you?" he said, a smirk tilting up his perfect mouth.

Ignoring his question, I focused on the one thing I could pick at. "Glasses, huh? I wouldn't have guessed you'd need them."

"One should always dress for the role they desire."

"Uh huh. And what role are you dressed for? Asshole of the Year?"

He chuckled, removing the glasses and setting them on the desk beside his typewriter. "Award-winning author, obviously."

"Why bother carrying on the facade?"

"What facade? I decided it was high time to write my memoir. Can you think of a more widely anticipated book?"

"Who's going to be left to read it? If you get your way, everyone will be dead."

Lucifer smiled at me, far too amused for someone I was trying to offend.

"What?" I snapped.

"Can't a man appreciate a woman?"

"A man, sure. Not you."

"Well, truthfully, I'm so much more than a man."

I rolled my eyes. "Ugh. That's something only a man would say. Next you'll tell me you're God's gift made special for me."

He cocked an eyebrow. "It would be true if you flipped it on its head. You're made for me, my sour little crabapple."

I'd been called a lot of things in my camming days, but that was a new one.

"Crabapple?"

"I am rather fond of apples, as you know, and you're just so delightfully prickly." His expression turned contemplative. "I suppose you can be my prickly pear if you prefer."

"No. I don't want to be your anything."

He gave me an almost comically exaggerated frown. "Well, it's a bit late for that. You may not have signed up for it, but you were born to be my *everything*."

"Stop trying to sway me with your silver tongue. Words are just that—empty promises when they're not backed up by actions."

His eyes widened, and he held his hands out as though to say, *but look at all of this*. "Haven't I shown you what I can do for you?"

"You mean lie, steal, and murder to get your way?"

"Don't forget the cookies."

Out of everything he could say, that took the wind from my righteously indignant sails. "Cookies laced with lies."

"They were not," he shot back, genuinely affronted. "They were made with love."

I laughed. "You wouldn't know love if it bit off your dick."

"Why would love do that? Seems a bit counterproductive. I think if you gave it a chance, that would be the last thing you'd want to do to it."

"Try me," I practically growled.

For a man who just got threatened with castration, he looked far too pleased with himself.

"Why are you smiling?"

"You're bantering with me."

"Threatening you, you mean."

"What's a little foreplay amongst star-crossed lovers?"

"Star-crossed lovers usually die in the end."

He shrugged. "I see it as progress. We're just another step closer to being where destiny wants."

"You're deluded."

"Thank you."

My God, he was infuriating. "That wasn't a compliment."

"It sounded like one. You're so cute when you flirt with me, crabapple."

"Stop calling me that."

"But it suits you so well. I rather like it."

I think I growled at him, but I couldn't be sure.

He stood from his seat to lean against the desk. "If you'd like, we can workshop your pet name for me. How about love of your life?"

I sneered at him.

"No? What about king of your heart?"

"More like pain in the ass."

"Mmm. I do love a pita, such a tasty treat. Especially with a little hummus. So yummy."

Frustration bubbled up in my chest. It was like talking to a handsome brick wall. "Oh my God, I think you're torturing me."

"Like I said, foreplay. There's a fine line between torture and edging. Think of how good it will be when you finally come to your senses and stop denying the chemistry between us."

Another harsh crack of laughter escaped me. "What fucking chemistry? This is *disdain*."

He waved a hand. "A rose by any other name . . ."

The Shakespeare reference made me think of Sin, and my heart gave a little pang.

"Speaking of cookies," I asked, trying to steer this conversation back to my original point, "Is there any fresh food here?"

Lucifer stood and made a show of stretching. "My lady love requires sustenance? The memoir of a fallen angel can wait. Come with me."

Okay, I could work with this. He was egotistical enough to want to be my sole provider. Following in his wake, we made our way into the kitchen. He was humming happily, as though I didn't hate him and wasn't his unwilling hostage.

"Alrighty, what does my tart little crabapple desire?" he asked as he opened the barren fridge. "Fresh fruit? A bit of veg? Perhaps pizza, or maybe fried chicken?"

As he spoke, ripe strawberries, pineapple, and blueberries appeared in a bowl in the refrigerator. Then a pizza box and a bucket of KFC showed up on the counter, the scents of melty cheese and pepperoni in addition to fried chicken filling the kitchen.

"I am rather fond of In-N-Out, if you wanted to go the burger route."

The mention of burgers had an image of Malice blazing to life in my mind. I had to squash the wave of sadness before Lucifer saw it on my face. He would too. The man was far too talented at reading me.

"So . . . the cookies. You didn't bake them?"

"Oh, I baked them for you, darling. But I manifested the ingredients."

"Wow," I said, leaning in to the opportunity to fawn. "That's amazing. What else can you do?"

He turned to face me fully. "What do you mean, love? I can do so many things. You might need to narrow down the question for me."

"Well, for example, I don't have many clothes here. Just what I arrived in and some of Cole's old sweats. Could you conjure some of those for me?"

"Of course I can."

"Does that only work on inanimate objects? Like, could you manifest a puppy?"

"Is my girl in need of a cuddle? All you have to do is ask," he said with a wink. Before he'd completed the move, a basket of golden retriever puppies appeared between us.

Apparently, I was weak because a basket of puppies had me sinking to my knees and scooping two of them into my arms. They were soft and warm and even smelled like puppies did. One immediately began licking my face, while the other promptly passed out in my arms. I was such a sucker.

"If I'd known that was the way to your heart, I'd have licked you days ago."

I glared at him behind my puppy shield. "It's cute when you're a furry baby. Less so when you're a slobbering idiot."

"I don't slobber, darling. I think you'll find me quite house-trained. Besides, I didn't say *where* I would lick you."

Fuck me, but I blushed. And all it took was puppies.

This was going to be so much harder than I thought.

Lucifer

Merri's attempts to suss out my limitations were transparent, but I didn't want to crush her spirit. She was finally out of that godforsaken room and willingly engaging with me. I wanted to prolong the moment as long as I possibly could. Besides, letting her think she was winning would just bring us closer.

I leaned casually against the counter while I watched her play with the puppies. They would have to go sooner rather than later, back to their demon owner and to their hellhound forms, but what she didn't know wouldn't hurt her. I certainly couldn't conjure living beings out of thin air, but transformation was much easier done. I deserved to take advantage of the moment and soak in the sight of her joy. I did that. I made her smile. I brought the light back into her eyes. Didn't I?

Hang on a tick.

Didn't I?

There was no denying that Merri looked good. Better than good. Better than she had since she arrived, actually.

It took every ounce of self-control not to grind my teeth to dust.

This wasn't the work of a few puppies. She'd been feeding.

Naughty girl.

Who the devil had she been feeding from? It most obviously wasn't the only devil she should want in her life—*me*.

"Horsemen. Bloody fucking menaces, the lot of them," I muttered under my breath.

She looked up as a puppy licked her neck. "What was that?"

"Who has been feeding you, crabapple?"

Eyes widening, she placed the puppies back in the basket before lifting her chin defiantly. "Why? Are you going to try and pretend to be him?"

Wanting her focus fully on me, I vanished the mongrels with a wave of my hand. "No. Those days are over."

"If only I believed you."

"Why shouldn't you? I've never lied to you."

Her mouth fell open, and a harsh bark of laughter escaped as she got to her feet. "Excuse me? What planet are you living on, buddy? All you've done since you came into my life is lie to me."

"Not about anything important."

"You don't think lying about who you are is important?"

"Not when the content of our conversations was pure."

I didn't understand why she was so upset about this. I may have used Cole's name and visage—okay, and his voice—but the man she interacted with was me. Everything I said to her was from the heart.

"Pure? You call trying to infiltrate my dreams, pretending to be someone else, and attempting to seduce me so I would fuck you and carry your devil spawn pure?"

"Well, yeah."

She laughed again.

"How else would I convince you? The world is filled with bullshit rumors about me. The only way to combat them was to have you get to know me, the real me, first. Otherwise you'd deny me from the jump. Unfairly, I might add."

"You'd be perfect on a dating app. In fact, you probably invented them."

I smirked. "Darling, I wish I could take credit for that one, but alas, I was imprisoned during the genesis of that particularly hellish experience."

"The fact that you want to take credit is telling."

"What do you want me to say, crabapple? I'm the world's favorite scapegoat. I get blamed for quite literally every misfortune that befalls humanity. Every now and then, it would be nice to actually be responsible for what I'm accused of."

"So you're saying you didn't give Eve the apple to force them from the garden? You didn't start a holy war against your father? You didn't whisper in the ears of your followers and encourage the Satanic panic?"

I snorted. "Why would I do any of that? Eve was hungry. That prat of a husband she was *forced* to be with, by the way, was hoarding all the food. What is it the bible says? For I was hungry and you fed me? Seems to me I was simply ahead of the curve. And it wasn't a holy war. I left home. Struck out on my own. Wanted to be my own angel. Daddy dearest didn't like that, so he disowned me. If you really think about it, he should be the one apologizing to me. Children are meant to fly the coop."

I took a deep breath before continuing. "As for the rest of it, why in the glorious skulled gates of hell would I be interested in ritual sacrifice? I have no use for goats, or babies, or even virgins, for that matter. I don't mind the blood, truth be told, but that was all them. I was merely a means for them to justify their bloodlust. And by them, I mean the Christian nationalist kooks who coined the term Satanic panic to fearmonger the general public. It wasn't ever real, you know. None of it. But they sure got people to fall in line with their anti-me propaganda."

Wow, I hadn't realized how much I was still carrying after all this time. It felt good to get it all off my chest. Perhaps I should kidnap a therapist after this was all over.

Merri was looking at me with a flood of conflicting emotions in her eyes. I could tell she wasn't sure what to believe, and that despite her very best efforts to the contrary, she sensed the thread of truth in my words.

"If all that's true, why bother with the apocalypse? Why use me to get your antichrist?"

Her question was valid, and before her, I may not have had the same answer. Originally, I wanted the apocalypse as a way to control everything my father loved and take it from him. Now? I wanted to prove myself worthy of his time and attention. I wanted to show him just how wrong he was about me as I led them into a new era.

I understood them—the humans—I saw them at their worst and didn't judge them. Perfection didn't exist, and that was what made them beautiful.

But all I said to her was, "Because we are destined, you and I. You were made to give me this."

"What happened to free will?"

"The two are not mutually exclusive."

"Aren't they?"

"Not at all. Free will ensures there are several paths to the same inevitable end."

"Why then?"

I cocked my head. "What do you mean?"

"Why take the time to get me on your side? You clearly could have taken me captive and just raped me the moment I walked into your trap. What's the point of this?" she asked, gesturing between us.

I stepped closer to her, reaching out and wrapping my hand around her nape as I pulled her to me. I didn't want her to see me as this monstrous creature hell-bent on getting my way. But she did. And she always might.

I leaned down until my face hovered just over hers, my voice whisper-soft but threaded with steel. "I have never raped a woman, and I don't intend to start now."

And then my lips slammed down on hers.

CHAPTER NINETEEN

MOIRA

"Festering goat balls," I grumbled as every candle I'd lit extinguished on its own, yet again. "You're supposed to be the head of the most powerful coven in the fucking world, Moira, but you can't even locate four stupid men?"

Closing my eyes, I willed the candles to light once more, anger causing the flames to blaze six inches high until I settled down. There was too much on my plate, as fucking usual. Life had been good—great even—until that bitch Death came in to ruin it all and throw a Lucifer-shaped wrench into my plans at a happily ever after.

Ash and I were in the middle of making a baby. I mean, not in the biblical sense, because yuck. No penis was going anywhere near my lady garden. But we had our sperm donor selected, and I'd already started preparing my temple, as they say. I was going to carry our first one, and she was on deck for baby number two. If we survived the first one. No one knew we were trying, and with everything going on, it never seemed like the right time to bring it up. But when I said I had a vested interest in ending this stupid apocalypse—a-fucking-gain, by the way—I wasn't kidding.

I rolled my gaze up to the sky, the alignment of the planets not visible through the flaming aurora streaking across the wide expanse. I could feel the energy, though. It radiated like a beacon, and time was ticking. This was the only shot we had at getting a lock on the people we needed to find. If I failed, we'd be SOL until fate stepped in. And, as we all knew, fate was a real bitch.

Closing one of my eyes, I glared up at the stars. "All right, we are going to reset and try this *again*. I've got the stupid item. We've got the celestial event with that mofo's arrival. WHAT ELSE DO YOU NEED, UNIVERSE? And yes, I used my shouty cap voice because come the fuck on."

A low snicker filtered through the treeline to my ears.

"Don't make me send you fleas, Kingston Farrell. Right to your balls."

He stepped out of the cover of trees and shook his head. "You wouldn't. You know you love me, witch."

"Debatable, but my bestie does, so I have to tolerate you."

Alek jumped down from the treetop where he'd been keeping watch, his big body leaving a dent in the softened earth. "Can you really do that? Give him fleas?"

"Of course I can. Are you really doubting me? After everything I've done for you, Brutus?"

"No, of course not. But I'd love to see how he'd handle that. He's a baby about most minor inconveniences."

"Rude," Kingston said, crossing his arms with a definite sulk marring his brow.

A new voice broke through the night, preceding the glow of purple eyes followed by a hunk of male specimen. If I were into that sort of thing. Which I was not. "This doesn't look like guard duty," Kai pointed out.

"It's not," Tor agreed, making it a four out of four on my guard dog bingo card. The only way they'd let me out here to attempt this spell was if the Brute Squad came with. I had to admit, it made a gal feel special.

"If you can give me fleas, Glinda, you can do this." I was pretty sure that was Kingston's way of encouraging me.

"How can we help?" Kai asked.

"Probably by keeping Kingston quiet," Tor offered.

"That is nearly impossible."

"Et tu, Alek? I thought we were friends."

I snickered at Kingston's echo of my earlier joke. I don't even know if he realized he'd done it. I'd probably subliminally implanted it there when I called Alek Brutus. I really was magic.

Rolling my neck out, I shook my arms and attempted to relax my posture. "I'm not sure what the deal is, honestly. By all accounts, this *should* work. I don't know why I can't find them. It's like the spell snuffs out before it has a chance to take hold."

"Maybe they don't want to be found," another voice said, joining us.

"Asher? You're not supposed to be out here," Tor chided, still a stickler for the rules.

"In case you haven't noticed, the world is ending. I can do whatever the fuck I want. Moira, I came to tell you my theory on the horsemen. I've been working it out with Gavin, and we realized that they've never been locatable in their entire existence. Not them. Not the horsewomen."

I stood and brushed the dirt off my ass. "What do you mean?"

"I think it's in their genetic makeup. They're naturally shrouded. You won't be able to break through it. Not with any Earth-based magic, anyway."

A blur of motion caught my eye a second before Gavin appeared at Asher's side. "Did you tell her? Is it too late? Can she shift her focus?"

"Jesus, Count. I told you I could handle this on my own. You were supposed to stay back with Rosie while Ben and Remi are on patrol."

"Pan's with her, it's fine."

Asher raised a brow. "You really trust him to be a responsible adult on his own?"

"No more than I trust you, but thankfully there's a sea of other grown-ups around to lend a watchful eye."

I cleared my throat delicately. "Are you two done jerking each other off yet?"

Gavin shot me a glare, but I didn't back down. I wasn't afraid of him.

"I assure you we have not, nor will we ever, jerk each other off."

"There was that one time . . . " Asher started, but before he could finish, Kingston chimed in, "Never say never."

"Ugh, you dick swingers. Focus. Tell me what I need to know and get out of my hair. Please, for the love of the goddess."

Asher took a deep breath. "I think you need to change targets."

"Who—" I cut myself off, the answer obvious. The only other person we've been trying and failing to locate was Gabriel. This was a perfect opportunity to see if we could break through whatever dark magic Lucifer was using to hide him. "I didn't bring his feather."

Asher held it up. "Way ahead of you."

"What's going on?" Kingston stage whispered.

Kai patted the top of his head. "Shh, the grown-ups are talking."

Tor and Alek cackled.

"Hey, man. You're on Team Sunday, remember? You can't take the bully's side."

"She's going to find Gabriel," Alek said in a placating tone.

"Oh! Good old leather feathers. Would be nice to have his help. He usually comes in clutch when we need him."

Goddess, Kingston was the definition of a himbo. Pretty, kind, allegedly good in bed, but not a lot going on upstairs.

"Okay, I've got at most a few minutes left before this celestial event is past its max power surge. If I'm going to do this, it has to be now." I returned to my seated position and extinguished the candles before preparing to start the ritual again. "Everyone shut the hell up and let mama work."

"Should we chant or something?" Alek asked.

"Are you deaf? I said shut the fuck up."

Alek winced and mimed zipping his lips. The men stood in a loose circle around me, Tor and Kai eyeing the surrounding area like a couple of secret service agents, while the others watched me reset the spell for Gabriel.

I felt it the moment something changed. Instead of the sensation of coming up against a wall, my power kept moving, riding the energy like a wave or the tide as the spell searched for the wayward angel.

"Are the candles supposed to do that?" Kingston whispered, prompting me to open my eyes and observe the change in the flames. Where they'd once been a happy orange, they'd changed to pure white.

"Did it work?" Gavin asked.

"Beats me," Asher said with a shrug.

"I thought there was supposed to be a portal?" Alek asked, looking between Kingston and Tor. "I thought you guys said there was a portal the last time she did this spell."

"There was," I muttered. "But Gabriel is different from you. He's not a Novasgardian. He's a fucking angel."

"So . . . did you find him?" Asher asked.

"Kind of."

"How does one kind of find an angel?" Kai asked.

Reaching into my bag, I pulled out a clear crystal ball. "Very carefully. I'll need a few days—"

"We don't have a few days to sit around out here and guard you."

"Yes, Captain Obvious, I am well aware," I said to Kingston with a roll of my eyes. "Thankfully, now that the locator spell has been put into motion, all I have to do is transfer it to this orb. Once we have our answer, it will change color, and boom, we can go find him."

"Oh! So it's like baking sourdough."

We all looked at Kingston.

"What? You have to get the starter going before you can bake the bread. Everyone knows that. The orb is the starter. We have to wait for it to be ready. I have one at home. I named it Bread Sheeran. You know, like Ed Sheeran, but Bread."

"You're cute," I said with a shake of my head.

"So that's it?" Asher asked. "We just wait for the magic ball to finish baking and then we can poof off?"

"It's less of a poof and more of a shwoooop, but sure. Something like that."

"And it'll bring us to his doorstep?"

"Theoretically. It might be more like the neighborhood block, but you know, beggars can't be choosers. If we're lucky, though, it might place us quite literally on top of him. Which will be super fun to explain."

"I bet he'd love that," Kai muttered.

Gavin snickered. "Would serve the pompous arse right for all the times he'd barged in on us."

"Ohmygod, what if we catch him jerking off?" Kingston asked.

"Isn't he like a Ken doll?" Asher countered.

"You guys are way off topic. Also, isn't your whole dad an angel?" I asked. "How does that work if he doesn't have man parts?"

"Technically he's a fallen angel."

"So he lost his wings and grew a dick?" Kingston asked.

"How the fuck should I know?" Asher asked, nose crinkling like he smelled something foul.

"Personally, I'd rather have a dick than wings," Kingston said.

"I have both," Kai offered smugly. "They're excellent teammates."

Tor silently held up his hand for Kai to high-five. I shuddered.

"Annnd, that's about enough of that for me." Shoving the orb back in my bag, I stood. "Clean up after me, would you, boys? I've met my testosterone quota for the rest of my life."

"You're not going anywhere without us," Alek said. "If something happened to you, we'd never forgive ourselves."

"Aw, you're sweet. The duke is going to see me to safety. He's fast. I'll be back in the shelter before you can say abracadabra."

“Abracadabra,” Kingston shouted.

I shot him a hard side-eye before giving him the finger and climbing onto Gavin’s back like a much less clumsy Bella Swan. “Fuck off, Kingston.”

“Love you too, Elphie!”

Taking my life into my own hands, I leaned close to the vampire’s ear and said, “All right, Sparkles, let’s see how impossibly fast you are.”

“Fucking Twilight,” he grumbled, grabbing me under each knee as he started to run. “That book wasn’t even close to accurate.”

I snorted, but kept my comments to myself because he wasn’t kidding. Closing my eyes against the blur of the scenery, I made a mental note to make some corrections to vampire lore in fiction if we survived this. It was the least I could do.

CHAPTER TWENTY

SIN

The warm ocean breeze brought the scents of plumeria and sea salt to the forefront of my awareness as my dream came into focus. I knew the moment I turned my head I'd find Merri next to me, and I was right. Since coming to Malice, she hadn't missed a night. Loath as she'd be to admit it, she needed us. And I was not-so-secretly preening because if you counted my venture into her dream a few nights ago, I was the only horseman she'd talked to twice. Grim hadn't even gotten to see her once yet.

Not that anyone would be surprised she was avoiding him. The real question was whether she would visit him next or just circle straight back to Malice. It would serve that stuffed shirt right if she skipped him altogether.

My mouth ran dry at the sight of Merri, posed on a lounger in a tiny black bikini with her hair piled high on her head in a messy bun. She was reading a paperback, lower lip pulled between her teeth as she focused on the words on the page and ignored me.

"You need a cocktail, kitten. Can't be sitting poolside on a day like this without one."

Without missing a beat, she reached beside her and lifted a fruity umbrella drink, the glass dripping with condensation as she put the tiny straw between her lips.

I'm not ashamed to say my gaze followed a drop of water as it fell from the base of the glass and hit her chest, sliding slowly down her body until it disappeared in her bikini bottoms.

"You're drooling," she murmured.

"You're gorgeous."

She flipped a page, still mostly ignoring me. It might have hurt my feelings if Malice and Chaos hadn't both warned me that she was definitely still punishing us. And fair enough, honestly. We deserved it—some more than others. The difference between me and them? I wasn't going to roll over and take it.

No way. No how.

I was going to fight fire with fire. Or lust with love. The details were fuzzy, but I had the makings of a plan. The pieces, at least. Kind of like when you got a box from Ikea and you had it all laid out but still needed the instructions to help you put it all together.

Hmm. I wonder if they serve Swedish meatballs at this joint...

I supposed the best way to start was with the direct approach. I could seduce her better than anyone, but we already knew that.

Clearing my throat, I swung my legs over the side of my own lounger and faced her. I eyed the banana hammock she'd put me in with a twist of my lips. "You summoned me to this fancy resort. Are you just missing me? Need to breathe the same air as me for a while? Or can I help you with something you need?"

She turned another page and let out a soft, musing sound. "It doesn't have to be so one-sided, Sin. This can be a mutually beneficial arrangement."

"It's never one-sided. You get to feed. I get to come. Although I like it so much better when we feed from each other."

Putting down the book, she leveled her gaze on me. "That's what I meant."

"Does that mean you're going to unlock that chastity belt of yours?"

"Chastity belt?"

"They told me you're locked up tighter than the Vatican's secret archives."

"If they're a secret, how would you know?"

I gave her a pointed glance. "Is that really a question?"

She rolled her eyes and resumed her reading. "To answer your original question, I haven't decided yet."

My heart skipped a beat. If she hadn't already ruled out the possibility, it meant there was still a chance. The fact that it was with me when she'd been adamant about the others had me feeling some kind of way.

Then again, it shouldn't be a surprise. Merri and I had a thing for firsts.

I reached out and ran my fingertips along her leg. "Anything I can do to help you make up your mind?"

Vulnerability flickered in her eyes as she looked at me over the edge of the book. "Say you're sorry."

"I di—" I began, but the protest died on my tongue. Had I never actually apologized to her?

Shoulders slumping, I heaved a frustrated sigh. "Merri, I'm so fucking sorry for everything that happened. I'm sorry I hurt you by being silent. I'm sorry I let you down and didn't defend what we have immediately. I'm sorry I made you feel anything less than what you are: The most important person in my entire world."

She held my gaze, her eyes searching as her lower lip wobbled. "Do you really mean it?"

I wanted to tell her to check for herself, but I knew it was only natural to question everything after a betrayal like the one she'd suffered at our hands. Her gut had her believing one thing, and Grim was trying to gaslight her into something else. It would take a long time to repair the damage he'd caused.

Prick.

"You don't have to believe me. I know I don't deserve it, but, Merri, if I could go back in time and change the way everything played out, I would. I'd tell Grim how wrong he was and make sure you knew how proud I am to be your mate. I swear, if you give me the chance, I'll prove it to you with more than words."

Silence stretched between us as she weighed my vow. I knew she'd come to a decision when her expression cleared and she set down her book.

"Well, I guess you'd better get started then."

Okay, well, fuck. How did I go about doing that?

I glanced at the romance novel she'd placed on the table between our chairs. Right. Book boyfriend shit. I could do that. I was *made* for it.

As soon as I got to my feet, I leaned over her and scooped her into my arms, smirking at the little yelp of surprise she couldn't contain. I angled away from the loungers and headed for the cabana just a few feet behind them. The white fabric walls blew in the ocean breeze, revealing the two-person daybed within.

It was like she'd planned for this exact scenario. Which meant I was on the right track. Good job, Sin.

She didn't say a word as I laid her down in the nest of pillows and soft blankets, but her expression was less guarded, less reluctant. And then there was the lust coming off her that hadn't been there before. She wanted me—not just to feed from, but to connect with—and she couldn't hide it.

"I've missed you," I murmured, brushing a few fallen strands of hair off her face as I curled up beside her.

Her breath stuttered out, and for a second, I didn't think she was going to say anything, but then the words left her in a rush, "I missed you too."

Reaching for her, I cupped her chin and turned her to face me simply so I could gain access to her perfect lips. I hadn't kissed her in so long. It had been a special kind of agony to go without now that I'd found her.

I moved until I hovered just over her lips and then lifted my eyes to hers. "Stop me now if this isn't what you want."

She tilted her chin up, her lips feathering against mine in the palest imitation of a kiss. "Don't stop."

"I love you, Merri. It kills me that you had any reason to doubt me." Fuck, my voice was broken.

Close as we were, each word had my lips moving against hers. It was the biggest fucking tease.

Merri let out a soft hum as she threaded her fingers through my hair and tugged me that final centimeter down. Our mouths met in a gentle press that was rapidly replaced by a passionate and demanding kiss. All our pent-up longing, the hurt, the love, the need, culminated in this perfect reunion between us. I wanted to stay here forever. And wasn't that part of the danger of dreamwalking? We could trap ourselves in this haven we created and never leave. Even as the world was destroyed around us.

"I need you," she whispered after breaking our kiss, her fingers trailing down the back of my neck and over my shoulders possessively.

"Not as much as I need you."

Her lips twitched in a small smile. "Prove it."

I moved until I was above her, my aching cock pressed against her core. "How's that for proof?"

She leaned up and nipped my bottom lip. "You can do better."

Reaching between us, I untied her bikini bottoms and let the fabric fall away. My fingers drifted over her hip and to the apex of her thighs, but all I could look at was her face as I touched her.

"You're wet for me," I whispered.

"Always."

"Good girl."

A ripple of lust poured out of her at my praise, and I had to fight back a smug grin. I was so fucking good at this.

"Stop teasing me. You know I'm ready." She slipped her hand under my bathing suit and grabbed hold of my throbbing length. "And I know you're ready."

I groaned, head falling back as she stroked me. "I've been ready since the moment I first saw you." The ghost of a breeze over my ass was the only hint she'd used her magic to take care of our clothing. I huffed out a laugh. "You really are in a hurry."

"Like you aren't?"

I made sure our gazes were locked when I admitted, "If I could make this last forever, I would. For a few days there, I thought I'd never get to have this with you again. It makes a guy selfish."

She didn't reply, simply wrapped her arms around the back of my neck and arched up so she could kiss me. I used that opportunity to fit myself between her thighs and sink into her warm, welcoming body. Her whimper sent a rush through me as the sensation of us being joined again took hold. This wasn't a frenzied fuck so we could power up. I was making love with the woman I wanted to keep for eternity.

A bit of soul-fucking, if you will.

Our bodies moved together in a sinuous dance, my thrusts slow but deep, our eyes focused on each other. Merri might not be using her succubus power, but it was a magic all on its own. Something I'd never experienced with anyone but her.

My Merri.

My mate.

I wasn't going to last much longer, and part of me wanted to fight the urge to fill her with my cum so soon, but a bigger part knew this was the plan all along. She needed this from me so she could be strong while we searched for a way to bring her back.

Her nails scored my ass and thighs as she cried out, an orgasm taking her by surprise if the look on her face was anything to go by. That was all it took for me to go over the edge right along with her. Pleasure turned my vision white as I gave her everything I had and delighted in knowing I'd help strengthen her.

I stayed planted inside her as we both came down from the high of our joint climax. She was running her fingers through my hair, her expression love-drunk and happy. I wished I could capture this moment, that there was a way to take a mental picture so I could come back to it over and over again. If heaven was something a horseman could experience, this was mine.

"I love you, Meredith Deveraux."

She blinked up at me, her smile stretching. "I love you too, Emmett Sinclair, Horseman of the Apocalypse and whatever other names you go by." Her brow furrowed, posture stiffening before she said, "I have to go. He's coming."

Merri being aware of what was happening outside the dream realm was a new development. I wondered if it was because her control of the dream realm was getting stronger, or if it was something she'd been capable of all along.

"We're doing everything we can to find you, Merri. I swear it."

"I know you are. I'm sorry I left you."

"I'm sorry you felt it was your only choice."

She brushed her lips over mine and I closed my eyes, enjoying one last kiss. When I opened them again, I was back in my bedroom at the château, staring up at a crack in the ceiling and hoping like hell she was okay.

CHAPTER TWENTY-ONE

ALEK

Our hunting party was larger than usual tonight, but this wasn't just about patrol or recon. We needed supplies. Those of us who required real food over blood couldn't survive on magically conjured sustenance for long. It was akin to attempting to nourish your body on nothing more than popped corn. Tasty, but not particularly healthy.

I did a quick headcount, ensuring everyone had safely made it out of the portal. Representing the Novasgardian contingent were Tor, myself, and Strega. For the vamps, we had Thorne, West, and Lucas Blackthorne. The fae volunteers included Kai and Finbar. And the wolves sent Briar—Lucas's star-crossed shifter mate—Dylan Farrell, and the Mercer twins.

"Do you think Lilith was making a joke when she chose the Alice in Wonderland statue for one of her tethers?" Remi asked, doing fuck all to keep his voice down.

Central Park at night wasn't somewhere the general public frequented, even when we weren't in the middle of an apocalypse, but I wasn't worried about humans at the moment. Demons hid in the shadows everywhere we went. We were prepared to fight them, but that didn't mean we should call attention to ourselves.

Before I could chastise the overexcited wolf, Tor spun around and hissed, "Quiet or we'll send you back."

Remi's eyes flared, and he glanced at his brother. "Was it something I said?"

Ben placed a hand on his shoulder. "Y-yes."

"Got it." Remi mimed locking his lips and handing Ben the key. "Mmm-mmmph-mmph-mm."

"What did he say?" I asked my twin.

"Who cares?" Strega answered for him.

I cracked a smile at my father's second-in-command. "Fair point."

Kai came up on my right, his eyes constantly scanning the horizon. "I don't like this. It's too quiet."

"This place is a damn ghost town. Of course it's quiet," Dylan Farrell said, adjusting his cowboy hat as he glanced across the park at the broken city skyline.

New York City hadn't fared well between the earthquakes and tsunamis and demon hordes. The city was barely recognizable. Many of the skyscrapers had come tumbling down, and Lady Liberty had taken a header a few weeks past and was now somewhere on the bottom of the Atlantic.

"I have a question," Briar asked, standing beside her mate Lucas Blackthorne. She narrowed her eyes as she returned to the statue we'd used as a portal and placed her palm on the largest of the bronze mushrooms. "The portal is closed. How the fuck are we supposed to get back? I doubt we're standing on top of the secret fight club."

"Lilith m-made sure w-we all h-had k-key cards," Ben answered, holding a black card up.

"We do?" she asked.

Lucas nodded, pulling out two more of the black keys. "Never doubt me, darling. I've got yours right here."

"Who has the supplies list? We don't want to stay out here long. We're sitting ducks at this point." Thorne's posture was tense as he took the lead, walking toward the city, eyes roaming every possible place a demon could lie in wait. "Vampires should hit the bodegas first. The wolves can collect the items on Moira's witchcraft list."

A low growl left Ben. "Who m-made you the l-leader?"

"Benny, now's not the time to alpha out on our brother-in-law." Remi placed a hand on his twin's shoulder as he spoke.

Ben stood down, his eyes returning to their typical blue rather than the vivid neon they'd just been. Not for the first time, I had the fleeting thought that alpha shifters and Berserkers weren't all that different.

"So what are *we* going to do?" Strega asked. "I didn't come out here to twiddle my thumbs."

Tor gave her a grin far too sinister to be mistaken as friendly. "We're going hunting."

"Oh, my favorite," she purred, pulling the broadsword out of its sheath and giving it a little flourish. "It's time to bless my blade with more of that demon filth's blood."

"Is that really a blessing?" Briar asked.

"Demon blood is only good for spilling. It tastes like arse," West said, looking at his sister-in-law before frowning at Thorne. "I'll never forget the time you tricked me into drinking from a demon."

Lucas snickered. "I did that to your father and Auntie Sorcha once as well."

"Rude," Remi said under his breath.

"It's a rite of passage. How else are we supposed to learn?" Thorne asked.

I shot him a look. "Did you ever learn?"

Shrugging, he adjusted his collar and said, "Didn't have to. I saw it, and that was enough for me."

My mind went back to the night we almost lost our Sunday to a demon attack. How Thorne willingly sucked out the poisoned blood to save her. He knew what would happen to him, and still he chose to do that for her. If I hadn't already known the depth of his commitment, I would now.

Finbar held up a hand, signaling for the rest of us to stop. "Someone's out here."

"Where?" Kai snarled, his eyes glowing in the darkness.

Finbar pointed to a park bench several feet away. It was a bit hard to make out the details from here, but it appeared as though a body was slumped across it.

"Are they alive?" Tor asked.

The wolves and vamps all collectively inhaled, and an involuntary shudder worked its way down my spine. It was easy to forget they weren't human until they went and did something like that.

"Yes and no," Lucas said.

"What the fuck does that mean?" Finbar asked.

"It means we need to move. Fast." Dylan picked up his pace. "The less interaction we have with anyone, the better."

"Wait," West called, his eyes narrowed. "What are they doing?"

"Fuck," I whispered, as the hitherto still form abruptly stood.

"I told you to keep it down," Tor muttered.

"I was quiet as a church mouse. It was these bozos," Remi said, pointing at the rest of us.

The mostly dead body moved toward us in jerky movements. Unnatural and eerie. Those were the best ways I could describe it. The closer it came, the better I could make out its features. I'd heard Tor's stories of the fight at Blackwood. The zombies Dahlia had raised with her power. This didn't look like a zombie. In fact, he looked like a mildly ill human man.

"He's possessed," Kai said.

"How can you tell?" Strega asked, moving into a defensive position.

"He smells wrong," Remi answered.

"Remi's r-right. Human but n-not." Ben's hands curled into fists as he stepped up beside his twin.

"Edgar suit," Remi muttered.

"A what suit?" I asked.

"Like Edgar in Men In Black. A demon is wearing him like a suit. It doesn't fit quite right, that's why he's so shambly and awkward."

Obviously he was referencing a film I hadn't seen yet. I added it to the never-ending list of movies we would be watching on one of Kingston's movie nights.

The half-dead possessed man grew closer, his stench now reaching my nostrils. One adversary, I could handle. One was manageable on my worst day.

I rolled my neck and readied to charge him, but as soon as I took a step forward he stopped. He was only a few feet away from us.

"What's he do—"

Before Briar finished asking her question, the man exploded, red mist and chunks of gore spraying out in every direction. Tor and I hit the ground out of instinct. Some of the others were not as lucky, the force of the unexpected blast sending them flying.

"Oh, gross," Remi complained, spitting out whatever he'd unfortunately gotten in his mouth. Perhaps if he kept it shut more often, things like this wouldn't happen to him.

"Everyone okay?" I called, pushing myself off the ground.

I glanced around, doing a quick headcount as the others gathered themselves.

"I wouldn't do that—" Thorne started, just as his brother licked at some of the blood coating his face.

West immediately grimaced and gagged. "Yup. Definitely demon."

"I tried to warn you," Thorne said with a barely contained smirk. It was a look only a smug older brother could pull off.

"What was the point of this?" Finbar asked, pulling a piece of entrails from his hair and flicking it to the ground with a disgusted look on his face.

"Have you never seen a bomb?" Lucas asked, his voice tight with pain as we all turned our attention to him. Briar gasped and rushed to his side when he gripped the large piece of what looked to be a femur and pulled it free from his gut.

Strega was similarly impaled by bone shrapnel, though she'd taken it to the neck.

"Maybe you should w—"

She tugged the shard free with barely a hiss before I could finish, blood blooming from the wound and running down her neck.

"Fucking hell," Thorne grumbled, blurring to Strega as the other two vampires stiffened and homed in on the waterfall of blood coming from her throat.

She had her fingers pressed to the wound, but it was doing nothing to stanch the flow. The bone had most likely nicked an artery. Stubborn woman.

"Wh-what," she spluttered, making a feeble attempt at fighting him off, but she didn't have healing magic. She was a formidable Novasgardian warrior, not immortal.

"Let him help you," I said with a nod for Thorne to continue. His blood would close the wound and speed up the healing process. It was that or abandon the hunt and get her back to sanctuary immediately.

She gave Thorne a wary side-eye before lowering her hand. "If you turn me, I will kill you before you have time to draw breath."

"As far as death threats go, it's one of the better ones to come my way," he said with a half-smile as he pierced the skin of his thumb and swiped his blood over the tear in her flesh.

Vampiric healing power never ceased to amaze me, no matter how many times I witnessed it in action.

As her skin knitted back together, her expression went from wary to grateful, and by the time she was fully healed, she had placed a palm on Thorne's shoulder in a gesture of thanks.

"This is really moving and all, but allow me to ring the alarm bells, because—"

"We've got company," Tor snarled, his transition to his Berserker form instantaneous.

"—we're fucked," Dylan finished.

More shambling figures stumbled out from every direction. First a handful, then a couple dozen, then at least a hundred.

"What are we doing here, guys?" Briar asked, her posturing defensive, but her expression tinged with fear.

"We fight," Kai snarled, black scales rippling down his exposed skin like reptilian armor.

"No," I said with a harsh shake of my head. "We have to retreat. This is a trap, and we're clearly outnumbered."

"But the supplies," West protested.

"Can wait. We aren't ready for this level of conflict."

"I can outrun them. If you guys distract them, Ben and I can make it into the city so we can complete our mission." Remi was visibly shaking with tension, eyes blazing electric blue with the need to shift.

"N-no. Don't b-be an idiot." Ben shook his head.

"What? You're just giving up?"

"D-don't make m-me explain to Rosie why y-you d-died."

Remi's shoulders slumped. "Fine."

"We need to go. They're closing in faster than the last one." Tor headed for the statue, Lilith's key card already in hand.

Thorne and I exchanged looks. "Go," I said. "I'm going to make sure the others are clear before I join you."

"But—"

"Get the fuck out of here, Noah."

He gave me a terse nod before he and his brother both popped out of existence. The others were quick to follow, blinking out of sight until only Tor and I remained.

"What are you doing, brother? Go."

"Not without you. Together, or not at all, remember?"

I sighed at my twin, but clasped his hand just as the first of the walking bombs got in range.

"I hate running," I grumbled.

"Me too, but there's nothing cowardly about living to fight another day."

With a final nod, we each activated our cards and got the fuck out of Dodge.

CHAPTER TWENTY-TWO

MERRI

The moment I stepped into the hall, I heard Lucifer humming from somewhere deeper inside the cabin. I'd been hiding since our confrontation, like the coward I was. But how was I supposed to look him in the face after he kissed me like that yesterday?

I wish I could say I hated it. That I'd instantly pushed him away or drawn blood, but the truth was I'd leaned in. Like the proverbial moth to a flame. I could blame being a succubus all I wanted, but there was a part of me—a teeny, tiny atom-sized piece—that was curious. No, that wasn't a strong enough word. That traitorous little slut *liked* it. But wasn't that the dangerous part of all of this? Just because we liked something, that didn't mean it was good for us. Lucifer wasn't good for me in any capacity. He wasn't good for anyone.

He was the freaking devil.

That's the antithesis of good. Well, unless you believed a word he said. Then he was actually the victim. Which felt like Gaslighting 101, or at the very least, some real NPD shit. If you've ever dated a narcissist, you'll know exactly what I mean.

Before I was halfway down the hall, Lucifer himself came around the corner, stopping in his tracks with a sly grin spreading across his lips.

"I was waiting to see how long it would take you to come out this time. Not even a full twenty-four hours. You're obsessed with me."

"You want to talk obsession? Who is holding whom captive, Lucifer?"

"Semantics."

"Details matter. I hear that's where the devil lives."

"If we're being technical, I have a very lovely castle in hell, as well as a condo in LA and a penthouse in Helsinki." He lifted a hand and started counting on his fingers. "All of Manhattan. An adorable little pub in Glasgow. Plus the high rise in Dubai. A couple of islands." He snapped. "Oh, and that sheep farm in New Zealand."

"Not Vegas? That seems right up your alley."

He sneered. "No, thank you. Too obvious."

I opened my mouth, but shut it again immediately when he sucked in a sharp breath.

"I almost forgot the best one of all. My koala sanctuary in Australia."

"I'm sorry, did you just say you have a koala sanctuary?" This had to be a lie. Why would Lucifer Morningstar rescue anything?

"Koalas are going to be extinct in the wild in your lifetime, Merri."

"The world is literally ending. Everything is going to be extinct in my lifetime."

He waved a hand. "But not because of chlamydia."

"And that's an upside because . . ."

"They deserve better."

I stared at him. Was the devil actually debating the finer points of koalas with me? It was so reminiscent of the time Cole went off about camel mating facts that I had to blink a couple of times and force myself to focus.

"Don't look at me like that. All they do is eat, sleep, and fornicate. That's all. They're the most innocent of creatures."

"I guess I'm just . . . confused."

"About what?"

"About who you really are."

He grinned and held his arms out wide, as though he were saying *I'm here, you're welcome.*

"My darling little crabapple, I contain multitudes."

I was starting to see that, but saying so out loud felt like surrender, so instead I didn't say anything.

"I don't see why you struggle with the reality of me so much. I know everyone makes me out to be the bad guy—"

"You *are* a bad guy."

"—the root of all evil," he continued, as if I hadn't contradicted him. "But I'm so much more than that. Just like you are so much more than a sex demon. No one, not even the most beautiful of angels, is only one thing."

My head was spinning as I attempted to process and filter the truth from his well-crafted lies. *Was* he all bad? Surely he must be if the horsemen were working so hard to keep me from him, to defeat him.

"Stop trying to talk circles around me. I see what you're doing." I shoved past him, holding my breath so I couldn't inhale the scent of him. He had this delicious manly campfire thing going on that I absolutely refused to admit I enjoyed.

"And what is it I'm doing? Besides getting to know the future mother of my child?"

I spun back around and shoved my finger in his chest. "No. I am not your future anything."

"Of course you are. We've been over this." He lifted his hand and made his fingers dance like he was finger painting in the air. "We're written in the stars, crabapple. You and I are a done deal. Sealed by destiny before you were even born."

"That's creepy."

He scoffed and rolled his eyes. "Don't be puritanical about this. Not after everything we've shared already."

"We haven't shared a single thing."

"I beg to differ. You've listened to me come on more than one occasion. I've watched you touch yourself. And then there's the little matter of our kiss yesterday. That one wasn't even over a screen. We shared that . . . IRL, as the kids say."

"You know what else the kids say?"

"I'm sure you're about to tell me."

"You give me the ick."

"Liar."

"That would be you."

"Now, now, Merri. Let's be honest with each other, if nothing else. I initiated said kiss, but you, my darling, were the one who leaned in."

"I also slapped you."

It's true. I had. Just about thirty seconds and one damp pair of panties later than I should have. But the point was, I did it.

"I like a feisty woman. Lucifer doesn't run from a challenge."

"Ew," I said, backing away, but there was a small part of me that lit up at his persistence. What the fuck was wrong with her?

"I am not a challenge, Lucifer. I am a dead fucking end. You and me? Never gonna happen. The sooner you realize that, the sooner we can both go home and get on with what's left of our lives. I don't fuck with liars."

His fingers encircled my wrist as I spun away and made to storm into the living room, stopping me with very little effort. Before I could wriggle free, he had my back pulled against his front and his lips were at my ear, voice low and measured.

"You keep harping on that word. Liar. How many times do I have to tell you that I do not need to lie to get you to want me?"

"All you do is lie!" I shouted, spinning back around to glare up at him, suddenly furious with the both of us. Him for being him, and me for forgetting far more often than I should that he was the enemy.

"No!" he shouted back, getting down in my face. His eyes searched mine for several heartbeats before he shook his head and said much more softly. "No. I've been more myself with you than anyone I've ever known. Anyone, Merri. Do you know how long I've lived? How fucking rare it is that I can drop the mask and just exist? That's the real privilege of being human, you know. That ability to simply be whatever it is you are. Unapologetically. Authentically. And so many of you take it for granted, trying to squeeze yourselves into boxes that don't fit just to please other people. Wearing a mask is exhausting. Taking it off is the real gift."

That brought me up short. As much as I didn't want to, I could relate. I understood exactly what he was saying because I had lived my life with the same mask. But while I'd only lived a quarter of a century, he'd lived millennia. A reality I couldn't comprehend. I'd struggled with my mask after a couple decades; I couldn't imagine the burden of wearing it as long as he's had to.

But again, admitting any of that felt like a loss I could not afford. So I did what I accused him of. I lied.

"I don't believe you."

His gaze seared into mine, but his expression was gentle as he reached up and tucked a stray piece of hair behind my ear. "I think the thing you're struggling with, crabapple, is that you do."

As I looked into his eyes, I released a flare of my power, intentionally using it on him for the first time. I needed to know if he was being truthful. If he noticed, he didn't give any indication, but sincerity coated his aura. I didn't think even *he* could fake that.

It wasn't a perfect test, but it certainly seemed to back up his assertions.

I had a sudden flash of Andi whispering in my ear: *You in danger, girl.*

"Merri, you say I lied, but you need to accept that we've shared countless intimate moments together already. Conversations I may have had using a different accent, but not a different truth. I sounded like Cole," he said, the last sentence coming out in Cole's voice. "But I was always me. Everything I told you came from here." The man took my hand and rested it over his heart.

"Don't you see how manipulative that is? You pretended to be someone to further your psycho plot, which, for the record, is. a. lie. And speaking of that, let's address the real elephant in the room, shall we?"

His lips twitched with amusement. For someone being called out, he looked like he was enjoying himself. "By all means, let's."

"What happens to me after you get what you want?"

"You'll need to be more specific."

"If you knock me up—"

"*When* I knock you up."

"Whatever. What happens after?"

He pinched the bridge of his nose and closed his eyes as he took a long breath. "Well . . . I ascend to the throne as ruler of all and—"

"No. Not what happens for you, asshole. What happens to me? What happens to the child we have?"

He floundered. I'd actually stumped him.

I snorted a laugh. It was so completely in character for him to be so self-absorbed that he'd never considered what would happen to us.

"I suppose you'll rule at my side, or do whatever it is you want to do."

"Because I'll have served my purpose and you'll have no need for either of us? Typical."

"No. Why must you always insist on seeing the absolute worst side of things?"

"Is there an upside here?"

He huffed. "Did you ever consider that maybe I wasn't going to force a role on you because you'd have earned the right to choose for yourself what part you wanted to play? Just because I'm orchestrating a brilliant takeover does not mean I want to control every aspect of our lives. I do still believe in free will, you know. That might be one of the only things Daddy dearest got right."

I wasn't expecting that. I figured he'd throw me away like yesterday's takeout and be done with me once I gave him what he wanted. And he still might. His energy gave off sincerity, but Lucifer could be sincere in the moment and change his tune later. Both things could be true.

"And what happens if I never give you my body, or I do, but you can't get me pregnant?"

His grin was absolutely sinful. "I never miss."

"I hate to break it to you, but I'm not particularly fertile. I don't think your skill matters much against genetics."

He snickered. "Darling, your fertility is a non-issue. I'm more virile than any man you've ever been with. You're probably ovulating right now, simply being in my proximity. All it will take is one time, and my little astronauts will walk on the moon, as they say."

"No one says that."

"They'll discover Atlantis."

"Still not a thing."

"You will get pregnant with my child, Merri. There is no doubt in the matter. You could only have a .001 percent chance, and the second I fill you with my seed, it'll be well over a hundred. You could be on every birth control known in this universe and every other, and it would *still* happen."

Well, that settled it. He was never getting the chance to slip one past the goalie. Even if the determination in his voice made things tighten low in my belly.

"Does it matter what I want?"

"Of course it does. We've been over this."

"What if I don't *want* to have your child, Lucifer? What then?"

Confusion furrowed his brow. "Why wouldn't you? Look at me."

"Because you're evil."

A flash of hurt radiated from him, so quickly I would've missed it if I hadn't still been locked in on his emotions. Then he huffed out a light laugh and brought my knuckles to his lips. "Don't be silly, darling. Everyone loves a bad boy."

Without another word, he left me there in the hallway staring at the swinging screen door as he bounded outside. If my brain weren't so scrambled from the twists and turns of that conversation, I might have taken a second to enjoy my win. It was the first time I'd gotten Lucifer to run away from *me*.

Too bad the victory would be short-lived. Because if nothing else, one thing was abundantly clear.

He wasn't going to give up. And unless I figured out where he was keeping me, I wasn't going anywhere. Which meant we'd keep facing off like this, over and over again. And if that was the case, I didn't feel good about my odds.

I didn't want to admit it, but I might be starting to *like* him, and that was exactly what he wanted.

At the very least, I understood him, and that was dangerous because it left room for empathy. And once there was empathy, it was impossible for hate. And if I couldn't hate the devil, the world's biggest enemy, then how could I possibly hope to keep myself from the inevitable fall?

CHAPTER TWENTY-THREE

LILITH

"Well, I must say, I think you made the right call," I murmured, having just listened to Alek's full report from their aborted supply run. "We haven't seen a mass possession used like that since before the Princes were locked away."

"So it was demons," Alek murmured. "I didn't realize they were so willing to work together to possess armies."

"I believe this to be the work of Sloth," Evander murmured from his perch in the corner. I'd invited the angel to be part of this meeting due to his unique insights. My Drystan was still sulking and hadn't stopped shooting daggers at him with his eyes. Possessive little poppet.

"He's done this before?" I asked, even though I knew the answer. I wanted Evander to share what I'd already learned so as to keep from giving all my secrets away in front of the angel. We may currently be working on the same side, but we would always play for different teams.

"Once, right after the Fall. When the Princes went unchecked and Lucifer attempted to strike on the heels of being cast out."

"What makes you sure it's him?" Alek asked.

"The pope."

"What about him?"

I sat back and waited for Evander to relay the information I already had.

"He is under Sloth's control. He used his influence to possess the surviving humans in Vatican City as they flocked to him for guidance and salvation. The sloth demons are spreading faster than a plague. Before long, humanity won't exist, and all of those souls will be lost to hell."

"Why not wait a few more weeks? Seems like a big risk when they're going to be wiped out anyway," Drystan asked.

This one I had no trouble answering.

"It's the difference between a guaranteed payday and a potential windfall. If left to die of 'natural causes,' most of those humans would inevitably end up in heaven, but by getting them to agree to possession, they signed their souls over to the other side."

"What use will anyone have for souls if all this comes to an end?" Alek asked.

Evander spoke before I could. "Souls have power. Lucifer wants to shore up as much power as possible. Life finds a way, Alek. The humans may die, but new life will come crawling out of the primordial soup before long. If Lucifer has control, he will claim them as his people, and heaven ceases to exist."

The Novasgardian grunted. "And so what happened in Central Park was what? A precursor? A test of some kind?"

"Not quite," I said. "If I had to guess, I'd say it's the next wave of attacks against you and your fellow . . ." I struggled to find the appropriate word. What did one call a collection of people persecuted both for random blood ties and who they dared to love? "Family members," I eventually said.

"This was about us?"

"Darling boy, haven't you been paying attention? It's always been about you. And Sunday. And dare I say, little Eden. Your connection to the horsewomen has painted a lovely target on your back. Yours as well as your brother's and everyone else you love in this world."

"So we will never be safe? That's what you're telling me."

"I—"

"I did it! I did it! Call me Moira-the-fucking-exploira, because I did it!" Moira burst into the room with the glowing crystal orb between her palms, excitement blazing in her eyes.

Thunder shook the room as my Drystan surged to his feet. "Normally I'd not let this interruption stand, but something tells me we need to see what she's prattling on about."

"The spell worked?" Alek asked, clearly recognizing the orb in her hands.

"You bet your man titties it did."

I pressed my lips together to avoid laughing at the incredulous look on the demigod's face.

"Man titties?" he parroted.

"You could hide a pencil under those things. Hell, you have better cleavage than me," the witch continued with a pointed look at his tight-fitting shirt.

"You've found him," I stated, snatching the orb from her hands and staring into the swirling gold mist within.

"Yep. And I locked in on him good too."

"Then let's go. We need him on our side," Alek said, shoulders back as he clearly was preparing himself for a conflict.

"That's the only problem. This isn't like the spell I used to open a portal to Novasgard. It can't transport a bunch of us."

"How many of us can go?" Alek asked.

I could already tell what was coming, but I waited for her to say it.

"One."

Predictably, the room devolved into everyone vying for the opportunity.

"I'll go," Alek offered, all heroic bluster and bravado.

"Why would you go?" Evander pressed. "You don't know him beyond a few encounters. How could you even help him? I will go."

The stench of testosterone was more than I could bear. We didn't have time for this, and the longer Gabriel was gone, the less aid he could provide.

I threw the orb onto the stone floor hard enough to shatter it into dust, and before the two of them even noticed, I was stepping through the portal.

"Lilypad," Drystan called, alarm ringing in the lone word.

I'd have to explain myself to him when I returned, and I *never* explained myself to anyone. But that was a problem for future me.

Between one step and the next, I left my temporary office and vexed lover behind. When my new surroundings took shape around me, I was only mildly surprised. It was not all doom and torture dungeon as one might picture. It was giving Rapunzel locked in her tower, which was somehow wholly unexpected and completely on the nose all at the same time.

Some sort of vine grew up one side and gracefully framed the door. No doubt during the summer months, it would bloom with fragrant blossoms and give this structure an even stronger fairytale vibe.

"Fucking Lucifer," I muttered. "Always has to be a bloody show pony."

The thick wood and iron door beckoned, and I reached for the handle, not quite knowing what to brace myself for. Would an army of minions rush out at me? Would Lucifer be waiting on the other side?

But no. It was none of those things.

The door swung open with nary a squeak.

The bastard hadn't even bothered to lock it. The knowledge did not fill me with comfort. One would expect all manner of security and defenses, but Lucifer had done the opposite. He was either overly confident Gabriel would never be found, or this was a trap, and the angel was the bait.

But what he hadn't planned on was me. It didn't matter what he had waiting on the other side of the threshold. He couldn't catch me. I was most concerned about the state in which I'd find Gabriel. I was limited in my abilities to render emergency first aid. My kind wasn't exactly known for healing. That said, depending on the state of him, I should be able to get us both safely away in time for others to do what needed to be done.

Inside the tower, I found very little aside from a dust and cobweb-covered table with an empty vase in the center and two wooden chairs, but that wasn't of interest to me. The spiral staircase that led up to the top was my goal, especially after the soft sound of chains rattling overhead caught my ear.

I grimaced at the seemingly never-ending staircase, but begrudgingly made my way up.

"Who's there?"

My heart lurched at the weak sound of Gabriel's fearful voice.

"He's not getting what he wants, so he's sent his lackey this time?"

Now, even through the rasp, I heard anger. He'd endured something awful, that much was certain, but Gabriel wasn't broken.

"It's me," I called, just as I'd hit the top.

He scoffed, clearly thinking it was a trick, until I stepped into his line of sight. The door to his prison had been left open, and sunlight currently streamed through the room's several arrow slits. He was slumped on the floor, bound by thick chains. Physically he looked well enough, though there was so much dried blood caked on him and staining the floor, it was a little hard to tell.

Narrowed eyes searched my face. "What are you doing here?"

I cocked my hip and smirked. "Rescuing you, of course."

"Why?"

"Because you're being held prisoner. That is generally what rescue missions are about."

"You're a demon."

Perhaps I'd been wrong and Lucifer had broken him.

"I'm neutral. You should know this after all our years."

"If that were true, you'd do nothing. Your arrival here clearly indicates that you've chosen a side. Neutral parties do not choose sides."

For a single instant, I regretted coming here. "You're insufferable, you do know that, don't you?"

"I've been told." Without waiting for a response, he let out a soft groan as he lifted his arm. "The chains are enchanted. I cannot break them."

"Are you healing still? Is there damage to your body we need to address?"

He shook his head. "I'm physically weakened by my bindings, but Lucifer is sadistic enough to allow me to heal so he can inflict wounds over and over."

Yes, that did sound like him.

"Unless you have the key, I don't see how you can help me."

I narrowed my eyes at him. "You know, for someone in your position, you are quite ungrateful. Do you really have so little faith?"

His jaw flexed, and when his eyes returned to mine, they were blazing with an emotion I could not recall ever seeing from him. "And why should I have faith? And in what? I have been Lucifer's captive for weeks and suffered every indignity at his hand, and the only one who came for me was a demon. Not my brothers. Not my father—though he sacrificed his only flesh and blood child, so I guess I shouldn't be surprised he'd leave me to rot. Tell me, Lilith. What good is faith to me? I have been forsaken."

I gave the moment the weight it deserved before I burst his bubble with a derisive snort. "Don't cry to me about being forsaken. You're needed. I'm here to bring you back to the fight, but if you're going to wallow in self-pity and let the world burn around us, I'll just leave you be."

"The fight?" he asked, a small light in his eyes now.

"Yes. The time for neutrality has passed for us both. We can't continue to sit idly by while the world we've both grown so attached to is snuffed out. No matter how you feel about your brethren, or heaven, or . . . Him, we cannot let Lucifer win this."

He held my gaze for an uncomfortably long time. I knew this was a big decision for him. It went against the moral code he's clung to for centuries. Longer, really. But I also knew I was right.

His expression didn't change, but he held out his hands. "Can you do something about this?"

"Is that your way of saying you'll join us?"

"I can't exactly help you from here, can I?"

A little flicker of hope curled in my belly, but I kept my expression neutral as I rolled my eyes. "See? Insufferable. Just say thank you, Gabriel. It's really not that hard."

"Thank you, Gabriel," he teased, though his heart wasn't in it.

I leaned close and flicked him on the nose. "Don't be cute. Now's not the time."

The spell on the chains was intricate, each link coated in power beyond my own. It made sense; Lucifer was the oldest of us and filled with his own warped type of angelic grace, but after a short inspection, I was able to recognize the magic.

"Do you know where he is?" I asked as I prepared to unravel the enchantment. I may not be strong enough to cast it, but spells were easy enough to undo if you knew what to look for. And I'd had the best possible teacher.

"No. He left me here suddenly a few days ago, or maybe it was a week. The days blur together."

"Does he do that often?"

"He usually didn't leave me alone for more than a few days. He wanted me to join him."

I snorted. "Of course he did. He loves to have an audience witness his *victories*." Reaching for Gabriel, I said. "Give me your hand."

He did, but wariness crossed his face. "Why?"

With one razor-sharp nail, I sliced across his palm, making him flinch. "Because, you twat, your blood is the key. You could have freed yourself at any time if you'd known the incantation."

"Well, I didn't. What is it?"

"Ephphatha," I said, grinning as the shackles opened and the chains fell to the floor. "You're welcome."

He rubbed his wrist with a rueful smirk. "I should have known."

"Truly," I agreed, offering him a hand up.

"Now what?" he asked, still holding on to me.

"Well, as lovely as our little reunion has been, we are in the middle of a war, darling. So off we pop."

We materialized in my temporary office at our underground sanctuary. Drystan was seated at my desk, fury burning in his eyes that promised a very entertaining session later. But it was the others who were scattered around that really caught my attention. Ben and Remi, Sunday and her priest, as well as Hades, all stared at me and my charge.

"What the devil are you all doing in here?" I drawled, turning my attention to my petulant prince.

"Deciding whether we needed to send out a rescue team," he countered coolly, leaning back in my chair with his arms crossed.

He could be so pouty. It was adorable.

"Hey, leather feathers! Glad you could finally make it," Remi said, striding up to us and clapping a hand on Gabriel's shoulder. He leaned in and murmured, "I've gotta say, you've looked better. You might wanna take a minute and get cleaned up before you make your rounds."

"Excuse the hell out of me. I've only been tortured for weeks on end by the actual devil. But sure. Let me get right on that. I wouldn't want to offend anyone's delicate sensibilities," he snarled before storming out of the room.

"Does he even know where he's going?" Hades asked, amusement coloring his tone.

Remi bolted for the door, calling behind him, "I'm on it! I've got a romance novel I want to talk about."

"Do try not to piss him off this time. We need him to stay," I shouted after him.

Before anyone could say another word, the lights flickered and the air grew thick with electricity. Drystan was standing now, palms flat on the top of my desk.

"All right, that's enough. Everyone is where they belong, and the mission is accomplished. Now, unless your name is Lilith, I'll thank you to see yourselves the fuck out." His silver eyes locked on me. "We need to talk."

Sunday snickered as they all stood and made for the door. "Usually that means she's in trouble, but I'm pretty sure it's code for fucking."

Caleb chuckled. "And what makes you think so, *a stor*?"

"It's all in the body language. And look at those fuck-me eyes." Sunday gave me a wink as they reached the door. "They're totally about to do it."

She wasn't wrong. But I shot her a disdainful glare anyway. "You heard him. Out."

As soon as the door shut behind the last of them, Drystan rounded the desk and snagged me by the nape. "Never do that to me again," he growled.

"Or what?"

His nostrils flared at the challenge in my voice.

"Bend over the desk and I'll show you."

"Is this supposed to be a deterrent?"

"Not even close."

I wouldn't typically let him take the lead, but he'd been genuinely concerned for me, and now that he wasn't wearing my collar, all bets were off. So I did as he told me, offering him my leather-clad arse.

"Are you going to spank me, Drystan?"

"I should." He ran his palm down my back until he circled one of my toned arse cheeks. Then he leaned over me until his lips were at my ear. "But I think I'll edge you instead. Brats don't get what they want."

And then he was gone, his warmth and weight an unwelcome absence as the door opened and closed behind him. Now I was alone, turned on beyond belief, and uncharacteristically frustrated.

"Bloody hell, you do one good deed . . ."

CHAPTER TWENTY-FOUR

MERRI

I swirled my fingers in the hot water, bubbles breaking with the contact as I settled into my bath. There was nothing better to do here in my Lucifer-made prison, and I wasn't in a state to talk to him again.

For the hundredth time, I wished I were the sort of supernatural who might stand a chance against him in a fight. Not that I knew of any offhand strong enough to withstand that sort of physical confrontation, but it didn't stop me from wishing it was possible. I despised the idea of being stuck here, like a fly in a spider's web.

I didn't let myself think too hard about how Lucifer knew what scents I liked or the fact that I preferred bubbles to a bath bomb, even though deep in my heart I knew. I'd handed it over freely during one of my chats with Cole. The depths of his manipulation were staggering when I allowed myself to dwell on it, which was part of the reason I couldn't. I was in survival mode. Processing would come later. Assuming there was a later.

So, I laid my head back and breathed in the scents of strawberries and champagne, let the luxurious bubbles soften my skin, and tried not to think about my precarious predicament.

I was supposed to dreamwalk tonight. Sin made it clear to me that they were all expecting me to visit Grim. If we set everything aside for the moment, I understood why. Splitting my feeding between all four of them was the safest for all involved.

At least, that was our working theory.

Sin still maintained I could feed from him every day and it wouldn't cause any lasting harm. The biggest issue he wasn't focusing on was that my body craved them all. It had to be because we were bound to one another. The magic connecting us made us stronger in some ways, more stable, but needed to be fortified regularly.

Which meant avoiding Grim would create ripples, the effects of which I could only assume would grow exponentially the longer I did so.

But I just wasn't ready to face him.

The others were complicit, sure, but he was the one who took my heart and stomped on it without a second's hesitation.

"Ugh," I groaned, taking a hot washcloth and plopping it over my face in yet another effort to distract myself. "Don't think about them. It's fine. You're fine. You don't need them right now. You've gone days and days without feeding before. Everyone deserves a night off, especially from heartbreak."

Even as I said the words, I didn't fully believe them, but I clung to the excuse anyway. Two things could be true. I could need to feed, but also not want to. And I didn't owe anybody explanations. It was my body, my power, and only I got to decide the whens and hows of what they did and didn't do.

In what had become a bit of a habit in the last few days, Andi's voice floated through my mind. *Amen, sister.*

I wasn't sure if this was a Jiminy Cricket sort of thing, and she was now the voice of my conscience, or if it was simply a coping mechanism to deal with my current isolation from any kind of support system. Either way, I'd been through hell in the last few weeks, or was it months now since I'd been thrust into this apocalypse? I'd more than earned a little *me* time.

With a heavy sigh, I sank deeper into the hot water and let it soothe my tense muscles. It wasn't long before I drifted into a fantasy with no one around me. Not overbearing horsemen, not a world on fire. Just a beautiful garden at night, the fresh, clean air, and a sky filled with countless stars.

"Pretty," I murmured as I started following a path that led deeper into the foliage. I could still see the stars twinkling above, but there were sections of the sky obscured by a canopy created by the trees. It was magical in a way that had nothing to do with actual magic. The sort of fairy-tale setting that could only exist in dreams. The warmth of the night air coated me like a soft blanket, and I tipped my head up as I breathed in the rich scents of earth and night-blooming jasmine. Crickets chirped in the distance, adding gentle ambiance to an already idyllic setting.

Walking along the mossy path, I ran my fingers over blossoms that seemed to glow when the moon's rays hit them, my pace slow and relaxed. This was a sanctuary. A safe place for me to retreat when the world outside became too much.

The path veered to the left, and as I followed the slight curve, a new tree came into view. It was planted in such a way that it clearly took pride of place in the garden. It was massive, far larger than any other. It also exuded ancient power, which made zero sense, but this was a dream, so natural laws didn't exactly apply.

When a familiar blond head caught my eye, I suddenly realized exactly where I was and what I was looking at.

"Are you kidding me?" I muttered. "The Garden of fucking Eden?"

Lucifer was dressed all in black, his golden hair standing out starkly against the darkness he draped himself in. There was never any doubt he was beautiful. But as a cloud shifted and moonlight spilled over him, he was simply mesmerizing. I'd never seen a man glow the way he did.

The snake.

The morning star.

I huffed, annoyed that in avoiding one dark and broody ass's dream I'd landed smack dab in the middle of another's.

Lucifer smirked at me, a brilliantly red and perfectly ripe apple in his hand. "The Garden of Fucking? Hmm, I quite like the sound of that."

"Well, this has been fun, but I'll be leaving now."

I turned to go back the way I came, but the sound of his footsteps followed, and his fingers encircled my wrist. "Wait, please don't. I was only having a laugh."

Spinning to face him, I searched his eyes. "Why would I want to be here with you? This is the place you started the fucking patriarchy."

"I beg your finest pardon. I did not."

"Yes, you did. That apple? Consider it your boot on Eve's neck. You haven't let up since."

The apple dropped from his hand and he glared at me. "The woman was starving. All I did was offer her a choice. What happened next was up to her. And that bootprint you're accusing me of? It was definitely Adam's. He has much smaller feet."

I softened just a hair, latching onto the knowledge I could leave this dream any time I wanted. Perhaps this encounter was an opportunity rather than a problem. So I began a slow stroll toward the tree, allowing my curiosity to take the lead rather than my fear.

"Why?" I asked as he came up next to me.

"Why what?"

"Why all of it? Why fall? Why sabotage the humans? Why try to take control of the world?"

He sighed and plopped down on a bench that had appeared out of nowhere. "Haven't we already been over all of this? Why the incessant need to rehash ancient history?"

"Because at best you've given me half-answers. When you give me a straight answer at all."

Lucifer groaned and allowed his head to fall back. The angle gave me a surprisingly erotic view of his throat, and I hated myself for not only clocking it, but also the resulting lady tingles.

"You are nothing if not persistent."

I flashed him a bright smile. "You're welcome."

"I fell because I saw the writing on the wall."

"What does that mean?"

"He loved the humans more than us. He replaced us the same way one replaces a toy they've lost interest in. No worse than that. Like a dog whose humans decided to have a baby and no longer had the time or inclination to care for their first child. We were cast aside. Abandoned. Made to play babysitter to the siblings we never wanted."

"So you have daddy issues. That doesn't exactly make you special, Lucifer. Lots of us have trauma, you don't see everyone else trying to start an uprising and overthrow the natural order."

"How would you feel if you were told you were the favorite, only to be demoted when someone else came along, and *then,* insult to injury, you're expected to *guard* them as well?"

I thought for a moment. I was an only child. I'd wished for siblings when I was younger, but now I was incredibly thankful that never happened. How would I feel if I'd been in his shoes?

"Jealous."

"Ding, ding. We have a winner."

"But my point still stands. Plenty of people are jealous, and they don't destroy their whole lives."

He cackled. "Clearly you've never heard of a midlife crisis. It happens all the time, crabapple. Every fucking day."

"Buying a sports car or cheating on your wife is hardly the same as causing a full-scale rebellion."

"Isn't it? I was fighting for all of us, railing against the circumstances He forced us into. I am not a guardian angel. I'm more than the keeper of his precious humans. All I did was point out his error in judgment. I told my father how much he'd hurt us *all.* But only a handful of my brothers stood with me. As such, we were easily cast out. Which, when you take a look at *your* history, is a very typical move made by dictators and monarchs when they are confronted with the displeasure of their subjects. Hello, American Revolution. Isn't one of the tenets of your kind to rise up against tyranny? To oppose fascism in all its forms? How can you judge me so harshly for being the embodiment of heroism?"

"Are you really comparing God to a fascist?"

"I mean, they use him as an excuse all the time. So I say, if the iron fist fits."

His feelings on this issue were much bigger than I'd expected. Honestly, I'd assumed what I'd get from him was more bravado and bluster, not bare honesty.

"So . . . you didn't abandon heaven to come rule in hell?"

"No, darling. That was simply a side effect of my charisma. Free will isn't something angels are encouraged to push for. But it is something well worth fighting to keep." He heaved another sigh, suddenly looking exhausted. "And those who fell with me were lost. I'd been the face of our little revolution, so they turned to me expecting answers and direction. I couldn't abandon them. Not when I knew just how deeply that sort of injury cuts."

"So you ruled out of necessity, not selfishness?"

"All the best leaders rise to the occasion. Never trust someone who desires that much power over others."

"And now?"

"What?"

"Do you enjoy stealing souls and ruling the damned?"

He smirked. "I don't steal anything. If a soul finds its way to me, it was freely given. Once again, that pesky free will comes into play."

Now I was thoroughly confused. Was he right? Was God oppressing the angels the cause of all of this? Were we all working for the wrong side?

"I have another question."

"Of course you do," he said, but he didn't seem annoyed. More like he was resigned.

"If the whole point of this apocalypse is to get some sort of revenge for casting you out, how do you justify all the casualties? You claim you're different from Him. That you are not the callous leader you make Him out to be, but aren't you sort of doing the same thing you're accusing Him of?"

"I have never forced any creature to do my bidding against their will."

I cocked a brow.

"Okay, maybe I have a time or two, but it was for a good reason."

Shaking my head, I walked away from him. "You're a hypocrite, Lucifer. Your mission may have started in a noble place, but you've turned into someone worse than He ever was."

He'd caught up to me, clearly not ready to let this topic drop. "How can you possibly say that? I make people's dreams come true."

"You trick them into giving up their immortal souls in exchange for trinkets. If they understood what they were giving up, they would never agree."

"Don't be so sure about that."

"Fine. We'll set that point aside. You claim you're a hero, but when I look at what you are doing, the destruction you've already caused, there's nothing heroic about it. You are worse than any dictator or awful leader I've ever read about by a freaking landslide. It's not even close."

He went uncharacteristically quiet but continued walking the path with me. We strolled in silence a long while, until we reached a beautiful brook, the water silver in the night as it bubbled over stones.

"What would you have me do, Merri?"

I looked at him, his expression earnest. Pure sincerity radiated from every word. I wished I could truly believe he had the capacity for change, but he was the devil. The antithesis of goodness. "Stop it all. Put an end to this destruction and death. Give the world back to the humans and put aside your hatred of them."

"I don't hate them. Not anymore."

"Then how can you do this to them?"

"I'm setting them free."

"No. You're not. You're killing them. And if you get your way, you're going to be the meteor that renders them extinct."

Hurt flashed in his eyes. "So that's it then. I'm nothing more than your villain."

"You could be so much more, Luc. If you let yourself remove the mask of vengeance. You spoke about how heavy masks are. That the true gift is in setting them aside. I bet if you actually sat down and thought about what you truly wanted, this path you're on isn't it. Not anymore."

His expression changed from one of openness and honesty to cruelty almost in an instant. "You know nothing about what I truly want. Why shouldn't I have vengeance? My existence as I knew it was ripped from me simply for stating my concerns. The one person I trusted above all threw me away like so much rubbish. You'll do the same if I give you an inch."

I didn't even know what to say to that until suddenly, I did.

"How can I throw away something that isn't even mine?"

He dropped the mask of indifference as quickly as he'd adopted it and stared at me again with raw vulnerability. It made my pulse race and my stomach tighten in anticipation.

"Merri . . ." he whispered, looking into my soul. "Don't you understand? I could be yours. All you have to do is let me."

My heart lurched. That was a powerful statement, and one I never expected to hear from him. Being mine was very different from knocking me up. How had I gone from being rejected by the four horsemen to having Lucifer practically begging me to let him be mine?

He reached for me, his fingers brushing my cheek as he moved to close the distance between us. Something inside wanted the contact, craved the kiss I knew he was going for. But I couldn't give in. Not now.

I tore myself from the dream, coming to with a sputtering gasp as I sank into the now-cool water of my bath. I sat up with a start, sending bubbles and water flying.

"Holy. Fucking. Shit."

CHAPTER
TWENTY-FIVE
MALICE

This tightness in my chest wasn't something I was accustomed to. I think they call it anxiety, and I have realized quickly that I am not a fan of it in the least. Merri hadn't shown up for last night's dreamwalk, at least so far as I could tell. She certainly hadn't come to visit me, nor had I heard an update from any of the others.

My internal alarms had been sounding all night, going from a general sense of unease to a full-blown klaxon drowning out all other thoughts. Was this what dysregulation felt like? How did people exist in this state? I'd damn near paced a hole in the rug over the last hour.

"Fuck it," I grumbled when I made yet another full circuit of my bedroom.

I was driving myself mad, waiting to see if she was going to call me to her. I needed answers.

Chaos's room was closest to mine, so I stormed down the hall like a man possessed and pounded on the door. I wasn't even finished knocking before the door swung open and Chaos greeted me with his own anxious frown.

"Did she come to you?" I asked, already knowing the answer.

"No. You?"

"No."

"Fuck."

Without another word, the two of us hauled arse to Sin's room. This time, Chaos hit the door, and it was a frantic Sin on the other side.

"Any word?" he asked.

"No," Chaos replied.

"She didn't visit either of us," I confirmed.

"Do you think she went to Grim?" Sin asked.

We all exchanged glances containing varying degrees of hope.

"Only one way to know for sure," Sin said.

The three of us went down the hall to visit Death, which was never a good idea. Grimsby didn't welcome anyone into his space uninvited, no matter how long he'd known them.

But his room was empty.

"Where could he be?" Chaos asked.

"The study?" I guessed. He certainly spent a lot of time there.

"Grimsby!" Sin bellowed, not content to blindly continue our search. "Where the fuck are you hiding?"

No response came from anywhere on the estate. I wasn't surprised; Grim wouldn't be summoned for anything less than the end of the world. Which really made his silence concerning, come to think of it.

"Grim!" I shouted, adding my voice to Sin's as the three of us trotted down the stairs and made our way to his usual haunt.

I didn't realize how badly I was hoping we'd find him knocked out due to being pulled into a dreamwalk with Merri until the sight of him sipping his stupid overpriced whiskey sent my heart plummeting to my feet.

"Are you fucking joking right now?" I asked, slapping the glass out of his hand mid-sip.

"I beg your pardon." Grim's voice was low and threatening as he rose to his full height.

"Didn't you hear us calling for you?"

"When have I ever resorted to bellowing through a house like some sort of town crier? If you want to speak to me, you can come find me like the civilized being you're supposed to be."

"Spare me the fucking lecture on proper decorum. This is serious. Merri didn't show up for any of us tonight."

"And?" he asked, one brow lifted. So help me, I was about to throttle him.

"And that means she's either purposely avoiding us or something is wrong. You are such an unbelievable prick," Chaos said.

"Unless there's something you haven't told us," Sin added.

"No. Nothing of note."

"Of fucking course not."

The three of us stood as a united front, frustrated, angry, and at a loss for what to do now. Grim had two choices before him: join us and save her, or leave. I needed him to understand the damage his indifference was doing to not only his relationship with Merri, but his relationship with us. We were, and always had been, meant to be a team. The horsemen didn't ride alone.

Grim's choice to be down here instead of his room suddenly struck me. He never believed he had a chance of being the one Merri came to visit. He'd already removed himself from the equation because he fucked up so badly.

"When we get her back, you will fix this with her," I said, walking across the room and picking up the glass I'd sent flying. Lucky for me, it was high quality and the carpet was soft. Not even a crack.

I refilled his drink and poured one for myself, then returned it to him.

"She won't want me to fix anything."

"She may not, but you'll try anyway. And you'll keep trying until you can't anymore." Chaos must've picked up on the same thing I did because his voice was gentler than I'd ever heard from him.

Grim's expression didn't change, but his posture lost some of its rigid tension.

Taking that as my cue, I pressed on. "We have to figure out what's going on. She could be hurt. We can't keep waiting for her to come to us with information. We need to get it for ourselves. She's depending on us."

Chaos nodded along. "It's time to go on the offensive."

"Have you already tried to reach her through your access to the dream realm?" Grim asked Sinclair.

"Me? It's not my turn."

"How bloody thick are you?" Grim muttered. "She's not reachable by anyone in this room other than you. Now's not the time to wait your fucking turn."

Sin's mouth fell open, eyes wide as Grim's words registered.

"He's right, Sin. You need to go after her and make sure she's okay." Chaos dragged a hand through his hair and sighed. "I hate this. Knowing he has her and could hurt her whenever he wants."

Sin flopped into the closest chair, immediately leaning his head back and closing his eyes. The rest of us just sort of stared at him, waiting for something to happen.

He peeled one eye open. "Can you all do something else? It's super hard to concentrate when I can feel you all looking at me. I know I'm the most gorgeous man in the room, but this is a personal moment."

"No," I said. "Get on with it."

He sighed and settled in, wiggling his shoulders and fidgeting until he seemed fully comfortable. The three of us watched on, and if Grim and Chaos felt anywhere near the tension I did, they were buzzing with anticipation. Sin's brows drew together, a deep groove forming between them. It softened for just a moment before it returned, followed by the distinct downturn of his lips.

I already knew what he was going to say before he opened his eyes.

"She's alive, but I can't reach her. It's like she super reinforced her mental barricade or something."

"Isn't that a good thing?" I asked.

Chaos tilted his head in a considering way. "It could be. I'm more interested in the reason she'd need such strong defenses."

"You think it's protection against Lucifer?"

This time, Grim answered my question. "We all know he can reach her there, especially now that he's physically with her."

"Fuck."

Chaos took the word right out of my mouth.

"What is our next step? If she has to keep her walls up, we won't stand a chance at finding her without outside intervention," Sin asked.

"It's unlikely Lucifer is ever going to divulge that information, even if she hadn't put her defenses in place. It's like Chaos said, we need to make a move. No more waiting for her to tell us how to find her." I was already filtering through potential allies in my mind, hoping we could find at least one of them.

"Lilith," Grim murmured, almost like an afterthought.

"What about her?" Sin asked.

"She's our only link to both Merri and Lucifer. If anyone knows where he could be keeping her, or the best way to go about tracking them down, it will be her."

"Great, but isn't she in hiding too?" Chaos asked.

"She is, but I know a surefire way to reach her," Grim said.

"Well, don't leave us waiting," I said.

"It's time for the four horsemen to pay a visit to The Den of Iniquity."

CHAPTER TWENTY-SIX

GRIM

My brothers all stared at me like I'd just suggested we all ride llamas into battle instead of our horses. Choosing to ignore their disbelief, I got to my feet and adjusted the cuffs of my shirt before clearing my throat.

"Shall we be off then?"

"All right, I'll address the kitten in the corner."

I raised a brow at Sin. "Pardon?"

"What makes you think Lilith will be at *Iniquity?* Isn't that like the very first place anyone would think to look?"

"I never said she'd be there."

"Why go then?" Sin asked.

Chaos shrugged. "Not like we have any other pressing engagements. Might as well check it out."

"Does it even still exist? London was decimated," Malice added.

"If you think Lilith doesn't have protections in place as well as eyes and ears everywhere, you have another think coming."

Malice made a musing sound. "Fair point."

"Any other stupid questions, or can we be off?"

Proving that he was still the reigning king of stupid questions,

Sin cleared his throat. "Did you say *think* coming? Isn't it another *thing* coming?" he asked, brow furrowed.

I sighed and rolled my eyes. "I'm not going to take the time to educate you on basic grammar, Sinclair. You can Google it when this is all over."

"If we ever get the internet back," Malice said under his breath.

Chaos locked eyes with me. "That's the least of our worries. You're right, Lilith is our best chance at this point. We need to find her. *Iniquity* is a strong start."

Sin made a circling gesture with his hand.

I raised a brow. "What's that supposed to mean?"

He snorted, muttering, "Now who needs Google?" Then he rolled his eyes and explained with exaggerated patience, "Let's get on with it. After you. Keep calm and carry on. Allons-y."

"Someone stop him. He's going to get stuck on a loop if we let him continue," Malice said.

I simply popped out of the room and into a strangely humid London alleyway. The street was littered with rubbish and debris. Most of the businesses were boarded up, and the ones that weren't had been looted of everything that wasn't bolted down. The scent of what had to be burning garbage filled the air, and as I looked around what used to be a bustling metropolis, it wasn't hard to confirm my suspicions. Here and there, orange glows emanated from alleys, and on one corner in plain view, a large skip bin burned nearly out of control.

"They'd better be careful," Chaos whispered, eyes on the three emaciated humans huddling around the fire. "If the flames don't get them, the demons will."

From a bit further down the alleyway, a lone figure rose and shambled our way. He wore layers of tattered and grimy clothes, his skin weathered and dirt-streaked. As he passed one of the flickering bins, his eyes flared, and I was struck by a fleeting sense of familiarity. Whatever he was, it wasn't human. I took a moment to suss him out. Not a demon, that was certain, but something . . . other.

"They'll get them eventually. They're picking them off slowly. One by one," the man muttered, as if he were part of our conversation.

"How do you know?" Sin asked.

"I've been watching. That's what I do. Watch. Wait."

"From where?" Chaos asked.

The man coughed out a phlegmy laugh. "From my corner office." Then he laughed again and gave a mocking bow.

Iniquity's entrance was next to his "corner office," which consisted of a heap of dirty, stinking rags beside a trolley filled with empty cans and plastic bags.

"How long have you been camped out there?" I asked, eyeing him carefully.

He shrugged. "Long enough."

"When was the last time anyone came or went through that door?" I pointed to the nondescript entrance to the club, though it was now painted over with graffiti, rusted chains strung across and secured with a padlock.

"Ages," the man said. "Ages and ages."

"Fuck," Chaos grunted. "So much for that plan. Now how are we supposed to get word to Lilith that Lucifer has Merri?"

Sin gave Chaos an incredulous look. "Since when is the God of War afraid of a little padlock?"

"I am not the God of War."

"Might as well be, dude. But back to the point. Are you really telling me a little metal is going to keep us out?"

"No," I growled.

My brothers materialized beside me in the belly of Lilith's club. What had once been a den for all manner of depravity, frequented by every species of supernatural creature in existence, was now in shambles. Tables overturned, glasses shattered on the floor, cracks spiderwebbing the walls, and the mirrored ceiling broken, with deadly shards hanging by a thread.

"Hello?" Sin shouted. "Anybody home?"

"Do you really expect that to work?" Malice asked.

"Worth a shot, ri—" Sin's response was cut off by an undignified scream as a shard of glass from the ceiling came crashing down, narrowly missing his head. "Motherfucker," he panted. "That was some real Final Destination bullshit. It nearly sliced me in two."

Chaos sighed. "Don't be so dramatic. You would have healed."

"Do you have any idea how long it takes to regrow an entire brain? Also, I'm tired of always being the one who has to heal. Why aren't you guys ever on the receiving end of a fatal blow?"

Chaos smirked. "You do have the most punchable face."

"Is that supposed to make me feel better?"

"Well, you always wanted to be the best at something," Malice offered.

"Being punchable is hardly an achievement."

I huffed a frustrated sigh. We didn't have time to go on a tangent. Not with the humans being picked off for sport, Merri gone, and all the Princes released. "She's not here."

"How do you know? We haven't checked her private rooms. Her office." Malice took a step toward the stairs that would take us to her voyeur rooms and office, but I stopped him with a hand on his shoulder.

"Can't you sense the emptiness? She's not here. The only flickers of life in this tomb are coming from us." I cocked my head. "And maybe a couple of rats."

"Great, so this was a colossal waste of time. What now, Columbo?" Sin asked.

"Maybe that watcher knows more than he let on," Chaos suggested.

Malice frowned. "You think so? He seemed like a nutter to me."

"You have a better idea?" I challenged.

"Nope."

"Then interrogation it is."

Once again we teleported, this time back to our original location on the street.

The man let out a sinister laugh as soon as we reappeared. "No luck, eh, boys?"

"No," I muttered, turning to fully face him, but he was gone. Vanished into thin air. "I fucking knew it."

"Fuck," Chaos snarled at the same time Sin asked, "Where'd he go?"

"To tattle on us, most likely."

"Tattle to who?" Malice asked.

"That's the question."

CHAPTER TWENTY-SEVEN

BEN

"A-are you s-sure he'll l-like this one, sugar? It's about a p-priest," I asked Rosie under my breath as I followed her across the room toward her quarry.

Gabriel was deep in conversation with Lilith, Crombie, Caleb, and Gavin. The five of them had their heads bowed close together and were chatting in hushed tones while looking over something Gavin had marked up for them. The fact that they were out here and not locked away in Lilith's office meant it wasn't necessarily a private conversation, though their body language indicated otherwise.

We'd adopted this space as a sort of living area, furniture arranged in conversational pods, all put together piecemeal using small bits of magic from those who had extra to spare. Alek's mother, Lina, offered to weave a space—her power giving her the ability to permanently alter reality however she wanted—but after a pretty heated discussion, it was determined that no one should use excessive amounts of their power. Period. We didn't know when we might be called on to fight, and the last thing we could afford was to have the most powerful among us at a disadvantage in any way.

"Remi said he'd love it. Apparently Gabriel has a touch of bad boy in him no one knew about." Rosie squeezed my hand.

She knew I wasn't just worried about her offending an angel. I didn't trust anyone new to our group. It had grown larger than I could manage. Too many alpha personalities in one space. Add in an archangel with a bit of a God complex, and I worried we were asking for internal conflict. The last thing any of us needed was a ticking time bomb around our pregnant mates.

"Did I hear my name?" Remi asked, sauntering over to join us.

Rosie smirked at him. "You did."

He leaned down to give her a quick kiss. "You were sharing good things, I hope, baby girl."

"Mmm, doubtful," she teased. "That would require you to behave."

"Yeah, fair enough."

We shared a laugh before Remi spotted the novel in Rosie's hands. "You haven't given it to him yet?"

"W-we're going n-now," I grumbled, gesturing at the group a little ways away.

Remi's eyes widened as he looked at the paperback more closely. "Who took out my tabs? I marked all the best parts for him."

The way Rosie's cheeks turned pink gave her away. "I thought those were for me. Things you wanted to reenact."

Remi winked at her, dropping his voice to a seductive croon. "I mean, yes. Absolutely. But they were also for leather feathers. How else is he going to know where the good bits are?"

"I-I'm s-sure he c-can figure it o-out."

"Siiiigh. You two are no fun." He yanked the book out of Rosie's grip. "Now I have to mark it up all over again."

Before he could turn to leave, the air shifted in the room, putting us all on edge at the exact same time. I saw it in the collective tensing of everyone's posture. They felt it too. The pressure change that made my ears pop, and the weight of power.

"Who the devil is that?" Rosie whispered, halting her steps before I had to stop her.

"I h-have no idea, sugar. Get behind me." My voice went from human to wolf as I put myself in front of her.

Several things happened at once.

Caleb and Gavin tensed, ready for a fight. Lilith stood carefully, surprise lifting her eyebrows nearly to her hairline. Crombie joined her with barely leashed power crackling around him. But it was Gabriel who pulled my focus. His arms were folded across his chest, eyes narrowed, fury written on his features.

"Michael, how very unlike you to grace us with your presence." Then he added under his breath, "Finally."

"You know what they say, brother. Better late than never." The stranger—Michael—said, his lips curling in a smug grin. He was dressed like someone who'd been living on the streets, his clothing tattered and stained. Hardly what you'd expect from an angel, but then, Gabriel and his motorcycle leathers didn't fit the bill either.

"That remains to be seen. We've gotten along just fine without you all these years."

"Is that any way to say hello?"

"I take it this is some sort of family spat?" Remi said, speaking close to my ear.

"L-looks like," I said, my wolf stepping down now that it seemed we weren't actually under attack.

Michael took a step forward, and I swear, if vampires really did hiss, Caleb and Gavin would have. Unsettled wasn't a strong enough word to describe their energy.

"Lilypad, I need you to tell me if this angel is a threat or a friend before I vaporize him," Crombie warned. "He's already too close to you for comfort."

"As Gabriel said, that remains to be seen, pet. But for the moment, I think we're safe."

"You know what they say about assuming," Remi offered unhelpfully.

"Remington, be a dear, and shut up," Lilith snapped, then returned her attention to Michael. "Why are you here?"

His appearance changed as we all watched on, the torn and stained clothing turning into a meticulously tailored three-piece suit in charcoal gray. The rough beard and matted hair morphed into slicked-back dark locks and a clean-shaven jaw. His eyes were the only things that didn't change. They remained molten gold.

"Angels really are beautiful," Rosie murmured, and if I'd been less secure in our relationship, I might've been jealous.

"And dickless. Don't forget dickless," Remi said.

"Th-that wasn't c-confirmed," I reminded him.

"Challenge accepted."

"No, Remi," Rosie said.

My twin pouted. "Fine. Nobody lets me have any fun."

"Think how Asher would feel about you getting that up close and personal with another male," Rosie pointed out.

Remi took a second to consider it. "You're right. Dickless or not, I'd feel pretty murdery if he was in range of another dude's crotch."

I cocked a brow at that. We'd all been in range of plenty of dicks during our group time with Rosie.

Catching my expression, he waved a hand. "Present company excluded. Members of the group chat don't count."

While we'd been side chatting, Michael had moved closer to the others. His eyes lingered on Gabriel, though he seemed to be addressing Lilith.

"I have a message for you."

"Wait, isn't that Gabe's job?" Remi whispered loudly before shouting, "Gabe! He took your job too?"

Gabriel flinched, but didn't respond, his eyes carefully leveled on Michael. "Go on then."

"The horsemen are currently just outside of *Iniquity*. They were searching for you, Lilith. The final battle is on the horizon. It's time for everyone to come together."

Caleb cleared his throat. "Can I ask what might be seen as a daft question?"

"That's usually my job," Remi murmured.

Michael stared Caleb down. "Go on, priest."

"Why are you suddenly involving yourself in all this?"

Gabriel nodded. "Yes, why? You've been firmly against our interference. I believe the words, on your own head be it, were used when I gave Caleb his mark."

"Yes, well. Times have changed, haven't they? The apocalypse looms, war is brewing . . ." He sighed and gave Gabriel a pointed look. "And I haven't been as removed as you might believe. Did you really think I didn't know you had my sword? That I couldn't have taken it from you at any time I so desired?"

"You expect me to believe that when you left me to rot at Lucifer's hand?" Gabriel spat, his temper flaring.

"We all have our parts to play."

Remi nudged me. "Burn. But also . . . Oh no, he didn't."

Gavin blurred across the distance until he loomed over my twin. "Remington, if you do not shut the fuck up, I will make you."

"Oh yeah? How you gonna do that, Daddy G?"

Gavin's teeth ground together. "I'd threaten to shut you up with my dick in your mouth, but you'd enjoy it too much."

Remi was momentarily stunned, his mouth gaping open.

Rosie put her hand on his chest, her arousal scenting the air. "Careful, my lord. We don't have the capacity for that level of privacy."

"Oh, she means the sexy dungeon," Remi whispered to me. "God, I miss the sexy dungeon."

I shook my head at my twin. He'd hinted more than once that he wanted to play with Gavin. *For the plot,* he'd said. I'm pretty sure he was just a horny fuck, but if Asher and Rosie were okay with it, then who was I to say so?

"If you four are quite finished with whatever is happening over there, we have the small matter of the horsemen to attend to," Lilith said, the steel in her voice effectively cutting through our banter.

"Where do you need us?" Caleb asked.

"At her side, of course," Crombie scoffed. "Are they alone?"

Michael nodded. "Aside from the human stragglers, they are alone. I'm not sure how much longer they will be outside the club. They were quite . . . frustrated."

"About what?" Gavin asked.

"Lucifer. He has Merri."

"And you didn't think to lead with that?" Lilith snarled, her fury making me tense. If I'd been in my wolf form, my tail would have been tucked firmly between my legs.

"I'm here, aren't I?" Michael snapped. "A guy can't win for trying. You should be thanking me. If I hadn't been keeping watch, you wouldn't know any of this. Where's my thank you?"

"They rarely say thank you," Gabriel murmured.

Lilith's gaze snapped to us. "Rosie, darling, you can't come on this mission. Be a love and go get Hades for me? The rest of you, get ready. We are going to wrangle some horsemen."

CHAPTER TWENTY-EIGHT

CHAOS

"That's the question."

Grim's words sat heavy between us, the air filled with both anticipation and dread. For a city overrun with demons, it was decidedly quiet. A calm before the storm, perhaps.

"Those humans aren't going to make it through the night," Sin murmured as he leaned against the wall and pulled a chrome lighter from his pocket. He began flicking it open, then closing it, over and over. A nervous habit he'd picked up from his days as a rock star.

"And we care, why?" Malice asked.

"We don't, I was just stating facts," Sin murmured, his eyes still focused on the trio at the far end of the alley.

As I followed his gaze, I saw what appeared to be a shadow peeling away from one of the brick walls.

"Case in point." Sin stiffened as he pushed himself upright and put away the lighter. "Do we help?"

"No." Grim's attention was trained on the humans as well, his brows pulled together with a look one might consider concern. "They made their beds."

"Does this mean we *aren't* the good guys? Cause I thought we were the good guys now. You know, because we're trying to save humanity instead of damn it this time."

Sin's question brought me up short. Could horsemen ever be considered good? We were morally gray antiheroes at best, and outright villains to most.

"He has a point," Malice murmured. "Maybe we should . . ."

"Shiiit, that's a lot of them." Sin's words echoed my thoughts exactly, which was a rare occurrence.

A hundred or more demons crawled, slithered, and flew out of the shadows, all converging on the three humans in mere seconds. They didn't even have time to scream before they were dead, their souls forfeit to hell.

"What are we doing, guys?" I asked, adrenaline surging through me at the promise of a fight. It had been a long time since I'd got to use my full strength, most match-ups rarely requiring me to break a sweat. But as I clocked several monsters that I knew hadn't seen the light of the human realm in several centuries, I realized we were in for a serious battle.

These weren't your run-of-the-mill minor demons. Some of them were known as lesser gods back when I'd been alive. They had the ability to do damage to the most powerful beings . . . even us. The leather-skinned creatures stalking across the street were probably the least of a threat to us. They were a mixture of a panther and a squid, with barbed tentacles extending along their spines like wings. The claws and fangs were tipped in venom that would bring down a shifter in his prime, but would only sting one of us. I knew that personally.

I was a little more concerned about the floating eyeballs the size of cantaloupes. They too had tentacles, these ones attached like legs. I'd never fought one, but I'd heard stories of them. Soldiers returning from battles, shells of themselves, plagued with nightmares of the effects these monsters had. If the creatures locked you in their sight, they could manipulate your mind, forcing you to believe whatever they chose. Then, once you'd served your purpose, they'd finish you with their tentacles. If the tales were to be believed, this was generally done with a very unpleasant hug around the face, so the tentacle could penetrate all available orifices, before sucking the brain out until the skull collapsed and their victim was nothing but a husk.

"Should've brought my pickleball paddle," Sin muttered. "They're almost the perfect size."

"Looks like we know who our spy was working for," Grim said. "Fucking Lucifer."

"That was fast," Malice muttered beside him.

"Armor up!" I shouted, knowing the decision had been made for us. Our chance to flee was long gone. We were in this fight whether we wanted to be or not. "We have to kill them. Every last one."

We all acted as one, calling our armor and weapons to us in a move too polished to be coincidence. We'd done this exact thing countless times before.

"Spread out. Take them down. Don't let them touch you. Especially not the brain suckers. Avoid line of sight if you can, they have psychic attacks. Then they'll suck your brain out, and we can't afford to wait for you to regenerate."

Sin shuddered. "It hurt plenty when my throat was ripped out. I can't imagine how much it would sting to have my brain eaten."

Grim was the first of us to stalk into battle, and I followed on his heels, albeit in a different direction. A cluster of winged gargoyle-like demons hissed as they prepared to lob what appeared to be balls of fire they'd summoned. Fire would be a nightmare, an added element for us to dance around when we could ill afford it.

The comforting weight of my sword in my palm helped me shore up my focus with every step toward the enemy. Mow them down. Send them back to hell where they belonged. Don't let a single one survive.

Easy.

By the time I reached the first one, my grin had to be just this side of sane. I needed this release for more reasons than one. Violence coiled in my belly, deadly and ready to be unleashed. It was time for me to prove why War hand-selected me to be his replacement.

Swinging my blade in a powerful arc, I sliced the demon's head clean off its shoulders, the stinking, acrid scent of the monster's blood only serving to amp up my bloodlust. On the return swing, I caught another in the belly, her humanoid form making her an easy target as I cleaved her in two.

Just that quickly, I was lost to the thrill of the fight, mowing down foes until I had to literally tread over the smoldering remains of their bodies.

"Has anyone ever told you you stink, you weird cat thing?" Sin shouted as a tentacle lashed out at him from where the displacer beast had appeared. He swung his weapon and attempted a strike, but the creature disappeared before he could make contact. "You stink, but you're fast as fuck. I'll give you that."

He had no clue just how much danger he was in.

But I did.

The beast appeared behind him, one of its razor-sharp tentacles already snapping forward to stab him.

I started moving before the creature fully manifested, placing me in range to swing my sword as it appeared. I severed the tentacle before it could land its sneak attack, then quickly lobbed off the others before they could strike.

The beast howled, baring its teeth in a feral snarl. Saliva dripped from its teeth, little drops of acidic spit falling to the ground where they immediately started to sizzle and eat through the asphalt.

"Not today, Satan!" Sin shouted, swinging his double-headed flail and bashing the fucker's head in.

"That was fucking awesome!"

The voice came from behind me, pulling my attention and setting me on edge. I was millimeters away from taking his head before I clocked Hades beside him and realized he wasn't a threat. He was with our allies.

"Now's not the time to fanboy, Remington," Lilith said, her hand on one hip, brows lifted. "It seems we've appeared in the midst of a fray."

Usually I wasn't one to need backup, but I wasn't about to turn down eight able-bodied fighters. For as many demons as we'd already taken out, several more swarmed to replace them. More fighters meant we would be able to end this sooner.

I quickly shouted out orders. "Stay away from the brain suckers! Don't look at them. Focus on the lesser demons, let us handle the others."

"How are we supposed to tell them apart?" the one called Remington asked, glancing around.

"Follow my lead," Gabriel said, his eyes glowing with his angelic grace.

I couldn't say I had the Messenger of God showing up on my apocalypse bingo card, but I wasn't going to bitch about an angel fighting on my side.

"Ben . . . Did he say brain sucker?" Remington asked a man who looked identical to him.

"Y-yes."

Heaving a sigh, I struck down an approaching brain sucker, slicing it straight down the middle. It fell to the ground with a disgusting squelching sound. "That is a brain sucker."

"Noted," the man said, his eyes glowing as he shifted into a massive alpha wolf. His twin followed suit, and together they dove toward a smaller group of what appeared to be pestilence demons.

From the corner of my eye, I caught sight of Grim and Malice, backs to each other as they fought a group of gluttony demons. They were deceptively slovenly, waddling as they approached, but their wide, toad-like mouths could swallow down anything, the acidity of their saliva able to dissolve down to the bone.

I was about to shout out another warning to the newcomers, amongst them two vampires and the fae beside Lilith, who I vaguely recalled meeting, but they didn't need my help. The vampires worked together to dismember the demons gathered closest to them while Lilith and Drystan used a combination of their skills I couldn't quite pinpoint to deal with several others.

My curiosity was piqued, but now was hardly the time to sit back and watch. My blood was calling for me to rejoin the fight.

"Watch yourselves," Hades warned from across the street as he caught three demons in his shadows and squeezed until their eyes popped from their sockets.

My attention snapped to where he was looking and who he was attempting to warn, but I was too late. Grim was face-to-face with a gorgon, her hood already dropping as she used her snake-like bottom half to raise her eyes to his.

"Don't!" I shouted, but it was futile. As I watched on, his skin turned to stone and she smiled.

Throwing my blade with all the force I had in me. It landed in her chest, knocking her to the ground, but I knew she wasn't finished. Nothing short of removing her eyes would stop her.

What the fuck was it about eyes tonight?

Charging forward, I rapidly closed the distance between us, pulling my sword free and closing my eyes in one fluid movement. Then I knelt down, pinning her serpentine body to the ground with a knee to her chest. She writhed beneath me, but I used one hand to hold her head in place, quickly sheathing my sword with the other. Pain bloomed across my forearms as she clawed at me, long, sharp nails scoring my skin. I would not be deterred. My thumbs found their home in her wicked eyes, and I shoved them deep, well past the point of feeling them pop, until she ceased all movement.

Threat handled, I allowed my eyes to open.

The scene around me was grisly, to say the least. Everyone was fighting, except Grim, who was stuck playing statue. His stone form would eventually fade, but there was no way to know how long that would take. On a mortal, a gorgon's gaze was fatal, but he was a horseman. It was simply—and unfortunately—a matter of time.

From my knees, I swept my gaze over the melee. The demons just kept coming, more and more pouring in. A harsh bark came from my left, calling my attention to one of our wolves, pinned on his back by a displacer beast, a tentacle shoved into his chest.

"No!" I called out, helpless as I watched him shift from wolf to human, the shock of the attack clearly forcing him to revert.

A pulse of power washed over us, the air growing thick with it as everything around us stopped. For a second, I thought we were all frozen in place, but then I heard a strangled shout.

"Ben!"

Someone had frozen everything other than the fighters on our side. That was some powerful fucking magic. I didn't know of a single being capable of such a move. My eyes darted between the newcomers, trying to suss out who was the source.

When my gaze landed on the fae, I knew I'd found my answer. He was not simply a weather fae as I assumed, but something far greater. He had to be royalty of some kind; they were the only ones with access to the type of power required for such a feat.

"I can't hold them much longer. There's too many," he gritted out, sweat dotting his brow.

"We have to retreat," Lilith said.

"We can't leave Ben. We fucking can't." Remington raced to his brother's side and moved to rip the beast off him.

"Stop." Drystan was trembling now, but his voice was forceful. "If you remove that tentacle, you risk doing more harm."

"What the fuck do you suggest we do then?"

As they shouted at each other, Sin and Malice moved to my side. The three of us exchanged wary glances.

"This didn't go exactly as planned, did it?" Sin asked softly.

"When does anything go according to plan?" Malice muttered, eyeing the others with interest.

Drystan swallowed, seeming to have considered the shifter's question before biting out, "We portal out of here together and leave the monster behind. As soon as we're safe, one of the vampires can heal him."

"I'll do it," one with an Irish accent offered.

"There's no way he'll let anyone other than Rosie do it," the other countered. "He has trust issues with vampires."

"Work that out between yourselves." Lilith leveled her gaze at me. "Come with us. This fight isn't winnable in our current state."

Everything in me protested the thought of a retreat. War did not retreat. War razed entire armies to the ground single-handedly.

Reading the conflict on my face, Lilith snapped, "What's more important to you, Chaos? Getting Merri back or staying to finish this?"

Grim's voice broke through my thoughts. "Merri. Let's go."

"Oh, he's back. Have a nice little nap?" Sin quipped.

"Where are we going?" Malice asked.

Lilith shook her head. "If I told you, I'd have to kill you." Then she opened a portal and stepped through, leaving the rest of us to follow in her wake.

The vampires were quick to slip through, followed by Gabriel. Hades hung back until the four of us reached the shimmering air, pausing only long enough to slap a hand to my shoulder.

"It's fucking good to see you boys."

"We have a lot to catch up on," I said, and he nodded before ducking through the portal.

"Wait!" Remington called. "Do you really just expect me to leave him?"

"I've got him," Drystan said. "Trust me."

With no little uncertainty in his eyes, Remington went through the portal.

Drystan looked to us. "Go on. I will be there with him. I swear it."

"We really doing this?" Sin asked.

"We came here to find Lilith and get help finding Merri. I'd say we've accomplished the first part," I pointed out.

The others exchanged glances and nodded before we all jumped through the portal.

The magic closed behind us, sealing us in an unfamiliar place. The instant it was closed, Remington began panicking.

"Fuck! Ben! Oh fuck!"

There was a moment when I thought perhaps we might have to restrain him, but the fae appeared with Ben in his arms.

"See? I told you to trust me."

CHAPTER TWENTY-NINE

SUNDAY

It was always unsettling when my mates were gone, but after the last supply run had ended with a shambling possessed zombie attack, I was completely on edge knowing Kingston, Noah, and Alek were out there. Sure, they were strong and capable. I didn't doubt them. But they weren't immortal. I'd nearly lost each of them more than once.

I didn't realize I'd started pacing until the walkie-talkie crackled to life and I found myself on the far side of the suite Lilith had set aside for me and my mates. We'd taken to using the little radios to stay in communication while groups patrolled the perimeter. The Belladonna coven had found a way to make the signals work across realms. I couldn't pretend to understand how the magic worked, but I wasn't complaining about the results. Once, when Kingston had asked Moira how she'd done something, she simply looked at him, shrugged, and said *Because witches,* and that had been the end of it.

"Mayday, mayday, mayday. We've got missing persons out here. We need relief."

I raced to the walkie, heart in my throat. Not knowing which group had called in for aid had my stomach knotting with dread.

"This is home base. What's your location?"

The radio crackled again. "Outside of Aurora Springs. Timmy and Zed are missing. They were supposed to meet us thirty minutes ago, but they're MIA. We need backup so we can do a proper search."

Relief hit me hard, and I sank down onto the bed, even as guilt churned in my belly. My mates were safe, but Timmy and Zed were two of my pack members. As happy as I was my men weren't in trouble, I still had a duty to see these guys safely home. Not just as tonight's watch commander but as co-head of the Farrell pack.

"Do you suspect an attack?" I asked.

"No, it's been quiet. Well, as quiet as we can expect." The radio crackled and then went silent for a heartbeat, then came to life again. "I'm worried they got trapped in a mudslide near the hellmouth. The ground here is treacherous after the eruptions."

That made sense. The groups patrolling that area had been complaining about the degraded terrain all week.

Before I could reply, Sally continued, "Carl and I want to go check, but we can't leave this spot unmanned."

It was vital that our entry points around the globe weren't exposed to our countless enemies. Sally was right; there wasn't an option for the two of them to execute a search and rescue mission without someone else taking over guard duty.

"All right, let me see who I can send. Give me ten minutes."

"Copy."

Shoving the walkie into my hoodie's oversized pocket, I scrambled out the door to the common area. Caleb had stayed behind with me while everyone else went out so he could strategize with Lilith. He would be an ideal candidate for such a mission.

But when I got there, Caleb, Gavin, Lilith, and Crombie were all gone.

"Shit," I muttered. "Where the hell are you guys?"

Turning on my heel, I made a beeline for the most likely place I'd find Caleb since he wasn't here. Asher's command center, complete with murder board. When he wasn't with me, that's usually where he spent his time.

I took off at a slight jog, a sense of urgency propelling me down the hall. The soft murmur of voices met my ear as I pushed open the door, but my heart sank when the only two people I found inside were Rosie and Pan.

"Look at you," Pan crooned. "Even now with the world ending, you're still my dirty little slut."

Rosie giggled as Pan kissed his way down her neck, but at my sudden intrusion, her eyes went wide and she sat up straight. "Sunday! I was just about to come find you."

I cocked one brow. "Sure looks like it."

"Sorry, Pan distracted me." She righted her clothes. "Caleb asked me to tell you he had an unexpected meeting. He and the others stepped out, but they should be back soon."

Crap on a cracker. There went that plan.

"Everyone is gone," I said under my breath.

Pan scoffed. "I beg your pardon. I am right bloody here."

"I just mean . . . all my mates. The shifters, the Novasgardians, the fae. And the vampires are useless right now because it's still light out in Alaska, so unless they have the blood of the sun, they're stuck inside until the sun goes down. I don't know who else I can possibly send . . ." I chewed on my bottom lip as I tried to come up with an alternative, but there wasn't one. "It's going to have to be me."

"What the fork are you talking about, Sunday?" Rosie rested one palm on her growing belly and frowned at me. "You're not making sense."

"There's a problem with the patrol in Aurora Springs. Two of my wolves are missing. They don't think it was an attack. They're pretty sure they got stranded somewhere due to the eruptions."

"And what does that have to do with you?"

I pulled the walkie out of my hoodie and waved it at them. "I'm in charge right now."

"Then ask Asher to go. Or Caspian."

Pan snorted. "Caspian is good at captaining a ship. He's terrible at being on watch. And Asher needs to stay here for a multitude of reasons, the least of which is keeping you safe."

"As I said, it's going to have to be me." I pulled my hair back into a low knot at the base of my skull and lifted my hood over my head. "I'll be back soon."

Rosie awkwardly started to get to her feet. "I'll go with you."

"The hell you will," Pan snarled.

She gave her mate a sharp look. "If Sunday can go, so can I."

I understood the sentiment, but actually sided with Pan. I was pregnant, but Rosie was *pregnant*. Because she was carrying twins, she looked way farther along, and she'd been struggling. Not just with her rapidly changing body, but all the associated side effects. The safest place for her and her pups was here.

But I was also smart enough to know I couldn't say any of that. Rosie wanted to feel useful, not like a burden.

"Actually, I need you to man the walkie while I'm gone." I held the little radio out to her with a wave.

She took it, her shoulders straightening as she looked down at the device. "Just press this button and talk, yeah?"

"Exactly."

"Go find Asher, ma petite monstre. I'll accompany Sunday, and we will ensure the portal is protected." Pan's tone was far gentler than usual as he ushered her out of the room. "Let them know assistance is on the way."

"Stay safe," she urged, pressing a quick kiss to his lips before rushing off.

"Thanks for doing this," I said as he followed me to the portal room.

"It's entirely selfish, I promise. Your mates would skin me alive if anything happened to you."

As we approached the exit chamber, my belly fluttered in apprehension. "It'll be just a few minutes once they can get out there and help. All it will be is a locator spell. That doesn't take any time at all. They'll find them, and then we can come back."

"Are you telling me, or yourself?" he asked as we stood in front of the portal that led to Aurora Springs.

"Both?"

"Brilliant. Let's get on with this."

We walked through together, the smoky air stinging my eyes almost instantly as we appeared in the middle of the wooded area.

"Hello, daughter. It's good to see you."

A chill ran down my spine as my mother, the horsewoman War, wrapped her fingers around my wrist. I had barely a moment to register the bodies of every member of this patrol group crumpled at her feet.

Pan's hand grasped my free one and I felt him tug hard, but it was too late. My mother let out a dark chuckle and said, "Two for one. I do love a bargain."

Then the world went dark.

CHAPTER THIRTY

MALICE

"What the fuck are we waiting for? He's bleeding out in front of us!" Remington screamed at anyone who would listen as he tore his twin out of Drystan's arms.

"Remi?" a posh and pregnant British woman cried, rushing into the room. "What happened? What's wrong?"

"He's dying. I need . . . you have to . . ." Remi spluttered, unable to finish his sentence as emotion took hold. "Gavin, tell her."

"He needs your blood, petal. It has to be you, and it has to be now." This came from the vampire who'd remained mostly quiet until now.

Without question, the woman dropped to her knees beside who I was beginning to assume was her mate. Hades mentioned there were others in pods similar to ours. I suspected this was one of them.

In a quick move, her fangs flashed, and she tore open the skin of her wrist before pressing the bloody appendage to the dying wolf's lips. The slight nod Grim gave me when we made eye contact as he pulled his gloves over his bare hands confirmed my suspicions that Ben would survive.

"Where are we, Lilith?" Grim asked, calm but pointed at the same time.

"That I can't tell you, Grimsby. It's not only for our own safety, but because it technically doesn't exist in any realm."

Hades rolled his eyes, arms crossed as he muttered, "I'm pretty sure it's some kind of pocket dimension or realm. It can be anchored to multiple realms—regardless of whether they are connected to each other—and accessed only by those given permission." He flashed a little black card. "We will get some made for you."

Lilith, who'd begun a slow stalk down the hall, turned on us. "*I* will get them made for you, as it is *my* realm."

"What was the name of our little society, darlin'? The Lilith Society?" He tapped his lip as if considering before his eyes flashed with wicked delight and he smirked. "Oh, that's right. We're the Hades Society."

"Careful, you let it get any bigger and your head won't fit through the gates of the underworld."

He smirked but followed along as she resumed walking her original path. "That's a real spitfire you've got there," he murmured to Drystan as we all fell into step.

"I'm aware."

"How many creatures does this realm house?" I asked, dubiously taking in the narrow corridor.

"As many as are required." Lilith flicked her hair over one shoulder, not sparing me a glance as she answered. "All of the horsewomen's progeny and their mates. Save Merri, of course."

My stomach dropped, a pit of apprehension forming as her words registered.

Pan. Pan was here.

My son was *here.*

I stumbled, only staying upright because of Chaos's firm grip on my shoulder.

"You okay?" he asked, voice pitched low.

No. I decidedly was not. In all the madness of the battle and trying to find Lilith to get a lead on Merri, I'd forgotten Pan was linked to this band of rebels. It hadn't even crossed my mind that I might see him. Would he recognize himself in me? Would he even have a clue who I was? Would he hate me?

"My son is here," I whispered.

"Yes."

Hades turned his head, locking gazes with me. "I haven't told him who you are. He believes his father is a demon cast off by his mother before he was born."

That was half correct. She cast me off as soon as she got what she wanted, but I was no demon. Technically, neither was my son, despite his preference for that hulking purple form. In truth, he was the only one of his kind, the first being ever created by two horsepersons. But that was a conversation for another time.

"Where is he?" I asked.

A low groan from behind us pulled our focus to Ben, who stirred in his brother's hold. Vampire blood stained his lips, but the wound in his chest was slowly knitting together.

"Rosie will know. She's his mate." Hades jerked his chin back toward the slight woman. The sight of her swollen belly took on new weight. She was carrying my grandchild. If not biologically, at least in name.

"Are you sure you're ready to do this right now, Mal? That's a big step. Maybe we save the world first?" Sin asked, one hand landing on my shoulder.

"No. I need to know him now. I've waited too long already. Pan is my son."

"What about Odette?" Grim asked.

"What about her? She's a cunt."

"We've established that. They all are," Chaos agreed. "I think he was more concerned about her threats to harm him if you made contact."

"She's not here. They defeated her."

My brothers exchanged hesitant glances before Sin cleared his throat. "At the risk of being Captain Obvious, you know nothing keeps our kind down for long."

A handsome fae swanned into the hallway. "Did someone call for a captain?"

"No. If we call for you, you'll know it. Where's Sunday?" the vampire with an Irish accent asked, irritation sparking in his tone.

"Gone."

"What?"

"She's gone. Off on a walkabout with Pan. She left Rosie the walkie-talkie, but then the sweet girl gave it to me to take over once Remi started shouting in her head about needing help." The pirate held up a small handheld radio and waved it back and forth. "Crickets so far, so I'd wager all is well."

"Give it to me," the vampire snarled, dashing forward in a blur of speed and snatching the device from his hand. "Sunday, report," he demanded, holding it up to his mouth.

There was nothing but deafening silence.

Knowing that my son was with her, that there was no answer, sent my head swimming. I can't have gotten this close only to lose him again.

"Try again," I snapped.

The vampire glared at me. Fair enough, he had no idea why I'd be so invested.

"Sunday? Talk to me, darlin'."

He was met only with more silence.

"Where did she go?" he asked, rounding on Rosie, which only served to make the other vampire and Remi bristle.

"Aurora Springs. There was a problem with two of the patrol groups. She and Pan went to guard the portal, nothing more, Caleb, I promise."

"Are the others back?" he asked, stalking off in the opposite direction.

"No, not yet," Rosie answered.

"At least she didn't go alone," he grumbled, adding under his breath, "I'm still going to pinken her arse for scaring me though."

In a blur of motion, he left, and before we could discuss anything further, we'd entered a large common area filled with shifters, witches, vampires, and more. The low hum of their pockets of conversation held a tension I remembered feeling during times of plague, when people stayed consistently on edge, waiting for a cough, a sneeze, or complaints of fever.

We neared an empty sofa, and Lilith stopped, leaning her hip against the back of it. "Do the four of you have anything you'd like to tell me?" she asked, voice deceptively soft.

I knew a trap when I heard one.

"Besides go fuck yourself for getting us into this mess?" Grim shot back.

Drystan lost his shit, and thunder growled, causing everyone in the room to glance around uneasily. "Watch your fucking mouth."

"You had one job. Protect her." Lilith stood to her full height and stared hard at us. "That was all."

"Technically we were supposed to knock her up too," Sin offered.

"And did you?" she hissed.

"Well . . . no. Not for lack of trying."

I nodded. "He's right."

"We gave it our all," Sin said. "We fed our succubus every chance we got. Even Grim."

If that was surprising news to the others, no one indicated so. For the most part, the group we'd arrived with had stayed back, allowing Lilith her interrogation without interference.

Lilith squinted her eyes and held a hand up to her forehead as if searching for something. Or someone.

"I can't help but notice Merri isn't with you, Grimsby. So where is she?"

Her voice was so filled with icy rage that I felt as if she should be the one named Malice.

"If we knew that, we'd be there right now bringing her home." Chaos's growl was so low I felt it in my chest.

"She's with Lucifer," Sin answered, bravely—or stupidly, depending on how you looked at it—placing himself in front of War.

Lilith's eyes were little more than slits. "This is very bad news, Sinclair."

"You think we don't fucking know that?" I snapped, too emotionally wound up to give a shit about upsetting her further.

"How long has she been gone?"

"Too long," I admitted. "But we have been able to reach her when she dreamwalks. She hasn't been able to tell us where he's truly keeping her."

Gabriel, who'd barely spoken a word since joining our demon fight, finally stepped forward. "He's likely holding her in a realm similar to this one."

He stared at us like that was supposed to be helpful.

"And?" Grim growled.

Gabriel rolled his eyes and turned his attention to Lilith. "What happens to this place if you are weakened?"

"All protections cease to exist."

"Meaning what?" Chaos asked, eyes flaring bright with interest. "Spell it out for us."

He was smart enough he likely already guessed the answer, but he wasn't about to take any chances. Not with Merri's life on the line.

"Meaning it can be found and accessed."

"That seems like a real security risk," Remi mumbled behind us.

My brothers and I shared a look, several unspoken messages passing between us.

"That's great and all, but how can we weaken someone we cannot locate?" Grim asked.

Lilith heaved a long-suffering sigh. "Honestly, do I have to do everything around here? All the clues are in front of them, and yet they still need me to hand them the answer." Then she leveled her gaze at Grim. "Dreamwalks are better than reality. Whatever happens there happens here. Merri controls the dream realm. And she isn't limited to one partner at a time."

"That's true! I've been in her dreams with Lucifer twice now," Sin piped up.

"So, we convince her to pull more than one of us in . . ." I began, trailing off as I couldn't fully connect the dots.

"And bring her into her full power so she can weaken him in a dream," Chaos finished for me.

"Now you're getting it. Well done, boys." Lilith brushed her hands off as though washing them clean of us. "You should probably find somewhere to sleep. You're all looking a little . . . tired."

Sin winced, but it was Remi who spoke.

"Oooh, that's the kiss of death. Everyone knows when someone says you look tired, they really mean you look like shit."

"They don't sleep. They fuck her in the dreams, Remington," Gavin muttered. "She's a succubus."

"Nice!"

I was about to infect him with a case of laryngitis when Caleb rushed into the room, eyes panicked, face even more pale than before he left. "They're gone. The patrol group is all dead, and Sunday and Pan are fecking gone."

The ground seemed to drop out from beneath me.

No.

Chaos was at my side, his arm wrapped tightly around me, keeping me upright.

"We'll find him," he promised.

"We can't even find Merri," I muttered, before my fury broke free and I kicked over the table next to me. "What fucking good is it being a horseman when we fail at every fucking turn?"

Chaos turned to me and let out a pulse of his power, the rage coming from him rattling me enough to pull my focus.

"Whoa, nelly," Remi whispered. "Did anyone else feel that?"

"It's l-like f-fight club on s-steroids," Ben said, speaking for the first time since he nearly died. Now he was standing with one arm slung over Rosie's shoulder, using her for support, but just barely.

Chaos ignored them, choosing to put every ounce of his attention on me. "We will find him, Malice. It's all connected. If we find Lucifer, we find your son."

The room had grown so quiet in the wake of my and Chaos's outbursts that you could have heard a pin drop. There was a soft gasp, and then Rosie straightened, taking a step toward me.

I squeezed my eyes shut, already knowing what was coming.

"Wait a second. Pan is your son?"

CHAPTER THIRTY-ONE

MERRI

The first thing I noticed when I entered the dream was the moon. It hung heavy and low, looking almost comically large in the star-spangled sky. The second thing I clocked was the château. Idyllic and beautiful, it made my chest ache with longing for the men I loved. I could be with them in dreams, sure, but I wanted every moment to be a reality. Instead, I'd gotten myself trapped.

As I wandered the property, I let my power guide me toward my goal. It wasn't the sprawling estate or the gardens I was searching for. It was *him*. Tall, broad, handsome, and brutal, Chaos stood near the trees at the back of the house. He took my breath away on a good day, but right now? The look on his face was so fierce my heart stuttered.

"Where were you last night?" he snapped, pulling me out of my reverie.

"Well, hello to you, too."

He made a rumbling sound I was pretty sure was a growl. Like an actual growl. The predator-stalking-prey kind.

So why were my panties damp?

"You didn't come to any of us. We had no way to find you. You blocked Sin from your dreams. Merri . . . We didn't know if you were—"

I reached out and cupped his cheek as his words took on a new meaning. He wasn't scolding me; he'd been worried for me. "I'm okay. I'm here now."

His posture softened, but he wasn't ready to let it go. "Where were you? Why did you block Sin?"

"The answer is the same for both, actually," I said with a sigh. I'd known there would be no way to keep this from them, but I'd sort of been hoping we could save this conversation for *after*. When he was calm from a couple of orgasms.

He raised a brow, silently demanding an answer.

"Lucifer."

Just like that, he was tense again. "Lucifer what?"

"I don't know how it happened, but I ended up in a dreamwalk with him."

A muscle in his jaw ticked as he ground his teeth and released another low growl, but I held up a hand to stop him.

"Nothing happened. We just . . . talked. But afterward, I had to shore up my defenses. If my walls are down for you, they're down for him too. It's complicated, and I'm not sure, but it might be that my power seeks the most easily available target if I'm not focused."

He grunted, clearly displeased with this turn of events.

I tried the hand on his cheek again. "I'm sorry. But I'm fine. I'm right here."

He held my gaze for several heartbeats before turning his head and kissing my palm. "We have some updates for you as well."

"You do?" I asked, hope making my heart speed up.

"First I think you should bring the others."

I snorted out a laugh. "Oh, yeah, okay. I can't do that."

"Yes you can."

"How do you know what I can and can't do?"

"That's part of what we need to talk to you about." Stepping even closer, he wrapped his hand around my nape and squeezed gently. "You can do so much more than you think, Red. You have power over us all. One crook of your finger, real or in a dream, and we will come running."

I wasn't sure what to do with those words. I was simultaneously filled with joy and despair. Because while I didn't doubt the sincerity in his voice, there was a very specific time in the not-so-distant past where that had been far from the case.

And the reminder made me think of Grim.

A stone of anxiety sat heavy in my stomach. The thought of seeing him again made my palms break out in sweat.

"I . . . I don't . . ." I couldn't finish the sentence, unsure of what I really wanted to say.

"We need you to do this. It's part of the plan."

"What plan is that?"

"Which one do you think?"

The way he said it, so matter-of-factly, left no room for doubt. It was about getting me back.

"I don't even know where to start."

"So what? You didn't know how to dreamwalk until you did. It's all instinct, Red. Just try. You might surprise yourself."

Thoughts racing, I bit my lower lip out of habit as I tried to figure out how to go about doing this. I'd never pulled someone into a dreamwalk that was already occupied by someone else. But Sin had joined more than once when Lucifer had me in one of his. Maybe I was overthinking it all.

Chaos was right. I was powerful—so powerful I'd been locked away by Lilith.

"Okay. I'll try."

I took a deep breath and closed my eyes, something in me relaxing when he threaded our fingers as if to share some of his strength. I released a second heavy exhale, this time picturing those golden threads I'd noticed ever since the mate bonds snapped into place. I basically just had to think of one of the four of them and the shimmery fiber would appear, like a rope I could follow . . . or tug.

At first the only one I saw was a bright, shiny gold, strong and thick like a rope woven from our bond. I wrapped my hand around it and heard Chaos let out a soft grunt even as his energy poured over me. On instinct I released it, confident he wasn't going anywhere. Chaos wouldn't leave this dream until I ended it. He was mine.

Sweeping my gaze farther through my consciousness, I found two more woven threads, not as vibrant, but still glowing and golden. It didn't take more than a passing thought to know Sin's was the one on the left and Malice the right. Without giving myself a chance to second-guess, I reached for both of them and tugged. Hard.

I felt their presence the moment they arrived, their ropes now shining as brightly as Chaos's.

That just left one more.

The one I dreaded.

But when I reached for Grim, his thread was wispy and dull. It was still there, but when I tried to touch it, my fingers moved through it as easily as if it were a cloud.

I knew this was a bad sign. Our bond was damaged.

But I didn't know if it was his fault for rejecting me, or mine for being so torn about seeing him again. Like a self-sabotaging thing. Or maybe I was just subconsciously protecting myself. No matter the reason, it seemed like a future Merri problem.

"She did it," Sin whispered as I opened my eyes and came face-to-face with him and Malice. "I knew she fucking could."

Malice didn't give me words right away; he chose instead to wrap me in a tight embrace. "Good job, hellcat," he murmured as he pressed a soft kiss to my temple.

Fuck, I'd missed them.

"Where's Grim?" Chaos asked.

"Stubborn ass probably refused to come on principle." Sin took the hand Chaos wasn't holding and brought it to his lips. "His loss."

I shook my head, stepping back as Malice released me from his embrace. "No. I tried. I couldn't grab hold of him. I think the bond is messed up."

The guys wore various expressions of anger, though I could tell none of it was directed at me. Despite seeming the most upset by my admission, Sin was the first to recover.

"That shouldn't matter, though, right?" He looked at the others. "Lilith didn't say anything about requiring a mate bond to bring people into the dream realm. I mean, for the plan to work, it literally can't be a requirement."

"Maybe you three should fill me in on this plan. I'll work out my Grim stuff on my own."

Malice nodded, taking a beat before he said, "You're strongest in the dream realm, especially when you keep yourself fed. Whatever happens in these dreamwalks happens in reality, so you cut me, I bleed, you drain me dry, I wither with a smile on my face."

I nodded, none of this information news to me.

"And now that we know you can bring as many people as you want—"

"That feels like a bit of a stretch, Sin," I said. "So far we can only confidently say I can bring three."

He waved my concern away. "That's just a matter of practice, and in reality, you only really need to be able to bring in a couple more."

I was about to ask who he meant, but it was obvious. They wanted to face off against Lucifer here, where we would have the upper hand.

"You can do this, Red," Chaos said.

Taking a fortifying breath, I straightened my posture and gave a curt nod. "Okay. When do you want to do this?"

They looked to each other again, silently communicating in that way of theirs.

"Soon," Malice murmured.

"I think we plan on practicing tomorrow. Making sure you can get Grim here and limit testing your power to see what you can really do when the training wheels come off," Chaos said.

Sin nodded his agreement. "And then if everything goes as well as expected, we pull the trigger the next day."

My belly churned with nerves. "Two days?" I squeaked. "You want me ready to face off with the devil in two days?"

"We don't have the luxury of time, Red."

"Besides, you already have everything you need. You just have to believe in yourself. That's what tomorrow is for. By the time we're done, you'll be as confident in your abilities as we are," Sin added.

"You have a lot of faith in me."

Had they forgotten how out of control I'd been only weeks earlier? That I'd nearly died multiple times because of my lack of understanding of my power?

"We do. And nothing is going to change that," Malice murmured, reaching for me and brushing a lock of hair behind my ear.

Hunger washed over me at their proximity. Three strong, virile horsemen in my dream realm after going a night without feeding were proving too tempting to resist.

"Did you guys feel that?" Sin asked, his pupils blown as my lust hit him.

"Yes." Chaos's voice was like gravel.

"Hungry, hellcat?"

"Famished."

"Then maybe we shelve talking and get to the feeding portion of the evening," Sin offered.

"Oh yeah?" I practically purred. "What did you have in mind?"

Sin's smile was pure sex. "Remember that time you said you wanted to be chased? How about a little hide and seek?"

CHAPTER THIRTY-TWO

SIN

Merri's answering flood of arousal told me she was more than down to play this game.

"Rules?" she asked, voice breathy.

"First one to catch you gets to have his way with you," I answered immediately.

"What about the others?" she asked, eyes darting to my brothers standing on either side of me.

"They can watch," Chaos growled, his body all coiled tension.

He'd so be eating those words. I knew in a usual footrace he would be the one to beat, but I had an ace up my sleeve. I was a fucking incubus. The dream realm was just as much mine as it was Merri's.

"Better get ready, kitten. It looks like we're all ready to hunt you down."

Malice huffed out a laugh. "Should we give her a head start? Ten seconds to run before we give chase?"

"That's barely any time at all," she protested.

"Silly of you to waste it then," Malice crooned, then he leaned toward her and whispered, "Run."

Without another word, Merri spun around and fled into the woods, her bright red hair a beacon.

"Good luck, lads. You're going to need it," Malice said with a smirk.

Chaos gave him a sidelong glance and shook his head. "Yeah. Luck."

I decided to remain silent. Little did they know, they were both about to be sidelined.

"Three," Chaos counted.

"Two," Malice continued.

"One."

I bolted, rushing forward while using my power to twist and warp the dream. Not a lot, just enough that my brothers would have their hands tied for a while.

And seriously, who didn't love a labyrinth moment? I even added a Minotaur in the middle just for Chaos. Consider it a consolation prize.

See? Wasn't I the most generous winner?

A creative genius, some might say.

I could simply lock onto my Merri's energy, but we were playing a game. She wanted me to hunt her, to catch her, to pin her, and claim her.

I was so fucking down.

"Come out, come out, wherever you are," I sing-songed.

Merri was just ahead, her breath hitching, giving away that she heard the fall of my footsteps gaining on hers.

I could easily end this little chase, but I wanted to give her the full effect.

She ran hard, but the rustle of leaves and cracks of twigs underfoot only helped me find her that much faster. I broke through the trees and came up right behind her, eliciting a high-pitched yelp of surprise and delight from her that I felt all the way down to my toes. She was thrilled in a way none of us had experienced before. Thrilled, and turned the fuck on.

And honestly? So was I.

"Gotcha," I growled, my hands tight on her hips as I pressed my erection against her ass.

She squirmed in my hold, but I clamped down on the back of her shoulder, biting just hard enough to leave a mark. "You heard the rules, pretty girl. I caught you, now I get to have my way with you."

Her breath stuttered. "W-what are you going to do to me?"

"Get on all fours. Now."

She did, her short skirt riding up and flashing her bare pink cunt. Fuck me. I loved dreams. If I wanted, I could have her naked right now, but I liked the idea of taking her raw out here with most of our clothes on. We had time to get undressed later.

"Jesus, you have such a pretty pussy. Look at her, already dripping for me."

A visible shiver raced down her spine at my words. My kitten loved it when I talked dirty.

"Stop teasing me. Fuck me."

I ran my palm over her ass as I opened my pants and took my dick in my other hand. Stroking the rock-hard length, I shuddered in anticipation. I wanted this as much as she did, but I was in charge here. Not her.

With a growl in my voice, I slapped her wet pussy and said, "You'll take what I give you."

Merri yelped, the sound so filled with raw need that beads of precum slid down my aching shaft. I wasn't going to be able to resist sinking inside her for much longer.

A roar came from somewhere to my left, either from Chaos or the Minotaur. My bet was on Chaos defeating the Minotaur, but I'd been wrong before. All I knew was if I wanted her alone, I couldn't wait any longer.

"How many Os do you think I can get out of you before we have company?"

Merri whimpered and pushed back against my hand, seeking out some relief. When I didn't give it to her, she shot me a glare over her shoulder. "Probably only the one, because we both know as soon as I come, so will you."

My answering chuckle was dark. "Oh, kitten, if you think that means I can't ruin you a hundred ways from Sunday, you really haven't been paying attention." I lined myself up with her soaked entrance and said, "I have a quick recovery period. Not to mention my fingers"—I slid my hand around her front to toy with her swollen clit—"my mouth"—I leaned down and pressed a kiss to her spine as my dick pressed inside—"and I bet if I tried hard enough, I could make you come with nothing but my voice."

The punch of her arousal hit me hard and fast.

I smirked. "See, you think so too."

"Stop playing with me," she whined, trying hard to force me to bottom out inside her.

"But we're just getting started," I teased, giving her barely an inch.

"Siiin."

"I love it when you say my name, baby."

"Sin," she whispered.

"Fuck."

"Emmett." That one got me. I nearly lost it as she moaned my real name. I had to grip her hips with both hands as I drove inside her hard and deep.

"Fuck yes," she groaned, matching my thrusts by pressing back into them.

The only sounds I was aware of were Merri's soft cries and our skin slapping against each other. This was what I wanted for the rest of my days.

Her.

In every way.

However I could get her.

~

GRIM

Chaos

"Fuck this," I snarled, throwing the bloody head of the Minotaur to the ground as I heard the unmistakable sounds of Merri's pleasure coming from just beyond the labyrinth's walls.

Not bothering to wipe the blood from my sword, I started hacking at the thick hedges keeping me here.

Sin was a clever motherfucker, I'd give him that. But I wasn't about to miss out on quality time with our girl just because he was being a selfish prick. This dreamwalk was supposed to be mine. Which meant this time with her was also mine.

As soon as there was enough space for me to shove my body through the gap, I did just that. Then I started the process all over on the next wall. I had no clue how Malice was faring, nor did I care. The only thing that mattered was getting to Merri.

I hacked through the final hedge and tumbled out into a clearing, moonlight spilling across the ground, and a vision of pure carnality lay out before me. Merri on her hands and knees, Sin balls deep inside her from behind. She had her head down, eyes closed, hair a mess of wild tangles.

He spotted me before she did, his smirk filled with smug pride.

Grabbing Merri by the hair, he tugged until she was kneeling in front of him, his mouth at her ear.

"Look who found you, kitten. Do you see how badly he wants you?"

Merri's eyes popped open, her gaze unerringly finding mine. She was too gone for words, but I saw the need blazing in her irises. She wanted me.

Not wasting a second, I tugged down my pants, pulling myself free.

"Hey! What happened to watching?" Sin asked.

"Fuck you," I snarled, stalking toward them.

Sin laughed. "That would be new for us."

I didn't spare him any attention. Instead, I grabbed her by the waist, pulled her off his dick, and kneeled.

"Wrap your legs around me, Red."

"Excuse you, I was in the middle of something," Sin protested.

Merri sank onto my dick, writhing as she did, and I groaned, "Either join in or take your bitching somewhere else. She has a sweet little ass just waiting for you to fill." As if to emphasize the point, I used the two hands palming the perfect globes of her ass to spread her wide for him.

Merri moaned. "Oh God."

"If you don't want this, baby, just say the word," Sin offered, already shuffling forward so he could have a better angle.

"I want it."

"I fucking love enthusiastic consent. Anyone who says consent can't be sexy doesn't know what they're missing."

He shut up the moment he drove home.

To be fair, so did I. It was a tight fit, and it had me momentarily seeing stars.

Merri whimpered in response, and I worried she was in pain, but then she said, "Fuck, it feels good."

I'd never been more thankful our mate was a succubus. It made things so much easier knowing her body was literally made for pleasure.

She began rolling her hips, doing the work for us, and I was just along for the best ride of my life. My body was on fire for her, ready to explode as she clawed at my shoulders and chased the releases we all wanted.

"Is there room for one more?" Malice drawled, his footsteps sounding off to my left.

"Pretty sure this seat's taken," Sin joked, though his voice was tight with need.

Merri's eyes flashed, and she licked her lips as she turned her head his way. "I always have room for you."

It was hard to pay attention to what everyone else was doing. I was too caught up in the feel of Merri in my arms and the squeeze of her inner muscles fluttering over my cock. When she moaned, the sound muffled and strange, I turned my head to find her mouth stuffed full of Malice's dick. He had one hand fisted in her hair, the other holding his length for her.

We weren't going to last much longer. There was no way. The physical sensations alone had me teetering on the brink, but when you added Merri's lust weaving through the four of us, it was a fucking powder keg.

"You suck me so good, hellcat. Keep going."

Merri must have done something with her mouth because Malice's eyes rolled back in his head, and he let out a long, strangled groan. At the same time, she clamped down on both me and Sin.

"I can't hold back any more, Merri. Fuck," Sin gritted out.

"I need to come," I panted, sweat rolling down my back as I tried to hold off.

"I'm so fucking close," Malice chimed in, his voice rough.

She couldn't answer with words, but something we said must've triggered her own pleasure because she came, taking us all with her in an explosion rivaling that of a supernova. My vision went white and I swear, when it came back, a golden glow radiated around us all as she fed.

I never imagined that I would be into group activities when it came to my woman, but sharing Merri with my brothers turned an already incredible experience into something otherworldly. The intensity of my climax alone was testament to that. I felt wrung out in the best possible way, but I also knew if she so much as hinted that she needed more I would be ready for her again in a heartbeat.

We ended up lying on the grass, gazing at the stars, sweaty, breathing heavily, and incredibly sated. Merri trailed her fingers over my chest and hummed softly.

"One," Sin said under his breath.

Merri giggled as he started laughing.

I was confused as hell. "One what?"

"I asked her how many orgasms I could get out of her."

"Technically you said before company joined us, so I'm pretty sure the real answer is none."

"Hey now, I did a lot of the heavy lifting. These two swanned in at the end and claimed my victory."

Malice and I rolled our eyes before I looked at Sin and shook my head. "Only one? You're such a fucking underachiever." Then I pulled Merri on top of me and grinned. "I think we can do better than that."

CHAPTER THIRTY-THREE

GRIM

One hour earlier

"Do you think she'll show up tonight?" Sin asked, pouring himself a drink.

"We can only hope," Chaos murmured, settling back into an oversized armchair.

"She can find us, right?"

"Of course she can," I said before bringing my drink to my lips. "It doesn't matter where we are—a château in France, Blackwood, or even here in Lilith's secret fight club. Merri can pull us to her dreams."

Sin glanced around the room Lilith had given us. Modest, clean, and large enough to house four hulking horsemen, she'd provided us with the essentials and nothing more. Apparently Pan had snuck in the brimstone whiskey on one of the supply runs. When he and Sunday were safely returned to the group, I'd have to thank him.

"Now we simply wait." Malice paced back and forth, his words not matching his attitude. He was on edge for more than one reason, and rightfully so. I wasn't a father, but if my child was missing, no matter how old he was, I'd be a bloody menace until he was found.

"Chaos—" I spun to ask him a question, but it died on my lips when I found him slumped backward, a soft snore leaving him. "Well, I guess that answers that," I murmured, my disappointment palpable. Once again, she'd selected one of them over me. I shouldn't be surprised. I deserved it. But it still cut deep.

"Thank fuck," Sin said on a relieved sigh. "I knew she wouldn't wait too long."

Malice briefly closed his eyes before pushing to his feet and joining Sin at the bar cart. "She's hungry. She can't wait much longer."

"And she loves us." Sin beamed as he said the words with such certainty.

The desiccated remains in my chest gave a savage lurch at his words. I was fairly certain Merri's silence where I was concerned proved just how untrue that sentiment was.

This is what you wanted. You needed to push her away. To save her.

Then why does it hurt so much?

"Against her better judge—" Malice began, but his eyes rolled back in his head, and he and Sin both crumpled to the floor, their glasses shattering as they hit the stone.

"Ah, looks like she was successful at bringing multiple people into the dream with her. That's my girl."

I smirked at their undignified sprawls, secretly enjoying the discomfort they'd feel when they returned. Then I settled in and waited to join them.

Any second now.

Any minute . . .

Annnny minute . . .

A pit formed in my stomach as time ticked by. She called them to her. She needed them. That meant she needed us. Us meant me as well.

Didn't it?

Why would it?

You denied her time and again.

The truth of my fall from grace hung heavy around me. I'd had her so briefly, but for those fleeting moments, I'd finally known true happiness. But the reality of our situation meant anything lasting was impossible.

And yet.

And yet . . .

I missed her with a hunger so fierce it damn near rent me in two.

The others believed her, so why couldn't I? Why was it so hard for me to entertain the idea that fate might have granted the four of us our perfect mate?

Because your kind are unworthy of happy endings.

I tapped my fingers on the arm of the chair, my thoughts chasing each other until one rang out so loudly I sat up straight from the force.

So become fucking worthy.

Shoving to my feet, I raked a hand through my hair and took a heavy breath. I'd sat idly by my entire existence, waiting for my time to come, only entering situations when Death was needed. Not any longer. Not when I could do something to help.

"Gabriel," I thundered as I left the room and stormed down the hall.

Unfortunately the angel did not miraculously appear at my summons. Several heads turned my way, though.

"What are you looking at?" I snapped, annoyed by the judgment and pity I found in their curious gazes.

Though the latter emotion might have been a bit of me projecting. It's not like anyone here knew me.

I pulled my leather gloves from my pocket and slid my hands into them just in case I needed to shove someone out of my way.

"Everything all right?" Hades called, standing off to the side with a dark-haired vampire I vaguely recognized.

"Where's that troublemaking angel?" I demanded, moving to join the twosome.

"You'll need to be more specific. We have a handful of angels in our ranks these days," the vampire said with a barely there smile, his Irish accent tinged with something close to amusement.

As my eyes landed on him, that sense of recognition deepened. I knew this man. And not just because he was part of the rescue party that came for us at *Iniquity*.

"I'm surprised to see you here. I recall greeting your soul."

Caleb's lips twitched. "You'll have to take that up with Gabriel. He gave it back."

"As I said, troublemaker."

Hades let out a low chuckle. "It was more like he gifted it to your mate, Caleb. Don't twist things around. Gabriel isn't in the business of just handing things like souls out willy-nilly."

Caleb shrugged. "There were a lot of moving parts to my resurrection." He narrowed his eyes at me, clearly attempting to comb his memory for a recollection of me. "I don't think we've met."

"We have. You won't remember me, though. The souls I claim rarely do."

Caleb looked between the two of us. "How does it work between the two of you? Don't you technically have the same job?"

Hades and I exchanged a knowing glance. We got this question frequently when we were together.

"He reaps them and then passes them on to me for judgment and sorting."

Caleb nodded as though he followed, but it was obvious he had more questions than answers. Most did when it came to all things death and afterlife.

"And you need Gabriel now? To what end?" Caleb asked.

"I have questions I suspect only he can answer for me."

At first I worried the two of them might stop me, that perhaps they'd keep me from the angel due to my occupation, but Hades gave a sharp jerk of his chin to the left. "He's probably in the witches' greenhouse. He's been spending time there since we brought him back."

"I think you mean hiding there," Caleb murmured.

"Hiding from who?" I asked, still woefully out of the loop when it came to the dramas of our new allies. Not that I much cared, but knowledge was a powerful weapon.

"His brethren. Michael and Evander have been around. Gabriel doesn't want to talk to them," Hades explained. "Think he's got a bit of a chip on his shoulder because they didn't come to his rescue."

That I could understand. My brothers hadn't been pleased with me since Merri left, but for centuries the four of us kept our distance for reasons too complicated to name. She had brought us back together. She was the reason for so many of the good things in my life.

"I see," I murmured, then gestured toward the greenhouse with my head. "I'll be going now."

I didn't wait for either of them to respond before turning and heading away. I did catch their parting remarks, though.

"Is he always like that?" Caleb asked.

"What do you mean?"

"Abrupt. Demanding. Ungrateful."

Hades snickered. "That was Death on a good day. They call him Grim for a reason."

I resisted the urge to turn around and offer a retort. It wouldn't achieve anything, and honestly, a lifetime with Sin taught me there was power in silence. Silence was as much a statement as anything.

The moment I rounded the corner and saw the greenhouse, something in me lightened. It had been too long since I'd been able to cultivate my own plants. A pang of loss struck my chest for the rooftop greenhouse I'd used as a personal sanctuary, destroyed by demons, ruined by this pissing apocalypse I was supposed to usher in.

Pushing my way inside, I paused briefly just to breathe in the familiar scent of dirt, fertilizer, and life. Just that quickly, a sense of calm descended, and a little of the weight I'd been carrying dropped away.

"I see you've stumbled upon my hiding place," Gabriel said.

My eyes snapped to him, and I fought back a smile. The vampire had been right.

"It's not a very good hiding spot when everyone knows where you are."

Gabriel shrugged. "Usually it's enough not to want to get on my bad side."

I nodded my agreement.

"What brings you here, Grimsby?"

"I need information."

"Don't we all?" He snapped shut the paperback he'd been reading and tucked it into the interior pocket of his leather jacket. But not before I caught the title: *The Sinner and the Priest.*

Cocking an eyebrow, I muttered, "Interesting genre for an angel."

"I heard that. Judge not lest ye be judged. Now what information could I possibly provide?"

"You're familiar with our plan to weaken Lucifer?" I asked as a way of gauging how much background he required.

"By bringing him to the dream realm? Yes, I've heard."

I ran a hand along my jaw, weighing my next words. "I suppose I'm wondering what the best and easiest way to weaken him is."

Gabriel peered at me. "Isn't that what your Merri is for?"

"So she's nothing but bait? Cannon fodder? Something you designed to take him down regardless of the outcome for her?" Anger burned through me.

There was a lot of talk about angels and demons, often placing angels on the side of the heroes, but they'd just as easily sacrifice a living being for their own gain as a demon would. Perhaps they were no better.

"To be clear, I did not design Merri any more than you did. I am not in charge of fate."

"No, you're just the Messenger."

Gabriel glared at my snide tone, but simply said, “Yes.”

“He will kill her once he realizes what she’s doing.”

“Perhaps.”

Releasing a heavy breath, I reined in my temper and tried again. “Isn’t there a scenario where we can do the heavy lifting for her? Where we can trap him, or I don’t know . . .”

Gabriel considered the suggestion before shrugging. “I’m sure there are plenty of scenarios, but the limitations of the dream realm will be your greatest deterrent. For instance, the last time Lucifer was trapped, it required the efforts of an entire coven. You could bring a coven into the realm, but anything they required for the spell outside of their innate power would not come with them. And dream elements are all figments of the dream realm.”

“They hold no actual power,” I said, stating what he had not.

“Precisely.”

“So we’re just meant to send her in to fight him alone?”

“Just as David fought Goliath. Your mate will face Lucifer.”

My heart stuttered. “She’s not my mate.”

There was far less conviction in the statement this time.

Gabriel sat up straight, leveling me with a dubious stare. “Isn’t she?”

“Horsemen don’t have mates. We have no souls. It’s impossible.” I’d come to understand the meaning of what a soul was very quickly. Reaping countless of them resulted in a deep and intimate knowledge of who did and did not possess one. I could touch my brothers. None of us had souls to be reaped.

Gabriel laughed. He fucking laughed at me. “Who told you that?”

“No one. I put it together easily.”

“Well, you’re wrong. You may not have a human soul, but I assure you, you’ve got one.”

“How can that be?”

“Likely much the same way it is for angels and all other supernatural creatures.”

“Angels can have mates?”

He nodded, some of the light leaving his eyes. "They can, though it requires them to fall."

"How is that fair?"

"Who said anything about fair, horseman? Love rarely is. Though it very well may be the only thing truly worth fighting for."

I didn't have any rebuttal. I was too rocked by his admission. I could have a soulmate. I could have Merri. She'd been right all this time, and I'd thrown her vulnerable confession back in her face and dismissed it as ridiculous.

Unable to fully wrap my head around the truth he'd just laid at my feet, I mutely shook my head and pulled myself back to my original purpose.

"So there's really nothing you can tell me that could help us against him?"

Gabriel tilted his head incredulously. "As if I did not just hand you the most important thing on a fucking platter?"

I opened my mouth to speak, but he held up a hand with a world-weary sigh.

"I explain, and explain, and explain, and no one ever *listens*." He pinched the bridge of his nose. "This must be how mothers feel. Constantly repeating themselves, always ignored."

Still staring at him, I waited for him to give me something useful.

Pinning me with his gaze, he groaned in pure frustration. "The answer is your mate. All paths lead to her. She is the final piece of the puzzle, and without her, we may as well hand the world over right now. Go to her. Support her. Strengthen her."

If only I could.

I had the sudden fear that I'd already ruined things beyond repair.

"It's never too late, Grimsby. Until it is."

I glared at him. "Fortune cookies are more helpful than you."

He flung his hands up. "You were the one who came to me."

"A lapse in judgment I will be sure not to repeat."

"Well, thank the Creator for that." Falling back into his seat, he pulled the paperback from his coat and began flipping through the pages until he found his spot. When I didn't move, he looked over the book with an eyebrow raised. "Is there anything else? I was just about to get to the good part."

"What do you consider the good part?"

He stared at me as if I were the stupidest being in all existence. "When he stops being an obtuse fool and confesses his love for her."

For some reason, I had the sense he wasn't talking about the book. I didn't say another word as I left the greenhouse, stalking my way back to the room where my brothers were currently under Merri's spell.

As if my presence summoned them back, the three all shot up as one.

"Enjoy your little nap?" I drawled, doing my level best to shove my jealousy down as far as it could possibly go whilst they got to their feet.

Sin smirked. "Fuck yeah."

"I've never felt so relaxed," Malice murmured, his eyes half-lidded.

She'd fed on them. All of them. And my stubborn arse hadn't been included.

"She tried, Grim." Chaos's words pulled me out of my one-man pity party. "She said your bond was too weak and she couldn't bring you in."

Fuck. I was right. This was all my fault.

I sat down with a groan. If only I'd had the clarity of Gabriel's words earlier. Everything would be different. Merri would have never fled. I'd have had the opportunity to collect more moments with her.

My mate.

"Is he . . . crying?" Sin asked.

I was so startled by the question I sat straight up and wiped at my face. There were no tears. I glared at Sin and chucked the first thing I could reach straight at his head.

Chaos caught the lamp before it could make contact.

"No, I'm not fucking crying, you twat. I'm frustrated with myself. I was wrong. So bloody wrong, and now I can't fix it."

"Well, you've been wrong about a lot of things lately, so could you maybe tighten that statement up a bit? What were you wrong about now?" Sin flinched when I looked at him, but I didn't throw anything this time.

"She is my mate."

Chaos cleared his throat. "*Our* mate."

I nodded. "Right. Merri is our mate."

Sin and Malice just looked at me.

"Well?" I said. "No reaction?"

"Was that supposed to be news or something? We already know. We've been telling you that for weeks now," Sin said.

"What made you finally accept it?" Malice asked, his gaze a bit softer than the others.

"Gabriel."

Chaos frowned. "The angel?"

"Yes. I always thought it was impossible for us to have a soulmate. We are horsemen. We have no human soul. Our purpose would be in jeopardy if we were distracted by having a mate. But I was wrong."

Again, none of them seemed as profoundly affected by the news as I'd been, but then I was the one who dealt most intimately with souls, so perhaps they had none of my preconceived notions to inform them.

Sin chuckled and came over to me, clapping me on the shoulder. "Welcome back to the team, buddy. Better late than never."

CHAPTER
THIRTY-FOUR
MERRI

With each passing day since my dreamwalk with Lucifer in the Garden of Eden, it was becoming easier and easier to slip into the role I needed to play. So much so I couldn't quite tell what was real and what was just an act.

Case in point: Lucifer was squeezing behind me to grab something out of the cabinet beside my head. I could have moved. I could have told him to knock it off. I could have stopped myself from closing my eyes and inhaling his sinful scent. But none of those things happened.

Instead, my breath hitched, and we sort of leaned into each other.

Fuck my life.

These fucking dreamwalks were so useful but also incredibly dangerous when the wrong person became my subconscious's focus. Every time I pulled him to me, whether on purpose or not, I strengthened a bond I didn't want.

"Well, isn't this cozy?" he breathed against my neck.

Don't enjoy this, you hussy.

Don't you dare shiver.

Fuck your hard nipples. It's just cold in here.

Without my permission, a little sigh escaped me, and Lucifer took that as an opening to slip his free hand around my waist. The mug he pulled down from the cabinet was perfectly oversized, black, and emblazoned with chrome lettering that read *The devil made me do it.*

I sucked in a gasp as he shifted his hips and I felt the swollen length of him brush against my ass.

Holy giant cock, Batman.

He chuckled in my ear, far too attuned to me for my liking. "Sorry."

"We both know you did that on purpose."

"Guilty as charged. Though I could argue he has a mind of his own."

Fucking men.

"Tell him to keep it to himself, would you?"

Lips brushing the shell of my ear, he whispered, "I did, this morning in the shower. Didn't you sense it?"

Heat flooded my cheeks as I recalled the sounds he'd made. I'd definitely enjoyed it far more than I was supposed to, but a succubus can only resist a free meal for so long before she samples the goods.

And damn it all to hell, Lucifer's lust was fucking delicious.

"Don't know what you're talking about," I muttered, finally pushing away from the counter. The relief was instant, my senses clearing of him, which brought a much-needed wave of clarity.

"Little liar," he teased, pouring hot water into his mug before plopping a tea bag inside. "If you didn't know, why are you blushing? And why can I smell your arousal?"

I flipped him off.

Was it effective? Of course not, the asshole laughed in my face and looked far too good doing it.

But he was right, and we both knew it. One couldn't argue pheromones.

"Just because you're baiting me with lust. I'm a succubus. I feed off the stuff."

"So you do want me. Good to know. Thank you for confirming."

"Put a starving vegetarian in a steakhouse and her tummy's gonna rumble. It's biology, simple as that."

He stepped closer to me, mimicking the position we were in the last time he kissed me, and God help me, I didn't back away.

Andi's voice echoed in my mind, like the guardian angel she'd become, though this time she was more of a naughty devil on my shoulder. *Come on, babes. Just give in already. Who's it gonna hurt? Him, that's who. And bonus, you'd have the answer to a question plaguing the rest of womankind. How good is Lucifer in bed? See? It's for science. Two birds, one bone.*

I was pretty sure that last part was something Sin said.

"I know you've been feeding from them, my sweet," Lucifer whispered, brushing his knuckles down my cheek. "You're not hungry. Not in the least. That desire you feel is all you. It's *us*. Why can't you admit you want me as I want you?"

Ugh.

He was too smart for his own good, and I had to abort this mission before he had his way with me on the kitchen island.

"I'd rather my fingers fall off from overuse than give in to you."

And with that rather snappy comeback, if I do say so myself, I spun around and all but ran from the kitchen.

"Don't sprain your wrist, darling!" he called, laughter threaded through his voice.

I was still grumbling under my breath when I kicked the bedroom door closed behind me. It wasn't until I stood in the middle of my room that I realized I was clutching an empty plate. I never did get what I'd gone in there for.

Shit.

Did he notice?

Of course he did.

I flopped onto the bed with a groan. This plan was backfiring spectacularly.

I might've been well fed, sated, and rebuilding the connections I needed with my men, but Lucifer still affected me. How could I tell them that? Should I? With everything they had going on, it might not be the wisest choice to add to their already overflowing burdens. Or maybe they already knew. They were the ones who stressed the need to act quickly. To make Lucifer think he stood a chance so he could be trapped.

During our dreamwalk last night, they'd been confident we would succeed. Confident or desperate? After we wore ourselves out, they filled me in on what they'd learned from Auntie Lilith, and more concerningly, how Malice's son had been taken along with Sunday Fallon, the daughter of War. Time was running out on all sides.

Malice put on a brave face, but I knew the truth. His emotions gave him away. His fear for his son was palpable. More than anything, I wanted to help right that wrong.

And, you know, save mankind.

Which meant I couldn't put this off any longer. All roads led to the dream realm. And to Grim. Tonight I had to put on my big-girl panties and face the horseman who rejected me. He might think he's not my mate, but I knew it.

That didn't mean I was ready to forgive him. But I *would* work with him.

For Malice.

To get free.

To finish what we started.

Locking my door—like it would do any good if Lucifer wanted in —I settled myself on the middle of my bed, eyes closed, breaths intentional and slow. I found their tethers all lined up in a row—three bright and shining, one stronger than before, but still a dull glow. Grim's. I grabbed his first, this time gaining purchase rather than slipping through it. Collecting all four, I pulled hard, bringing them to me instead of going to them.

Just like before, they appeared near instantly.

Chaos looked around with a chuckle. "The gym?"

"You said tonight was for practice." I shrugged. "It seemed appropriate." I was studiously ignoring Grim's presence to the left of him. But his gaze burned into the side of my face. I'd say he was ravenous and I was his meal of choice, but that was a dangerous thought leading to nothing but heartache, so I shut it down.

"You're not really dressed for the gym, kitten," Sin said, his lips curved into a smirk.

Glancing down at my jeans and crop top, I laughed. "It's my favorite." Did it say *Thug Life* across the chest with the Golden Girls posed underneath? Yes. Do you have a problem with that? I didn't think so.

"She's fine. We aren't working out our bodies. Just her mind." Malice closed the distance between us and pulled me against his chest before dropping his lips to my ear. "We can work our bodies after, if you'd like."

"If training here is anything like back at the château, I'm not sure I'll be up for it." Those sessions with Malice left my brain in a pudding-like state. All I ever wanted to do after was sleep.

But when Malice pulled away with a smirk, my lower belly tightened.

Then again . . .

"Okay, enough flirting. We haven't even acknowledged the huge hurdle Merri jumped over already," Sin said, taking my hand and tugging me out of Malice's embrace.

"What's that?" Chaos asked.

"She brought all four of us in at once. Didn't even break a sweat. Our girl is so fucking strong."

I stood a little straighter under his praise, but my gaze slid to Grim, whose focus never deviated from me. To say the vibe between us was tense would be an understatement. The usually polished and well-kept man was unkempt, hair a wild mess of silver waves, beard longer than the normally meticulously groomed version I was used to. He was still in his customary suit, but the jacket was gone, and his shirt sleeves were rolled up his forearms.

Didn't hate that. Nope. Not one bit.

It was obvious he'd struggled in my absence, and I wish I could pretend I was a better person and that the knowledge didn't fill me with a sense of victory. But that would be a lie.

I was a petty, petty bitch.

Eat your heart out, Grimsby.

Forcing myself to look away, I settled my attention on Chaos. "So how are we doing this? Is there an actual plan, or am I supposed to wing it?"

"You are the only one with enhanced power in these dreams," Malice said.

Sin raised his hand and cleared his throat. "Not true. I also get a boost in here. Incubus. Remember?"

"Right, but I doubt you'll have the chance to get one over on Lucifer the way Merri will. He suspects nothing but foul play from you. With her, it's different. He wants to believe her. That's his weakness. We need to exploit it."

His lips turned down in a frown, but he righted his expression a moment later. "Fine. But I'm here to help if we need it."

"No one is arguing that, Sin," Grim said, finally speaking for the first time.

His voice ran me through like a spear. Dammit.

"What do you want me to do?" I asked.

"Knock him back with your lust and seduction power, then weaken him by taking his life force with your Famine side."

I stared at Malice, eyes wide as he presented this plan like it was the easiest thing in the world.

"It might not hurt if she tried to compel him to reveal their location first. Or if she searched his mind for any useful details we could take back to the Hades Society. This may be our only chance to do some spying and stop playing defense," Chaos added.

I gave them a dubious stare. "This is Lucifer. Do you think any of that is going to be easy? We're lucky if *one* of those work against him, let alone all of them."

"That's what the practice is for," he reminded me.

Understanding dawned, and my eyes bugged out of my head.

"You want me to use my powers against *you*?"

The idea of hurting any of them repulsed me.

"You can't really hurt us, remember?" Sin's voice was soft. "We're the best choice."

Logically I knew he was right, but I still hated the idea. The only time I'd accessed my Famine side, it had been to protect him. I didn't know if I was capable of doing the opposite.

"Here, let's get into position. Don't tell us who you're targeting." Chaos turned to form a line, and the others followed.

Except Grim.

He came to me.

"Merri," he started, but his voice trailed off as uncertainty took hold. I could sense it in him.

"What?" I snapped.

"I'm so incredibly so—"

Holding up a hand, I stopped him. "No. Now's not the time. Besides, you made your feelings very clear."

He winced, but surprised me by not forcing the issue. "We'll talk once you're home."

That was a bit presumptuous of him, but it still made me feel squishy inside.

Shoving all of that away for now, I moved until I was standing across from the others.

"What do you want me to start with?"

"Lady's choice," Malice said.

"It's more of a true test if we don't know what's coming for us," Sin added.

Over what I assumed was the next hour, I took turns throwing my various powers at them without warning over and over again until I was breathing heavily and all four of them were on their knees, enthralled by me.

It was a heady feeling. It was also the first time I felt like a legitimate badass.

Lilith and Sin always told me how powerful I was, but I'd never believed it myself until now.

There was just something about having all four of the horsemen on their knees for you that made a girl feel good.

With an unnecessary flick of my wrist, I released them from my hold. They got to their feet, eyes no longer glazed over, but with very visible bulges in their pants. Chaos adjusted himself and let out a huff of laughter.

"I think she's going to do just fine, boys."

"Are we ready to call it?" Malice asked, glancing around to ensure we were all on the same page.

"Do you feel ready, kitten?" Sin asked, leaving the choice in my hands.

"She's ready," Grim said, surprising me with his confidence.

Usually his speaking for me would have rubbed me the wrong way, but this time it made me feel warm inside. Holding his gaze, I dipped my chin in a slow nod. "I'm ready. I'll see you boys tomorrow."

CHAPTER

THIRTY-FIVE

LUCIFER

"She wants me. Everything's falling into place."

CHAPTER THIRTY-SIX

MERRI

The last twenty-four hours went by entirely too quickly. I'd been on a high when we'd finished our practice the day before, but with every passing minute, it drained away until I was left an anxious mess. Would I be able to betray Lucifer so completely? More importantly, why did I feel like it was a betrayal? I was trying to escape. He had me in his clutches. Did I have Stockholm syndrome?

Fuck.

I'd already entered the dream realm, but I'd yet to pull anyone else. I just needed a second to get my bearings. The risk here was all mine. The horsemen couldn't die. Lucifer probably couldn't either. And if I didn't succeed in weakening him, he'd take it out on me in ways I could never imagine. He was Satan, after all. Despite his protests to the contrary, not every story about him could be false. There had to be kernels of truth in there somewhere, and those kernels were enough to keep me from underestimating him.

First and foremost, I needed to create a space for us that would make him feel connected to me. Give him some semblance of comfort and ease. The Garden of Eden was the first to come to mind.

Beautiful, serene, and most of all, important to him. I hoped it would signify my attentiveness to what he shared with me.

If there was any setting where he'd be more inclined to let down his guard, I truly hoped this would be it. I was gambling my life on it.

"Okay," I breathed, shaking out my sweaty palms and jumping around a bit like a boxer before a match.

From one moment to the next, I went from alone to surrounded by my four bodyguards. That's what they'd be tonight.

"Wow, you really piled on the ambiance for Old Scratch tonight, didn't you, kitten?" Sin muttered, clearly annoyed with the world around him.

"Listen," I started, already sensing how quickly this could devolve, "he needs to believe this is real. I'm going to have to do and say things you won't like, and you need to promise me you'll stay put until it's time, or all of this is for nothing. I doubt we'll get a second chance, so you're all going to have to keep your collective shit together."

"Well, you didn't mention you were going to look like a fucking goddess in the moonlight. I can see your nipples."

"Sin," I chastised.

"I'm sorry. Okay. I know. It's all part of the plan." He took a heaving breath and let it out on a gusty sigh.

Malice clapped him on the shoulder. "We don't have to like it, but we do have to trust her."

Chaos clenched and unclenched his fists but nodded his agreement. Grim remained silent, his gaze once again locked on me. I noted that he looked marginally more put together than the night before.

"Can I trust you four not to interfere?" I asked, looking at each of them in turn.

One by one, they nodded.

"As long as he keeps his hands to himself," Chaos snarled.

"No. That's not what I asked. I'm going to have to seduce him. That means getting close. There might be touching and sweet words and things you won't like to see or hear. You can't come barreling out of the trees to defend my honor."

"Merri," Chaos grumbled.

"You wanted me to do this. You have to *let* me do it."

"She's right," Grim said.

My eyebrows lifted. I didn't expect him to support me so readily, but I wasn't going to turn it down.

"I never thought Grimsby would become a yes man," Sin muttered.

Malice shook his head. "People do strange things when they're trying to get out of the doghouse. Trust me."

"Personally, I prefer make-up sex."

I rolled my eyes at Sin.

"You four should get into place. Remember what we practiced. I'll signal when I'm ready for you to jump in."

We'd decided their roles were primarily to observe and protect. The heavy lifting was on me, but if things went sideways, they'd be ready to come to my aid and do what they did best. Based on Gabriel's incredibly vague advice, we didn't think a physical attack would be enough to weaken him the way we needed, but it was our "shit's hit the fan" plan anyway.

Once they were in position, I adjusted my sheer, flowing gown and sat on a boulder directly under a ray of moonlight. Fireflies winked in and out of view all around the garden, and the scent of apples filled the warm air. All I needed was . . . him.

Lucifer came to me easily. Too easily, if I was honest.

"Ah, we meet again," he crooned, stalking into view. He glanced around the garden, smirking. "Feeling sentimental, crabapple?"

I couldn't play directly into his hand; he'd sniff me out in seconds. Instead I glared and lifted a shoulder. "Not my doing."

"You look . . . delightful. Is this a date?"

"I'm hungry. You've said you're willing."

Surprise flashed in his eyes, and I had a brief moment of panic before he began a slow saunter to me. "Don't you have four horsemen to help you with your appetite?"

"They're not mine anymore, Luc. You reminded me of the truth. They are my exes. Nothing more. Continuing to sleep with them complicates things more than they already are."

He made a musing sound as he joined me. There was barely enough room for the two of us on the boulder's surface, and the sides of our bodies pressed together from shoulder to knee.

"So you'd rather sleep with me now? I'm not buying it."

Reaching for his hand, I threaded our fingers and looked into his eyes. He really was beautiful to behold.

"I didn't say I would sleep with you."

A low laugh came from deep in his chest. "So what are we looking at here? Over the dress? Under the dress? Mouth stuff?"

Undeniable heat flooded me at the suggestions. I could so easily picture all of it. And I didn't hate what I pictured. Not even a little bit.

What did that say about me?

"I guess we'll have to see what happens."

He reached out and tucked a stray curl behind my ear, his fingers lingering on my jaw as if he wanted to pull me closer for a kiss.

I needed to let him. For multiple reasons, one of which I didn't want to admit.

"Kiss me, Merri. Put me out of my misery and let me have your lips again," he whispered.

My breath stuttered, and my eyes dropped to his lips. They were so very kissable.

Giving in to temptation, but telling myself it was only for the purposes of the mission, I closed the distance between us and pressed my lips to his.

He groaned at the same time a rumble radiated from the trees. Fucking Chaos. On instinct, I created a thunderstorm in the distance, hoping against hope it would cover any further sounds of protest from the warrior.

"You taste divine," he murmured against my mouth.

"I bet you say that to all the girls."

He ran a knuckle along my cheek, laughing softly. "Only the ones who matter."

His large palm cupped my nape and he yanked me to him again, stealing another kiss, but this time deepening it and stealing my breath as he did. His tongue slipped inside, body firmly pressing against mine before he pulled me onto his lap and ground his hard cock against me. It felt good. *He* felt good. He felt . . . right.

Admittedly, my experience with actual partners was limited. But being with Lucifer was as easy as being with Sin.

I didn't let myself dwell on the realization, because any shift in my focus would be our downfall.

This was the opening I needed.

Moving carefully, I slid my hand into his hair and gripped just tight enough to draw a needy groan from him. Pulling back, I looked into his eyes and began sending a slow pulse of power into him. His dick throbbed and swelled with every wave of lust that emanated from me until he was whimpering and rocking his hips up in search of what he was desperate for. With no reason to withhold any attention from him—if anything, it would only make completing my mission easier—I ground my pelvis against the ridge of his cock.

"Fuck, Merri. Yes," he moaned. "I knew this would be good between us."

Instinct had me wanting to deny the claim, but the little fireworks going off inside me agreed with him. There wasn't anything wrong with me finding a little pleasure here. That's what I was made for, right?

Lucifer pulled the long skirt of my dress up until it was around my waist, my bare cunt rubbing over his trousers, making a mess of the fabric. It was pure biology, a reaction caused by stimulation, not true arousal for this insanely attractive fallen angel.

"If you let me inside you, I swear you won't regret it. You want me, I can tell by how wet you are." Lucifer kissed my neck, biting down on the tender flesh and making me cry out.

There was another rumble followed by what I swear was a swell of shadow. The horsemen were feeling some kind of way about watching this. Curious about how Mal and Sin were taking it, I cast out my awareness only to be hit by twin waves of lust. I had to duck my head into Lucifer's neck to hide my surprise and subsequent excitement over the discovery. Everyone knew I had a bit of an exhibition kink, but learning that my mates might have a matching compersion kink filled a girl's mind with all kinds of sexy possibilities.

I continued grinding into Lucifer, using his harsh breaths and grunts as my guide. Simultaneously, I released more of my power, snaring him even deeper in my web. I needed him so mindless he wouldn't register my presence in his subconscious.

He was close, his rising climax setting off my predatory instinct to feed, because, let's not forget, a succubus is a predator. I needed him to orgasm for more reasons than one. He was willing prey.

"Come for me, Luc. I want to feel you," I whispered before taking his bottom lip between my teeth and biting down as I flooded him with arousal.

On a deep, guttural moan, he found his release, fingers digging into my ass hard enough I'd likely have bruises.

I fed.

Long and deep.

Pulling his essence from him in great draws as though I'd never fed before and wouldn't again.

He shuddered under me, his cock pulsing as his orgasm continued on and on.

Now.

Using his climax as my distraction, I dove into his mind the way Malice taught me, quickly sifting through everything I could find. I was looking for details about where he was keeping me, along with anything about his plans for the apocalypse, the final battle, safe houses, weapons . . . anything that might be useful to those in the resistance.

But Lucifer's mind was nothing like others I've visited.

Perhaps it was due to his age, or that he was still a full-blooded —albeit fallen—angel. Either way, the weight of his mind pressed against me, overwhelming me with its power. It was a bit how I imagined drowning might feel. That first deep pull of air, only to learn far too late it was actually water. I *was* drowning.

Drowning in him.

Little bits and pieces of information rushed by me, swirling in the eternity's worth of memories and experiences that made Lucifer who he was. I couldn't catch any of them, not long enough to gain anything useful. Until one flicker caught my attention, a whisper of a conversation between Luc and a woman I'd never met before. I reached out to latch onto it and pull it in.

A jolt of resistance knocked me around, making it even harder to get my bearings.

Naughty succubus. Lucifer's voice echoed through his mind, startling me.

I was out of time. I had to end this before he did.

Changing tactics, I retreated from his consciousness before gripping him by the shoulders and tapping into the part of myself I now recognized as my Famine side. It had been hard to locate this particular skill during practice, since the only time I'd ever used it had been borne out of my fear and rage. With a good amount of coaxing from the boys, I'd learned how to isolate and use it on purpose.

I did so now, opening my mouth and pulling Lucifer's life force into my body. If his lust was a meal, feeding on him like this was akin to taking Molly. It was addictive, an immediate rush, and way different from the last time I'd used this power. Euphoric was the only word to describe the sensation.

"No!" he snarled, fighting back as I attempted to hold him still.

He was too strong, even now. I needed help as he bucked under me.

Reaching for the tethers that connected me and my men, I tugged, sending up my version of the bat signal.

My gaze was locked onto Lucifer's, a requirement to make him malleable enough for me to do this, so I only noticed the horsemen in my periphery. They hadn't wasted a second charging to my rescue.

In other circumstances, I might have swooned.

Chaos and Malice got to me first, each of them taking a side to keep Luc from throwing me off him. Their presence strengthened me and revived something I hadn't realized was flagging. Grim's shadows ran across my body, then between me and Lucifer, sliding up until he encircled the man's throat. We had him.

I redoubled my efforts on a furious Lucifer. He struggled against their hold, but he was well and truly trapped. Our plan was working. I had no doubt that if I hadn't fed on him first, we never would have gotten to this point. Now I just had to land the finishing blow.

At first it was like before. The high, the euphoria. But it quickly changed. Sort of like sucking on a straw when the cup is empty. I couldn't seem to pull any more of him into me. But it wasn't because I'd taken everything. Lucifer was still very much alert.

Something was preventing me from draining him further.

Panicked, my gaze shot up and landed on Sin, who'd moved to stand behind Lucifer. The horseman Famine glowed with power as he reached down and laid his hands on Lucifer's shoulders. Our eyes locked as we held the devil down so we could feast and end this.

Well, that was the intention. Even with the addition of Sin's power, I still wasn't able to get more than a trickle out of Lucifer. But it was okay, because Sin was doing just fine draining Lucifer on his own.

It wasn't until this moment that I realized Sinclair had been running on a nearly empty tank as of late. Once he began to take in Luc's essence, Sin's hair grew luminous, his skin more vibrant and youthful. In fact, every part of him seemed refreshed and healthier.

Beneath me, Luc's struggling slowed until it stopped.

"Just a little more," Chaos coaxed.

"You can do it, wildflower."

I wanted to say this was all Sin, but I got distracted by an unexpected emotion in Lucifer's eyes. It was a cross between betrayal and acceptance, and it slammed into me like a hammer. I jolted, a heaviness that felt a whole lot like guilt settling in my chest.

"Merri . . ." Lucifer shuddered once, a ragged whisper escaping him before his eyes closed.

Instantly, I sagged over him, my body overcome with insurmountable exhaustion the likes of which I'd never felt. How was it Sin looked like he belonged on the cover of a magazine, and I couldn't even keep my head up?

"Hellcat?" Malice shouted, his fear pelting me like shards of ice.

"I'm sorry . . . I didn't get it . . ." It was nearly impossible to force out the words, but I was fading fast and couldn't be sure how much longer I could keep us all here together. They needed to know that I'd failed.

"It's okay, Merri," Sin said. "You were perfect. You did everything we needed. Let go now, we'll take care of the rest."

There wasn't any other option. I did as he said. I let go and fell into a darkness of my own making.

"We almost fucking killed him. Did you feel that?" Sin asked, bouncing off the walls after we all came back from our dreamwalk.

"We did exactly what we planned. We can't kill him, but we weakened him substantially." I rolled my shoulders and moved toward the door, filled with purpose as time ticked by.

"Where are you going? We need to debrief," Chaos demanded.

"Every second we stay in this room is time for him to recover," Grim said, answering before I could.

"Precisely. We need that witch, and we need her now. There's no telling how long this window will last, and the mission is only half completed as it stands."

"What are we standing around here for?" Sin asked, bolting past me like some sort of cartoon character.

I rolled my eyes and followed him, the other two on my heels.

"Moira! Hey, Belladonna. Where you at?" Sin shouted.

The tiny witch popped her head out of a doorway, her vibrant pink hair startlingly different from the pure white it had been the last time we'd spoken. "Exsqueeze me? Put some respect on my name, cowboys. I am the head of my coven. No one summons me."

"Are we supposed to be impressed? She does know we're the four horsemen, right? Pretty sure that trumps witch all day long," Sin asked under his breath.

Chaos slapped a large palm over Sin's mouth, stopping him from hurling any further insults Moira's way. "Don't piss off the one person who can help us, Sinclair."

The little firecracker of a woman smirked. "At least one of you has some sense." She eyed Chaos up and down. "Usually the bigger they are, the dumber they are. Way to break the stereotype, beefcake."

I snickered, but as enjoyable as this was, we didn't have time to waste.

"Can you perform a locator spell for us? It's a matter of some urgency," I said, trying my hardest to be polite.

It did *not* come easily.

Moira sighed. "When isn't it these days?"

I swallowed my retort and reached for her hand, carefully taking it in mine. "We need you. Please?"

Her expression softened. "That was hard for you, wasn't it? Okay. Who are we finding? You know the rules by now, right? Someone needs to get me something of your target's so I can lock onto their location."

"Fuck, I don't have anything of Merri's on me," Sin said, his eyes wide.

"Here, use this."

We all turned to face Grim, who was holding out what appeared to be a thin red braid in his gloved hand.

Moira took it and, if she were a character in an anime, her eyes would have turned to hearts. "Aww, you braided strands of her hair and carry it in your pocket? Aren't you just a big softie?"

Grim cleared his throat. "I thought we may need it."

"Sure, big guy. Keep telling yourself that."

Then she turned and gestured for us to follow. "We've done so many of these recently, I have a backstock of supplies and a whole altar setup ready to go. If she's no longer shrouded, we should have her location in just a few minutes."

The relief I felt at her promise was so potent I nearly crashed into Chaos.

We'd tried to locate Pan and Sunday, but they were hidden from us, much as Merri and Gabriel had been. Fucking Lucifer. It would be a welcome respite to have one of these fucking spells actually work as intended.

A loud crash had all of us stopping and craning our necks.

"What the fuck was that?" Sin asked.

"Alek," Moira said with a frown. "He's been in full beast-mode since he heard about Sunday. Tor has been doing his best, but . . ." She shrugged, drooping a little before she seemed to shake herself out of it. "Come on, the sooner we find your Merri, the sooner we get our people back."

In mere minutes, we were all stood in Moira's chambers, watching her perform a ritual we'd now witnessed far too many times. She stayed silent, brows pulled together in concentration, and when she looked up, a wicked smirk twisted her lips.

"Bingo."

CHAPTER
THIRTY-EIGHT
LUCIFER

Coming to in the middle of the kitchen with my trousers wet and cold from the nocturnal emission Merri pulled from me was disorienting to say the least.

Her little stunt had fury brewing within me. There was no way I could let her get away with such a betrayal. I'd thought I had her right where I wanted her. I thought everything was finally coming together. She'd bamboozled me. No one bamboozled me.

A reckoning was at hand.

Getting to my feet, I took a wobbly step, then another before I had to reach out and steady myself on the kitchen island. Pain lanced my palm as the sharp edge of a chef's knife I'd carelessly left out sliced into tender flesh.

"Fucking hell, what did you do to me, crabapple?"

I hadn't felt this weak since I was unceremoniously shoved out of heaven.

A glint of red had me doing a double-take. Blood?! I was bleeding?

What fresh hell was this?

"If you prick me, do I not bleed?" I intoned, more from shock than anything. Just as quickly, I snarled, my head snapping up and eyes narrowing with a single-minded focus. "No one makes me bleed my own blood."

Taking a steadying breath, I balled my hand into a fist and stumbled out of the kitchen, lumbering down the hall toward my target. "Merri!" I bellowed. "I know you're in there, you naughty, naughty girl."

The door to her room was already ajar, stealing some of my steam. So much for my dramatic entrance.

I pushed it open with as much flair as I could muster, but instead of finding Merri poised and ready for a fight, she was out cold on her bed.

"Well, now I can't be angry at you. Look at you. So innocent when you're unconscious." I stepped into the room, interest piqued. Perhaps this was my moment. She'd taken from me. I could take from her . . . if I wanted to. A kiss wouldn't be so terrible. We've done it before. And everyone knew you woke Sleeping Beauty with a kiss.

Moving to her side, I propped a knee on her mattress, one hand on either side of her face.

She really was ridiculously beautiful. Equal parts innocent and seductive all at once.

"Come on, crabapple. I need you to wake up so I can scold you properly."

Was I whispering tenderly at the woman who'd just tried to kill me?

Hmph.

My brain must be more dysfunctional than I'd realized. Somewhere along the way, I'd equated attempted murder with grand gestures. I suppose the key word was attempted. She hadn't actually gone through with it, and part of me knew, as ensnared as I'd been, she certainly could have.

As furious as I was, there was also a grudging amount of respect. No one had pulled one over on me like that before. Not even Lilith.

Leaning down, I brushed my lips over hers, a twist in my heart betraying how much I enjoyed showing her affection.

She sighed, and her eyes fluttered open, finding mine instantly.

"There you are. Now, it's time we had a chat about your choices."

There was a delicate flare of her nostrils followed by a sharp inhale. Before I could so much as draw breath, Merri's eyes transformed from a lovely shade of blue to pure, endless demonic black.

Startled, I sat back, but she followed me, snapping upright.

"Mate," she hissed, licking her lips.

For one second, all I could do was stare at her. Then a wicked smile stretched across my face.

"Well, isn't this a delicious turn of events?"

She didn't answer me with words. Instead my future demon queen launched herself at me, tearing at my clothes in a frantic attempt to get to me.

"Darling, calm down. You can have me whenever you desire, but I was rather fond of that shirt."

She continued to pluck and pull at my shirt until I was forced to take her wrists in my hands and bodily push her down, holding them high above her head.

"Someone is in a hurry all of a sudden."

Her hips rolled upward, searching for me as a whine escaped her lips. "Mine."

She was in quite a state. In fact, it was one I knew of but had never experienced. Demons like her needed to sate the craving for their mates. Their nature insisted on it. And *I* was her mate. She'd said it on pure instinct.

Oh, this was going so much better than I had anticipated. She finally understood what I'd been saying all this time. That meant I could get everything I wanted and more. I'd make my antichrist *and* have my queen at my side.

And here I'd thought I'd jinxed myself. I should have known better than to doubt.

Holding her wrists with one hand, I brought my other down to caress her cheek.

"Do you want me, Merri?"

"Yesss," she practically growled, writhing against me.

I leaned forward to run my nose along the length of hers. "Do you need me?"

She rocked her hips up, trying to dislodge me, but I kept her locked in place.

"Answer me, darling."

Her hand slipped between us, and she grabbed my swollen cock through my damp trousers, squeezing possessively. "Yes."

"Then take me."

Eyes black as pitch still somehow flashed with excitement as I allowed her to roll us so she sat astride me.

She was already bare beneath her microscopic nightie. Her heat practically seared me.

Fuck, this was already so much better than I'd hoped.

In one swift move, she tore the scrap of lace and silk up over her head, flinging it behind her. Before I could make a move to free myself, her nails turned into black-tipped claws, and she shredded the fabric into ribbons.

I jerked away from her hands. "Careful with those, sweetheart. You've left me fragile."

Holding up my still-bleeding palm, I grinned as she turned her focus to the line of crimson. She reached for me, grabbing me by the wrist and guiding my hand to her chest. If I weren't hard as stone already, I would have been as my blood stained her skin in a long line from sternum to cunt.

"You look perfect bathed in my blood."

She bared her teeth, petite demon fangs visible now. Oh, how I wanted her to mark my skin as I took her. I'd had countless lovers in my long life, but none that I'd let claim me in such a way. I wanted her to be the first.

The only.

Wrapping my hand in her long locks, I tugged her head down, pressing her lips against the skin I wanted her to mark. It wouldn't scar—actually, maybe it would. My angelic powers were still diminished, so this was uncharted territory for me.

My cock jerked at the idea of a permanent reminder of Merri.

"Claim me, my pretty succubus. Bite down while I fuck you full of me."

Letting out a little growl, she did as I asked. The sting of pain was blissfully acute, and I sheathed myself inside her in one perfect upward thrust.

Taking her hips in my hands, I moved her along my shaft, setting the pace I desired. But my greedy succubus did not like the slow, deep thrusts and kept trying to take control. She rolled her pelvis aggressively, attempting to place her feet on either side of my hips for leverage so she could move faster, but I was having none of it. I was in control, even if she thought she was topping me.

Sitting up, I got to my feet, holding on to her as I spun her around and slammed her against the mattress.

"Behave, precious one. We only get one first time. I want to make it count."

She whimpered, but didn't fight me as much as I anticipated. My arms braced on either side of her face, I moved in deep, purposeful thrusts. The way my hair fell forward offered us a sort of cocoon, adding to the intimacy between us in a way I'd not expected. She was mine. Only I understood her the way she deserved. Now she realized it as well.

Pain bloomed across my back where my wings would be if I released them. I didn't let them out often unless I was performing for the sake of showing my power to my enemies. And even then, they only saw what I wanted. The truth of my wings was a secret known only to me.

"More," Merri urged, her eyes locked onto mine.

I held her gaze, giving her everything as I drove into her.

I'd thought my climax in the dream had been the best I'd ever had, but it paled in comparison to the one building now. While I was inside her. Fuck. Leaving a piece of me behind had always been appealing, a goal to meet, but Merri being bonded to me in every way possible did something primal to me.

A golden glow emanated from between us, threads of magic starting and ending at our chests. Warmth suffused my veins, and Merri let out a shocked gasp, her eyes turning back to their beautiful blue for just a second before going demonic once more.

I was so bloody close. But there was no way I would let this moment pass without Merri coming all over my cock. I had to feel that telltale clenching, see her body tense, maybe hear her cry my name in ecstasy if I was lucky.

Holding myself up with one arm, I reached between us with the other, easily finding her swollen little nub.

Her breath hitched, and she pressed into my fingers, urging me to work her harder. Faster.

The build was exquisite. But the next time I fell, I wanted her to fall with me.

"Be a good girl and come for me, Merri."

She whimpered, then began trembling, and it was riiiiight there. Her orgasm washed over us both, taking me and throwing me off the cliff right alongside her. Just like before, in her dreamwalk, the waves of pleasure crashed into me without end. Even though she couldn't possibly be hungry, she still fed off my desire. Each pull from her had my eyes fluttering as I drifted along. Weakened as I was, I couldn't resist the pull, the additional drain on me forcing me to slip into unconsciousness.

I should have been worried after what happened in the dream.

But I knew something this time.

I'd found my mate, and she would be here when I woke up.

CHAPTER THIRTY-NINE

MERRI

I woke with so much energy rushing through my veins, I felt like a live wire. It didn't make sense, not really. I'd expended so much power in my dreamwalk to subdue Lucifer, feeding from him in real life shouldn't have supercharged me. But here I was, practically glowing.

The word triggered a memory of Lucifer and I entwined, golden light swirling around us.

Oh.

Oh no.

I bolted upright, Lucifer sprawled in a very undignified, unLucifer-like manner beside me.

Shit.

Fuck.

Damn. Motherfucking cock ass.

The reality of my situation required every curse word possible.

Lucifer Morningstar was mated to me. He'd gone on and on about how we were fated to be together, and I hadn't listened. I'd seen it as an overconfident fuckboi telling his future conquest whatever he needed to get what he wanted. But I hadn't realized he'd been warning me of the truth. My body knew, just like it had with the horsemen. And when I wouldn't give in, instinct took over, and the demon inside me helped fate along.

Shit. Fuck.

I slapped a hand to my forehead with a wince. How the hell was I supposed to explain this to the horsemen? They barely came around about the four of them being my mates, and now I was somehow supposed to tell them there was a fifth? And Lucifer, at that?

Oh, that was going to go over so well.

Not to mention the sleeping with him part.

Fuck my actual life.

Where was the apocalypse sinkhole when you needed one? It could swallow me right now and spare me from all of it.

Then another, far more terrifying thought took hold, my hands clutching my belly. Was I pregnant with his antichrist right now?

Oh noooooo.

Sonofabitch!

I couldn't even fully blame my demon side for this, because I *was* attracted to Luc. I always had been, and I knew I was playing with fire every time I dreamwalked with him.

My emotions were such a tangled mess, I didn't even know where to start with them. Guilt. Fear. Satisfaction. Relief. Affection.

Wait a damn minute, affection?

Gaze darting to Luc, I studied him for a second. He was a bloody, disheveled mess. The one-two punch of feeding on him in the dream and then again here had knocked him out cold.

At least the mission had been successful.

Apprehension streaked through me at that. The mission had been successful, which meant the horsemen were coming for me. Who knew how long Lucifer would be down? I had to get out while I could. If I didn't leave now, I was one hundred percent certain I would never escape.

As silently as possible, I swung my legs over the side of the bed, pausing only long enough to steal a peek at myself in the full-length mirror. Oh dear God. I was just as bloody as Luc. The memory of purposefully marking myself with his blood had my cheeks burning red, and I quickly dropped my eyes to pull on a pair of sweats and a T-shirt I'd left on the floor.

With each movement, each noise I made, my heart pounded harder. He could wake at any moment. He was the fucking devil. So powerful he could do almost anything.

And he's your mate.

Holding my breath, I pulled the door open wider, thankful he'd left it ajar when he'd come in and found me in my feral state. A soft creak made me wince, and I looked back to find him in the exact same position as I'd left him.

For the briefest second, something a whole lot like regret flickered through me. I didn't want to leave him here, so vulnerable and alone. He would be so hurt that I left him.

And what about me? I'd left my mates behind before, and the pain had been nearly unbearable. Could I really do it again? To myself *and* him.

As soon as the doubt registered, I steeled myself and shook my head.

No. Bad girl, Merri. He's still the bad guy, you have to get the fuck out of here.

Something that sounded a lot like a groan from the bedroom sent ice running through my veins, and without further hesitation, I sprinted for the front door.

Grim

I'd know hell from anywhere else, no matter the facade painted over its landscape. This was a corner of hell, to be sure. The lakeside cabin flickered in and out of existence, being replaced by the mouth of a dank cave cut into a volcanic mountain.

The second my horse's hooves hit the ground, I was off its back and running.

Distantly, I heard my brothers arrive, but my attention was pinned on the cabin's open door and the woman spilling out of it.

Merri.

She caught my gaze as she reached the edge of the porch, her expression frantic before she looked back into the house. Fuck, she was hurt. Blood stained her throat and the exposed skin of her chest. That bastard had harmed what was mine. I'd have his wings for trophies after this.

She pushed against an invisible barrier, glancing back again, panic flashing in her eyes as she returned her gaze to me.

The facade flickered once more, briefer this time, and just when the cabin started to reappear, Merri tumbled forward, whatever barrier had been keeping her in place giving way. She fell with a look of shock, and I bolted forward on pure instinct, my hands clutching her hips and holding her steady.

"Oh fuck," Sin gasped.

"Merri, no!" Malice shouted immediately after.

"Grim, put her down." Chaos's words were so forceful they might as well have been shot from a gun.

It was then I realized my dire mistake. She was still in my arms, her fingers lifelessly falling from the bare skin at the nape of my neck.

A roar filled my ears as panic unlike anything I'd ever known took over.

Oh no. No no no no no.

I'd killed her.

I finally got her back, and I killed her.

Clenching my eyes shut, I swallowed back a wail of denial.

But then she moved, burying her face in my chest.

"You came for me."

My knees nearly gave out as I opened my eyes and looked into her beautiful blue irises. She reached up and moved to touch my cheek, but I flinched away on instinct, grabbing her wrist with my gloved hand.

"It's okay, Grim. You're not going to hurt me. I promise."

"How can you know that?"

She looked at me as if it were the most obvious answer in the world. "Because you're my mate." Then she wrinkled her nose and held up a finger. "But if you need further proof, one: I *just* touched you without issue." A second finger joined the first. "Two: I am also part horseperson, ergo if you can touch them, you can touch me. Three: We touch just fine in the dream realm, and that's our coremost selves." She shrugged, dropping her hand. "So I really don't see why it's such—"

I kissed her.

I kissed her like I'd been dreaming of kissing her since the moment Lilith threw her at us.

Her lips were as soft and pillowy as they had been in our dreams, but this, having her with me while we were awake, was more powerful than anything we'd ever experienced. I could be with her like this whenever I wanted. I could have her skin on mine every waking moment.

If she would truly forgive me.

I pulled away, chest heaving as my eyes bore into hers. "I am so fucking sorry, wildflower. I never should have doubted you. I know different now. I know the truth. You were right. About everything."

Her lips twitched with the barest hint of a smile. "Took you long enough."

It was a teasing answer, but I knew it was only the tip of the iceberg when it came to making reparations for the damage I'd caused.

"Merri," Sin whispered, agonized and desperate.

My fingers dug into her hips. Selfishly, I didn't want to let her go, but this wasn't only about me. My brothers needed the reassurance that she was safe and whole as much as I did. So I released her and stepped away.

She fell into each of their embraces in turn, taking precious seconds to kiss and be held by them.

I listened as each of my brothers took time to let her know how important she was to them.

Sin held her face in his hands and said, "I knew you'd be trouble, but I never expected to ride through hell to get you back."

"To be fair, it was just supposed to be Chicago."

He laughed and brushed her lips with his. "There's nowhere I wouldn't go to be with you, Merri."

Malice tugged her out of his arms without apology. Kissing her hard before resting his forehead against hers. "Never leave me again."

"I promise," she whispered.

When Chaos finally got his turn, he seemed to have no words to give her. I knew my brother well, and the truth was, his emotions were so great he had no way to get them out. After a few ragged breaths, all he managed was, "Well done, Red."

Realizing the facade hadn't flickered in a while, I narrowed my eyes and studied it. Something had changed. If I had to guess, I'd say the illusion was growing stronger.

Clearing my throat, I looked back at Merri, still tangled up in Chaos. "I'm sorry to break this up, but we need to go."

She pulled back from him, her face paling as she looked beyond me and to the cabin.

I followed her gaze, instantly understanding her reaction as my focus landed on the man standing in the doorway.

Lucifer

"Merri?" I rasped as consciousness finally found me again.

I was weakened, most assuredly, but it had been fucking worth it to bond with my mate. I'd do it a hundred times over if she asked it of me. Did this make me a simp?

I stood, legs as weak as a newborn fawn. Reaching out, I pressed my palm against the wall to steady myself.

"Where did you run off to, crabapple?" I murmured, listening for any hint of her whereabouts as I staggered out of the bedroom. Snagging my dressing gown off the back of the bathroom door, I continued down the hall.

Bloody hell, I couldn't wait for my full power to restore itself. This being mostly human thing was exceedingly tedious. It was all I could do to make it to the living room without needing to stop and rest.

My stomach dropped at the sight of the open front door, revealing not the picturesque lake property I'd conjured for us, but hell.

"Bollocks," I huffed. "You let your mate drain your power one time, and you lose your grip on the alternate reality you're holding her captive in."

Luckily I knew she wouldn't get far. Not in my domain.

There was nowhere she'd ever be able to hide from me here. Or anywhere, for that matter.

I gave our bond a little tug, feeling the tether connecting us vibrating with awareness as I moved to the open door. What I saw when I got there hit me like a cricket bat to the face. Those pesky horsemen were here. Of bloody course they were. Well, they were in for a surprise when she chose me, weren't they?

Her mate.

Like the proverbial moth to a flame, Merri's gaze turned to me.

That's right, my darling.

But it wasn't happiness on her face. It was horror.

A discordant note rippled through the bond connecting us, and unease spread through my chest like acid, eating away at any certainty I'd had.

The familiar ring of steel had my eyes moving to War, his overcompensatingly large sword in his meaty hand.

"Protect our mate at all cost," he snarled.

I froze as everything I knew to be true crumbled before my eyes.

The last time I'd felt this lost, I'd just been shunned from heaven. That was the second time today I'd been brought back to that moment in my life, and I did not care for it one bit.

"Leave him be. Take me away from this place," she said, looking to Death as though he was the love of her life.

I beg your finest pardon, madam, that is moi.

Anger swiftly replaced every other emotion until all I knew was glittering black rage. Around me, the facade of the cabin fell completely, the earth rumbling beneath my feet.

The horsemen tensed, waiting to see what I was going to do.

But before I could give them the ending they so clearly deserved, Merri's eyes found mine. "Please," she whispered.

The word landed like a dagger to my heart.

She was choosing them.

She *wanted* to leave me.

The truth stared me in the face as she stood there, surrounded by the four of them, asking me for mercy. She was never going to love me like she loved them. I was the monster she ran from. They were the monsters she chose.

Everything I thought we shared was nothing more than a lie.

Except the mate bond.

That voice in my mind stabbed at the wound Merri had already dealt to my chest. The mate bond was very real, even if she wouldn't admit it.

I had to let her go.

For now.

But I *would* get her back. The devil always got his due.

Without a word, I spun on my heel and stalked into the cave, using what power I still had to seal it with a stone before leaving Merri and her horsemen behind.

CHAPTER
FORTY
MERRI

We arrived in an empty, sparsely decorated suite I'd never seen before. A small living area with a hallway that I assumed led to bedrooms. Upon further inspection, it was more like an apartment. All I knew was I recognized Auntie Lilith's magic at work.

"Where are we?" I breathed as Grim pulled me close.

"Lilith's secret lair. All of us are here, building an army." This came from Chaos, who gazed at me with yearning in his eyes.

"You found them?"

Sin chuckled. "More like they found us."

"There's much to discuss. We will bring you up to speed after you get settled in," Malice offered. He moved until he was at my side, running a hand down my hair. "I missed you, hellcat."

"I missed you too," I said, wrapping my arms around his waist and squeezing.

"We should let the others know we're back," Chaos said, clapping Sin on the shoulder while discreetly gesturing to the door.

I knew what he was doing, and I appreciated it. He wanted to give Grim and me some time alone. We were the ones who needed healing. The others and I had done the repair work already, and until the bond Grim and I shared wasn't at risk of breaking, we had to prioritize it. Now more than ever. Who knew when Lucifer would strike next? We needed to be strong, united. There was no room for any cracks between the five of us, or he'd exploit them.

It was impossible to know what having Lucifer as a mate meant. For me. For them. For this apocalypse. But I knew better than to underestimate him. This wasn't the end of anything.

They left us alone in a heavy silence, our breaths the only sound in the room. Grim turned me to face him, his jaw tight, eyes anguished as he took me in.

"I thought you'd never let me near you again, wildflower."

"I'd considered it." He winced right before I added, "But it proved harder than I thought."

He looked away, throat bobbing as he swallowed. "I know I deserve every ounce of your anger. You offered me something precious, something I probably will never truly deserve, and I was an absolute arse when I denied you."

"Yeah, you were."

His eyes lifted to mine. "Do you ever think you can forgive me? Is there any chance of me finding my way back into your heart?"

I stiffened as I sat with the words, wondering what the truth really was. Could I forgive him? Yes. Had he ever really been absent from my heart? No.

"Grim, you broke something inside me."

He hung his head before going to his knees before me. "I wish I could take it back. All of it. But Merri, I truly thought you had to be mistaken because there was no way someone like me would be gifted something so precious as a mate."

I ran my fingers through his hair, knowing he wasn't done.

"It's not an excuse, merely an explanation, but you have to understand I spent my entire existence believing the world to be one thing, only for you to come along and completely upend it. It's a lot of history to unlearn."

"A lifetime's worth," I said with a nod.

"More like several hundred lifetimes."

I released a breath and offered him a wobbly smile. "Then I suppose it's a good thing you're immortal and can spend the next several hundred making it up to me."

Reaching for his hand, I tugged until he got to his feet. Then, I slowly removed his glove and brought his fingers to my cheek.

"I . . . I love you, Merri. I never thought myself capable of love, but you proved me wrong."

There was no doubt in my mind he meant everything he said. Grim never intended to break my heart, not really. It was a painful accident, but it was still an accident, and I'd had my fair share of those. Everyone deserved a second chance, especially a horseman who was learning what it meant to be human. Well, human-ish.

Feelings were new to him, to all of them, really. They were going to make mistakes, and so was I, but we were a team and we would figure it out together.

Lifting onto my tiptoes, I pressed my lips to his and threaded my fingers behind his neck. Then I pulled back and stared into his mercurial eyes.

"I'll forgive you on one condition."

"Anything."

"Please don't break my heart again."

Grim

"Fuck, wildflower. It's the last thing I'll ever do."

Unable to keep from touching her for longer than a moment, I dragged my fingertips over her beloved face. I'd been forced to deny myself the sensation of touch with nearly every person in my life. So here, in this room with my . . . mate, I needed to commit to memory the feel of her. Silken skin, the rise of her cheekbones, the slope of her upturned nose, her soft lips, the gentle curve of her jaw. Each feature created the face I loved. Each one deserved attention.

She remained still under my ministrations, her eyes fluttering closed as she leaned into my touch. Merri understood without my having to say a word how much this moment meant to me. In all honesty, it was probably the most intimate moment of my entire life.

"You are so achingly beautiful, Merri," I murmured, replacing my fingers with my lips as I kissed a path along her jaw and down her neck.

"So are you, Grimsby. Every part of you."

I didn't deserve the words. I wasn't worthy of them. Or this woman. But I vowed then and there that I would strive to be. Reaching down with one arm, I scooped her up until she was cradled bridal style in my hold. Her answering giggle lightened something inside me. Maybe I wasn't such a miserable git after all.

"Where are you taking me?" she asked, toying with my hair as I carried her down the hall.

"My lair."

"Oooh, your lair? And what do you intend to do with me once you have me in your clutches?"

"I was intending to ravish you, but if there's something else you desire, all you have to do is ask."

"I'm all for a ravishing, but for our first time like this . . ." She didn't finish her sentence, instead burying her face in my neck.

Reaching my room, I used my shadows to open the door so I didn't have to release my hold on her. "What, love? What do you want? Would you like me to cherish you as you deserve?"

I placed her on the bed and waited as she brought her gaze up to meet mine.

"I need to know this is real. That I'm not going to wake up and find out this was all a dream."

My heart shattered at the raw vulnerability in her eyes. I'd done this to her, made her doubt herself and my love for her. I was such a fucking fool.

"It's real," I promised, my voice little more than a ragged whisper. "I'm not going anywhere. And I will remind you of that as often as you need me to."

"Good."

She reached for the hem of her T-shirt and pulled it over her head, revealing gorgeous, bare skin underneath. Covered in blood as she was, I held up a finger and went to the bathroom to get a warm, wet cloth so I could clean her before I made her mine.

Each stroke of the washcloth over her skin caused her nipples to tighten, and the way her eyes darkened made my cock harder than it had ever been. I'd seen her nude countless times, but knowing I had her all to myself and could take the weight of her breasts in my palms without fear of harming her made me itch to touch her again.

So I did.

I cupped the full globe and lowered my head, using my tongue to tease and taste, then my teeth.

Merri groaned and dragged her fingers through my hair, pressing me closer.

I laughed against her skin, delighting in the way my breath pebbled her flesh. "Need something, darling?"

"You. Just you."

"We have all the time in the world. What's the rush?" I pushed her back until she lay on the bed, sprawled out and at my mercy.

"*I* need *you* now."

I fucking loved the sound of that. And I would never deny my mate anything she needed. Not now, not ever again.

Tucking my fingers into the waistband of her sweats, I pulled them down her body. If you'd have told me even a year ago that the sight of a woman's body would render me speechless, I'd have laughed in your face. But I understood now, in a way I'd never been capable of, what Botticelli had sought to capture with his art. She wasn't just beautiful because of her body. She was beautiful because I loved her. Because she was *mine*.

Being with her like this was unlike anything I'd ever known. The magic of loving someone the way I loved her made everything before her seem unimportant.

I'd only had one other lover before her, but that had been transactional at best. Nothing compared to this. Merri was it for me. She was everything.

"I love you," I whispered, pressing my lips to her belly. "I love you," I said again, this time kissing her hip bone. I'd denied the truth of the words for so long that we both needed this. Her to hear them, and me to speak them.

She arched her back as I made my way up to her nipple and sucked on the taut peak. When I released her flesh, I rolled my gaze up to meet hers and said one final time, "I love you."

Merri's eyes shone with emotion as she tugged me up and pressed her lips to mine. We fit together like two puzzle pieces, my hips settling perfectly between her thighs. With a whimper, she ground her pelvis against mine, wordlessly begging me to give her what she needed.

Part of me wanted to draw this out, to spend hours mapping her body with my hands, lips, and tongue. But I'd be lying if I said I didn't crave the connection just as much as she did. I needed her.

Pulling back just enough to complete my task, I unbuttoned my shirt and tossed it on the floor, then moved to the zip of my trousers.

Impatient little thing that she was, Merri reached between us and grabbed my aching length as soon as I freed it from the fabric. I groaned, a pained sound I couldn't contain, as she stroked me from base to crown.

"Please, Grim," she begged, guiding my tip to her entrance.

I'd denied her too much for too long. I couldn't resist anymore. Not with her plaintive plea in my ear.

I slid home, my breath stalling in my chest at her perfect heat. I'd technically experienced this in our dreams, but it was different somehow, having her in my bed, watching her pulse thundering at the side of her throat, her hands roaming over my body in much the same way mine had hers.

Knowing that she was made for me and I for her.

Everything culminated in one overwhelming truth: I was exactly where fate wanted me to be.

We moved together in long, slow rolls of our hips, gentle touches, worshipful kisses, and ragged moans. But as it always did with Merri, pleasure built swiftly and undeniably, and I was on the precipice far too soon.

"I'm going to—"

Taking my face in her hands, she cut me off with the sweetest kiss. "I love you, Grimsby."

I was gone. Done for. Over the edge and spilling inside her as she followed me in ecstasy. There was nothing more perfect than Merri telling me she loved me. Nothing.

And I'd do everything within my power to ensure she'd have reason to tell me, and I her, as long as I existed.

CHAPTER FORTY-ONE

DEATH

"What are we supposed to be doing? You say Lucifer has gone silent. For all we know, he has been caged by the angels," Sloth growled, standing from his seat and pressing his palms to the table.

Famine stared at him like a cat in heat. Sabine was the thirstiest of us, to be sure. All she wanted was to feed and fuck. Fair enough, I guessed. She certainly lived up to her title.

Slamming his hand on the table, Wrath called everyone's attention to him. "Enough whining. The mission is clear. Take control. End the world. Rebuild in hell's image. We don't need Lucifer holding our hands for that."

"And who will lead if he doesn't return?" Envy asked, feet kicked up onto the table. "You?"

I stood, utterly annoyed by their conversation. "We will."

"We?" Envy stared daggers at me. "We, who?"

"My sisters and I." Sweeping my arms out to my sides, I gestured to the horsewomen in question. They joined me on their feet. "Just like we have this entire time."

The Princes fell silent before the room broke out in stunned laughs. I made a point to meet and hold each of their gazes until the laughter died off.

"You think Lucifer is the mastermind behind this apocalypse? You think *he* could have ever gotten this far on his own?" I scoffed. "If not for me and my sisters, you would all still be locked in your cages. This is *our* apocalypse. *Our* big showdown. We have been running this shindig since the beginning. Lucifer is nothing more than a puppet. A means to an end. And now that he's out of the way, we can finally step out of the shadows."

Chains rattled from the other side of the room, muffled cries of protest coming in their wake from the two captives we had shackled to the wall. Minerva's and Odette's progeny. We were terribly close to having a full set. I almost felt bad for my niece and nephew.

Almost.

"And you expect us to follow you?" Pride asked, one brow raised.

I giggled. "Of course. You have been since you got here, silly."

"You think Lucifer will simply allow you to take the reins and steal what he thinks is his apocalypse?"

Rolling my eyes, I sighed. "It's not a matter of allowing. We will overthrow him on his return. Take what is ours."

"What do we get in return for this mutiny?" Greed asked, tilting her head with more than a little curiosity.

"What everyone wants, my dear. Power," I said with a wink.

The Princes exchanged a series of dubious glances.

I sighed, bored with all of them. "Listen," I said, using my most reasonable tone. "The way I see it, the seven of you have two choices. You either fight by our side and join in the spoils of our victory, *or* . . ."

"Or what?" Gluttony snarled.

My grin was pure evil. "Or we'll do the same thing to you that we do to all our enemies."

"And that is?" Lust pressed, leaning forward with a hungry gleam in their eye.

My smile stretched, and I giggled. "We will destroy you."

The Mate Games: Apocalypse concludes with Lucifer, coming soon. You can pre-order your copy here but in the meantime, we have a little something for you.

Curious what Lucifer was really up to in Chapter 35? download your copy of his bonus scene at www.themategames.com/GrimBonus or you can download it on audio at www.themategames.com/GrimAudioBonus

The Mate Games Universe

By K. Loraine & Meg Anne

War

Obsession

Rejection

Possession

Temptation

Devotion

Pestilence

Promised to the Night (Prequel Novella)

Deal with the Demon

Claimed by the Shifters

Captive of the Night

Lost to the Moon

Death

Haunting Beauty

Hunted Beast

Hateful Prince

Heartless Villain

<u>Apocalypse</u>

Sin

Chaos

Malice

Grim

Lucifer

MORE BY MEG & KIM

Twisted Cross Ranch

A dark contemporary cowboy reverse harem

Sinner's Secret

Corruptor's Claim

Deadly Debt

Also by Meg Anne

Brotherhood of the Guardians/Novasgard Vikings

Undercover Magic *(Nord & Lina)*

A Sexy & Suspenseful Fated Mates PNR

Hint of Danger

Face of Danger

World of Danger

Promise of Danger

Call of Danger

Bound by Danger (Quinn & Finley)

The Chosen Universe

The Chosen

A Fated Mates High Fantasy Romance

Mother Of Shadows

Reign Of Ash

Crown Of Embers

Queen Of Light

The Chosen Boxset #1

The Chosen Boxset #2

The Keepers

A Guardian/Ward High Fantasy Romance

The Dreamer (A Keeper's Prequel)

The Keepers Legacy

The Keepers Retribution

The Keepers Vow

The Keepers Boxset

The Forsaken

A Rejected Mates/Enemies-To-Lovers Romantasy

Prisoner of Steel & Shadow

Queen of Whispers & Mist

Court of Death & Dreams

Standalones

My Soul To Take: A Forbidden Love Meets Fated Mates PNR

Also by K. Loraine

The Blackthorne Vampires

THE BLOOD TRILOGY

(Cashel & Olivia)

Blood Captive

Blood Traitor

Blood Heir

BLACKTHORNE BLOODLINES

(Lucas & Briar)

Midnight Prince

Midnight Hunger

THE WATCHER SERIES

Waking the Watcher

Denying the Watcher

Releasing the Watcher

THE SIREN COVEN

Eternal Desire (Shifter reluctant mates)

Cursed Heart (Hate to Lovers)

Broken Sword (MMF menage Arthurian)

STANDALONES

Cursed (MFM Sleeping Beauty Retelling)

REVERSE HAREM STANDALONES

Their Vampire Princess (A Reverse Harem Romance)

All the Queen's Men (A Fae Reverse Harem Romance)

About Meg Anne

USA Today and international bestselling paranormal and fantasy romance author Meg Anne has always had stories running on a loop in her head. They started off as daydreams about how the evil queen (aka Mom) had her slaving away doing chores, and more recently shifted into creating backgrounds about the people stuck beside her during rush hour. The stories have always been there; they were just waiting for her to tell them.

Like any true SoCal native, Meg enjoys staying inside curled up with a good book and her fur babies . . . or maybe that's just her. You can convince Meg to buy just about anything if it's covered in glitter or rhinestones, or make her laugh by sharing your favorite bad joke. She also accepts bribes in the form of baked goods and Mexican food.

Meg is best known for her leading men #MenbyMeg, her inevitable cliffhangers, and making her readers laugh out loud, all of which started with the bestselling Chosen series.

ABOUT K. LORAINE

USA Today Bestselling author Kim Loraine writes steamy contemporary and sexy paranormal romance. **You'll find her paranormal romances written under the name K. Loraine and her contemporaries as Kim Loraine.** Don't worry, you'll get the same level of swoon-worthy heroes, sassy heroines, and an eventual HEA.

When not writing, she's busy herding cats (raising kids), trying to keep her house sort of clean, and dreaming up ways for fictional couples to meet.

www.ingramcontent.com/pod-product-compliance
Lightning Source LLC
Chambersburg PA
CBHW020306030826
48979CB00029B/2256/J
9781961742604